She knew her brother was innocent but no one believed her. How could she make them see…

"No," Lizzie shrieked, leaping out of her chair, and knocking the table over.

She threw all the papers on the floor and tore everything from the shelves. Jen, her big sister, rushed in through the doorway and Lizzie could hear Dr. Stewart scolding her for interrupting. She still believed that she was in control of her patient, but Jen didn't care what she wanted. Jen grabbed Lizzie to stop her from thrashing, and she sank to the floor, realizing that James wasn't really there. They stayed there a moment, Jen rocking her in her arms while Lizzie kept yelling. "My brother loved my family, and he would never hurt me. He was protecting me, and that bastard killed him."

"Shhh…it's okay. Everything's going to be okay." Jen could always soothe her.

Lizzie knew how guilty her sister felt for allowing her therapy to go on, but she was running out of options. Lizzie sobbed loudly into Jen's blouse, the buttons bumping into her nose.

"Ms. Moore, can I please speak with you privately for a moment?" Dr. Stewart asked.

Jen nodded. She helped Lizzie, who was shaking, off the floor and pointed to the hallway. Lizzie shook her head, clinging to her sister's arm. She scrunched her body to make it as small as possible. She was taller than Jen, even though Jen was seven years older.

Any time Lizzie had a public breakdown, people would stare in bewilderment at this towering girl trying to nestle her body under the arm of someone at least five inches shorter than she.

"Lizzie, sweetheart, can you go wait out there for a second? I promise I'll be there very soon."

Jen gently pulled Lizzie off her arm, gathering Lizzie's hands together so she was left outside the doorway, hugging herself. They closed the door on her, leaving Lizzie sniffling on the other side, still shaking.

After his mother's death, Brian suffers severe trauma from his abusive father. When the abuse becomes too much, Brian's mind splits into multiple personalities and starts him down a path of murder and destruction. Lizzie's life is turned upside down when she is tortured by a serial killer. Now she has to learn to cope with a new school, new friends, and a new life with a sister that she didn't meet until recently. As Lizzie struggles to discover the identity of the man who ruined her life, people think she's crazy and suffering from delusions. But when Lizzie finally discovers that Brian was her attacker, the two collide in a battle of survival…

KUDOS for *The Blackbird's Song*

In *The Blackbird's Song* by Katie Marshall, Lizzie is trying to recover from being tortured by a serial killer. She knows the guy is still out there and he's still tormenting her, even though her family and friends think she's crazy. She and her sister move from California to Maine, but Lizzie isn't safe even there. The killer seems almost superhuman in his ability to mess with her mind. And she needs to discover his identity or she has no chance of surviving. But can she do it alone when no one will believe her, and she can barely cope with the day-to-day chore of living? A chillingly and intense psychological thriller, this story is not for the faint of heart. Marshall takes us into the mind of a killer with his twisted logic and horrific deeds, creating an unforgettable reading experience. ~ *Taylor Jones, The Review Team of Taylor Jones & Regan Murphy*

The Blackbird's Song by Katie Marshall is the story of a young man whose father turns abusive after the mother dies, taking his anger and grief out on the children, Brian and Shelly. Though only nine years old at the time, Brian tries to protect his sister from their father, earning even more abuse for himself. Then comes the moment when the abuse is too much. Brian's young mind can't handle it and splits into other personalities designed to protect him. However, as Brian grows up, his fractured mind becomes twisted until the only thing that makes sense is to kill. One of his victims is Lizzie, a sixteen-year-old girl who manages to survive the attack, but suffers from PTSD and paranoia. Or is it really paranoia? Lizzie is certain her attacker is still out there, but no one will listen. The *Blackbird's Song* is well written, fast-paced, and intense—a forceful look into the world of the mentally ill and how twisted and evil some people can be. Once you pick it up, you won't be able to put it down. ~ *Regan Murphy, The Review Team of Taylor Jones & Regan Murphy*

The
Blackbird's
Song

Katie Marshall

A Black Opal Books Publication

Black Opal Books

BECAUSE SOME STORIES JUST HAVE TO BE TOLD

GENRE: CRIME THRILLER/PSYCHOLOGICAL THRILLER

THE BLACKBIRD'S SONG
Copyright © 2017 by Katie Marshall
Cover Design by Jackson Cover Designs & Katie Marshall
All cover art copyright © 2017
All Rights Reserved
Print ISBN: 978-1-626948-05-1

First Publication: NOVEMBER 2017

Published by Black Opal Books **http://www.blackopalbooks.com**

DEDICATION

For Kayla,
who became a sister when I didn't have one.
I love you always.

Chapter 1

Brian

September 1999:

Brian raced down the soccer field. Behind him, his opponent was a mere seven years old, while Brian was a proud nine. Brian had the ball in front of him. He saw his mom on the sidelines waving her arms from side to side, lips moving but the words unclear. Brian looked up at his target, as he got close to the goal, only to see his best friend, Adam, waving him away. He ran in the wrong direction. As Brian tried to shift directions, his opponent gained on him, stealing the ball and propelling it into the goal. The opposing team rushed to their comrade as half the little boys began to cheer.

Reluctantly, he got in line behind Adam to give his good sportsmanship high fives. In the crowd, Brian's mother was directing him to smile with her fingers while his little sister, Michelle rolled on the bench with laughter. She wrapped her purple-sleeved arms around her stomach and threw her head back in exaggerated peals. When she was finished, she adjusted her pink tutu, straightening it before it wrinkled. His mother was always late because of her dance practices.

Brian sulked over to his mother and she tried to give him a hug. "Mom, quit it!"

"It's okay, honey. I thought you did really good." She smiled again, trying to make him feel better while she hustled him to the car.

"Yeah, Bub, you were the best player out there," Michelle said, but the smile she gave him traced an evil glint around her eyes. She started to laugh again before she managed to add, "for the other team."

"Shut up. You're too stupid to even know what a ball is."

"I'm seven not two, you butthead."

"Okay, you two. Let's try to be nice to each other," Mom said.

"I call driver's side."

His sister hopped into the seat behind her mother before he had time to object. His mother gave him the "You're older," look and he got into the other seat next to his sister. The seat had crumbs from the Saltines Michelle had been eating, so he brushed them to the floor and tugged his juice box from his backpack as his mother pulled into the downtown traffic.

Traffic was backed up on the main street, as it always was at four in the afternoon. While they were caught in the jam, Brian stared out the window at the buildings. They weren't as tall as the one his father worked in, in the heart of the city, skyscrapers, each one a million miles into the sky. He wondered what it would be like to work in a place like that, just like his dad.

His father worked long nights in the office and, some nights, Brian would wait up to see him. His father would stagger through the doorway at ten, stumbling with exhaustion. His nose was always tomato red, and his mouth curled into a half smile when he saw his son perched in his chair, trying to prevent his eyes from shutting by blinking rapidly. He would thump Brian hard on the head, his breath hot and smelling of alcohol, blowing into his face.

"You run along to bed, kiddo," he'd say, pulling Brian out of the chair and plopping into it, his body collapsing like a scarecrow.

Some nights, when he was younger, Brian would sneak back out to watch his father dance around the kitchen with his mother. Brian sat at the top of the stairs, peeking between the wooden pegs of the banister railing at the kitchen's cream colored walls with borders of little blue flowers. His mother hated to dance and tried to brace herself against the kitchen chairs. One night he saw his father scoop her up under her armpits, her legs and arms hanging down trying to make contact with a surface, and spun her in circles while she pleaded with him to be reasonable. Then he stopped and cornered her against the wall, breathing his filth into her ears and calling her "whore." Brian didn't know what that meant, but his mother never seemed happy to hear it.

"Hey, Mom, can Dad watch the birds fly by from his window?" Brian turned to see that she hadn't heard him over the incessant talking of Michelle.

"So Hannah has this brand new Rockstar Barbie that I really want for Christmas. See, Mom, it's right in this flyer. Mom? Mom!"

"Sweetheart, Mom is trying to watch the road." She inched the car forward to the intersection lights.

"But, Mom, just look at it for a second. It's Rockstar Barbie, Mom. She even has a guitar."

His mother quickly twisted around and gave Michelle a nod followed by a brief sigh. The light turned green and the car moved forward.

Instantly, he heard the clang of metal on metal. It shook the car, spinning it horizontally. The sound of the glass shattering and the honking of the horn rattled in his brain. His ears rang with a high-pitched squeal, echoing through him until he expected his body to explode. He felt the opening of his mouth as his jaw muscles worked against him and realized that part of the noise came from his own muffled scream that caught in his throat. It stunned him for a moment, but when he recovered he could hear nothing but his sister's screams.

"Oh, my arm! My arm really hurts. Mommy, my arm hurts!" Her tutu was dotted with shards of glass.

The front left side of the car was crumpled into itself. His mother sat silent in the seat. Brian scooted toward his sister and climbed across the center console. "Mom? Mom, are you okay? Mom, please wake up."

His mother's eyes were open, sparkling blue like the earrings in her ears. Surrounding her detached beauty were pools of scarlet running from and around her face. It trickled from her ear canal, coating the earring as her neck tilted sideways in the seat. It dripped from her nose and mouth, creating a puddle on the gearshift. Her eyes stared up at him blankly as he tried to find the soul that once was there. For a second, he thought he saw the twinkle reappear in her eyes, a slight indication that she was still there, that she still loved him, but then it vanished again.

Beside him, his sister's cries turned into incomprehensible screeches. He shook his mother's shoulder, but she felt so far away. He felt her arm, wondering if it was cold. He had heard that you're always cold when you die, but she still felt warm and all he wanted to do was crawl into her arms for comfort. Then someone was opening the door and pulling him from the car. He thrashed, screamed, and cried to be put back, but they wouldn't let him.

Chapter 2

Brian had never felt so stiff. He wriggled in his new suit, scratching at the tight collar around his neck.

"Hey, buddy, do me a favor and go check on your sister," his father said, tying his tie.

His father hadn't said much to either of them since the accident. He'd taken some time off from work and spent most of it on the phone, making arrangements. At night, he spent his time in the den with his door shut and the lights out. It was the one place in the house that Brian wasn't allowed to enter. He didn't know why he couldn't, but he obeyed his father anyway.

Brian walked into his sister's room, not bothering to knock. Michelle was sitting in the middle of her pink paradise, black dress on, arms folded, and lip quivering.

"What's wrong, Shelley?" Brian said, trying not to cry himself.

As long as he didn't cry again, his mother would come home and the whole thing would be just a horrible nightmare.

"I can't tie my ribbon. Mommy always tied my ribbon." She stood up and the black ribbon hung off the sides of her dress where it was sewn on.

Brian grabbed both ends of the ribbon, wrapping one

end under the other. "One goes under the other, pull tight, make the bunny's ears, and wrap one under the other and done." He smiled, admiring his work. It wasn't as neat as Mommy used to make it, but it'd have to do. "Let's go tell Dad we're ready."

Michelle nodded, sticking her thumb in her mouth. She hadn't sucked her thumb since she was four, but the habit had started again after the accident. Brian had teased her about it before, but this time he ignored it. He had started to see monsters under the bed and was having nightmares, but he didn't tell anyone. He didn't want his father to think he was a little kid. At night, when the house was still, Brian wished he could crawl into his mother's arms, to sleep in the protection of her love, but no matter how much he tried to deny it, he knew he'd never have that safety again.

When they came into the living room, they found it empty. Brian called to his father, but no one answered. Leaving his sister beside the couch, he checked the bathroom, the kitchen, and with a bit of reluctance, his parent's bedroom, but his father couldn't be found. He tapped lightly on the den door. It swung open, exposing Brian to the room's contents for the first time in years. He peeked in, but his father wasn't in there either. He looked up and down the hallway, but he didn't see or hear any signs of him. He stepped into the room and gently pushed the door back into place.

It wasn't anything like he imagined. As a child, his mind had wandered to mythical places to figure out what his father could possibly be hiding in this forbidden place, but the scene was much more ordinary than his mind had ever expected.

There were bookshelves, a desk, a couple chairs, and his father's laptop. No Christmas elves or secret spy gear, or whatever else a child could possibly come up with when given the opportunity to think about a locked door.

He sat in his father's computer chair, spinning it around a few times to make the room blur and refocus. As he was playing with the chair, a frame on the desk caught his attention. He let the chair spin to a stop and picked up the picture. It was of Shelley, Brian, and their mother on her last birthday. She had worn her blue cocktail dress, and the kids their best clothes because they decided to go out for dinner that year. He stared at it for a second, looking into his mother's eyes. They seemed so warm, full of life. Then he remembered the accident and the distance it had given them, and he felt sick. He laid the picture face down on the desk.

He opened the drawers, flipping through papers and remnants of candy wrappers. He picked up a bottle, half filled with liquid, taking the cap off and sniffing its contents. It reeked of that strong, fiery smell that his father always had on his breath, and Brian wondered what the big deal about the bottle was. It seemed to be as natural as anything else that was always in his life and yet he had a queasy feeling when he looked at it. It was the same feeling that gave his mother that look of disgust when she smelled its contents on his father's breath.

"What the hell are you doing in here?" His father's voice jumped him as the door swung open. He grabbed Brian by the collar, picking his little body off of the chair. Brian had never seen his father so angry, fiery glint in his eyes as he ripped the bottle from his son's hands. "I told you to never come in here. Boy, I should slap you so hard that you—"

Brian kept his head down, trying not to upset his father more. His head and neck were starting to hurt from where the shirt tightened around his body. He felt weightless, feet dangling in the air, but there was a fear and helplessness that Brian had never felt with his father before. When he paused in the middle of his sentence, his hand made a fist, and Brian winced. His father had never hit him before, but something about his threat made Brian believe that he might. His father stared at him for a minute then released him to the ground.

"I'm sorry, Brian. Dad's just having a hard day. But next time you need to listen to me, you understand," his father said, not looking at his son. Brian nodded, but his father wasn't paying attention anymore. "Let's grab your sister and get this over with."

At the funeral, the children saw little of their father. Michelle hid in the corner of the room, shy of all the strange faces that came through. Her thumb hadn't left her mouth since the drive over. She backed herself against one of the floral arrangements, peeking out over some of the thick leaves. Brian had stood with her for a little while, but he grew tired of standing in one spot so he moved around in the crowd instead. He didn't recognize most of the people. His mother had only one sister, Aunt Caroline, and she was standing beside his father, next to the box his mother was in. Brian didn't like to use or even think of the word coffin. He knew what that meant and his mind refused to accept that his mother could be spending all eternity in that wooden thing. As long as he denied it, he wouldn't cry, and he wasn't going to be a big baby by crying in front of all these people. Not that they would've noticed. Most of them were whispering among themselves and dabbing their eyes with handkerchiefs. The ones that did notice insisted on touching him in some fashion, whether it was by patting his head, giving him unwanted hugs, or smearing lipstick on his cheek.

"Oh, you poor thing," the ladies cooed as he passed, face in a hardened frown and eyes hiding unwanted tears. He swatted at their hands like one who is bothered by pesky mosquitoes, but his gestures didn't deter his sympathizers. After all, the poor thing had just lost his mother, an ordeal that had left his sister injured and the child distraught.

At his father's request, they had a closed casket service, a distress to Brian, who refused to believe his mother was in there to begin with. He never mentioned it out loud for fear of his father's reprimand, but he wanted to believe it so much that he had convinced himself that it was only a terrible dream. When it was all over, he would wake up and his mother would be downstairs making him smiley face waffles for breakfast. He knew that he had to be sure so, when the grownups were talking, he opened the casket slightly, catching a glimpse of his mother's blue cocktail dress. His body jolted away from the sight, releasing the coffin with a thud that attracted the people closest to him. His father gave him a glare before going back to talking to his friends. His Aunt Caroline kneeled down beside him.

"What are you doing, sweetie?" Her voice was sweet and gentle, parting her mouth slightly across her pink lips. Her face was soft and round like his mother's, with the same wavy, blonde hair that she had, but her eyes were amber. Brian had forgotten how similar the two had looked, and when he saw her, his body relaxed again. He reached his arms out to her like a toddler and she hugged him to her. "Oh, honey, I miss her too."

He burrowed his face in her hair and, in the comfort of her arms, he burst into tears. She patted his head, stroking his hair to put it back into place. When she released him, she dabbed his face with her handkerchief and grabbed hold of his hand. He smiled a little, not really feeling happy, but feeling better than he had in several days.

"They're going to take Mommy out to the cemetery

now, okay? Why don't we go get Shelley and the two of you can ride with me?" She gave him a slight smile, but Brian could see the tears in her eyes.

Brian nodded and the two of them picked up Michelle, who had begun to develop a crowd with her sobbing tears.

At the cemetery, Michelle clung to Aunt Caroline's leg as Brian clutched her hand in fear that she might disappear too. Their father stood over by himself, not attempting to soothe his children, or even acknowledge they were there. Brian swallowed hard, but the lump wouldn't go away as he saw them lowering the casket. It all seemed so confusing to process. His mother had been here on earth, a loving, breathing person, and now she was nothing but a pale body in a box becoming one with the ground. He couldn't understand the finality of it, that his mother wasn't coming home, that he would never see her face again or hear her laugh.

As he watched people gather to throw a handful of dirt over the coffin, he felt the need to throw himself between these people and his mother. They were throwing her away, disregarding her as some useless object they could leave here. The only thing that kept him from moving was his Aunt Caroline. If he went to his mother, he'd have to let go of Aunt Caroline's hand and he was too scared to leave her.

"You don't have to go up if you don't want to," Aunt Caroline told him. He hugged her other leg, imitating his sister, and Aunt Caroline sighed. "It'll all be over soon enough."

People were starting to disperse as the rest of the dirt was piled on the grave. Aunt Caroline nudged the two children toward their father, and he finally took notice of them again.

"It'll be your bedtime soon. We'd better get home,"

he said, his voice rough. "Say goodbye to your Aunt Caroline."

"You're not coming with us?" Brian asked, feeling uneasy about being alone with his father. He knew he would probably be reprimanded again for going in the den and he didn't like the look his father had when he was angry.

"No, sweetie. I have to catch my flight back to New York. Big hugs," she said, pulling him and Shelley close again. "I love you both very much."

Brian was angry that his aunt wouldn't stay to make sure they were okay. He had just lost his mother and now the one thread of her existence he had left was abandoning him, flying off to her home without so much as another thought about them. At first, when she hugged him, he clung to her, thinking maybe if he held on long enough she would change her mind. When he realized that wouldn't happen, his body stiffened and he looked away as she walked to her car. When she waved to them, he pretended as if he couldn't see her. Shelley waved back and he whacked her hand from the air. She stuck her tongue out at him and continued to wave goodbye. As he watched the car off in the distance, he had no idea that that would be the last time he'd see his Aunt Caroline, and was not aware that she was even sick, but two years later, his father casually mentioned that she had gotten cancer and died. She wasn't spoken of again.

After the funeral, his father poured himself a drink and never seemed to stop. He staggered around the house, bottle in hand, yelling at the air. When Brian asked him what was for dinner, his father had thumped him hard on the head and sent him to his room. Michelle curled herself into the corner of his bedroom to hide from their father's rage. Her arm was cushioned in a bright pink cast. The more Brian stared at it, the angrier he got. *It's all her fault. If she wasn't such a spoiled little brat, my mother would have been more careful. But she always has to get the attention. That's why Mom was late to all of my games.* The thoughts crept into his brain before he was able to stop them. He got down from his bed, crossed the room, and punched Michelle in the face. She squealed, holding her cheek as her eyes welled with tears. Something inside him, that tiny, snarling voice in the back of his brain told him she deserved it. *Mom loved her more.*

Immediately, his anger evaporated. He looked down at his sister, her blonde hair in pigtails with black ribbons, and her eyes, the same blue as his, the same blue as his mother's. He sat down next to her and gave her a hug.

"I'm sorry, Shelley," Brian said. "I'm mean."

"Well, duh." She sniffled and hugged him tightly.

They sat together through the night, singing "Mockingbird" like their mother used to. In the other room, their father crashed into the kitchen table and fell to the floor.

Chapter 3

Lizzie

April 2012:

Lizzie had spent these past few months hiding in her new room, while Jen struggled to make everything okay, even though she couldn't. Now they were moving clear across the country to a place where woods replaced ocean and cold surpassed the sun. Jen had gotten the idea after communicating her concerns to Lizzie's friend, Nick, and his parents, who suggested that what Lizzie really needed was a "change of scenery." His grandmother swore up and down that there was no better place to heal the soul than Maine. She had lived there many years herself and was more than happy to welcome some more familiar faces to her town.

Lizzie wondered what a small town in Maine would be like in comparison to her beautiful California. It didn't really matter anyway. Snowstorm or sunshine he would come for her and she would be dead before anyone could find out what happened.

Lizzie sat on the beach in California, looking around to make sure it was too early for anyone to be there besides her and Jen. She really wanted to see it again before she left, but feared the thought of sharing it with strangers. It was completely empty though, a wasteland until teenagers and tourists arose from their beds.

In her childhood, the ocean was soothing. The water was warm, gently splashing against her skin, cooling it with every touch. She used to collect creatures from the tide pools in her lemon-colored pail then return them to their homes before her father made her. The sun's rays pressed into her skin, turning it a light brown while the sand felt soft between her toes. Above, the sky was a brightened blue that seemed to meet the ocean, intermingling in a way on the horizon that left each part undefinable from the other.

Today, the water had turned from a soothing blue to a dull gray as the waves rocked violently in it. When they hit the shore, they slapped against Lizzie's toes. As she sat, she dug her hands into the sand, feeling the gritty texture of rocks and shells against her palms. After months of hiding, her pale skin felt scorched by the sun. She would probably be going to Maine with a nasty sunburn. She had spent the past three months in therapy, trying to eliminate what her therapist liked to call "irrational fears" from her life and to better herself for the future, but nothing seemed to work. Eventually, her doctor prescribed anti-psychotics to help with her delusions, but the flashbacks increased, and Jen decided moving would be good for a fresh start.

After her parents decided that Lizzie was too much to handle, they agreed to pay Jen for Lizzie's care so money would never be an issue, but Lizzie was still unsure of the change. She stared out across the darkening horizon and tried to find its comfort, but there was none, and she would probably never know that feeling again.

"What are you thinking about, kiddo?" Jen asked, watching her with her hands pressed into the sand. They had been sitting there in silence for several minutes.

"It's not the same as it used to be," Lizzie said, not sure what she should say.

"Nothing ever stays the same. Life will always be full of changes." Jen sighed. "I'm sorry that things had to change so quickly for you. I had hoped you could be happy a little longer."

"You said I was spoiled. Guess I won't get my way now, will I?"

"I never wanted this for you," Jen said, turning toward Lizzie. She rested her hands on her shoulders, turning Lizzie so that she had to look her in her eyes. "You know that everything's going to get better, I promise. Nobody is going to hurt you again."

"You can't protect me. No one can," Lizzie said, pulling away from her.

The two were quiet again for a while. Lizzie watched the seagulls circling the water overhead and thought of the life she used to know. An hour later, they arose from their spots as people began to gather for their morning excursions. Lizzie looked back several times, wishing for that one moment of comfort again.

Chapter 4

August 2012:

Lizzie hated Fridays. They reminded her of everything she hated most in the world: car rides with her sister lecturing her the entire way to the therapist's office about being a "good" girl who promptly and accurately answered all of Dr. Stewart's questions, minutes spent in a waiting room with people who stared at her wondering what kind of mental case she was in comparison to their own imperfections, and forty minutes in a stuffy office while her psychologist drilled her over and over again about the same things so that she could express her "true feelings."

Lizzie scanned the room, watching the bookcase filled with books by deep thinkers so intensely that sometimes they shifted in and out of their positions on the shelves in her mind. Anything was better than looking into Dr. Stewart's overly scrutinizing face. The doctor seemed to look at Lizzie like her own personal mountain to climb, a sixteen-year-old with a severe case of post-traumatic stress disorder. Lately, Lizzie had become Dr. Stewart's Achilles heel, but she was determined to make things easier for the child.

"How are you feeling today, Lizzie?" Dr. Stewart

asked Lizzie, pen tip pressed into her notebook page, waiting for an answer worth scribbling down.

"Not so good, Dr. Stewart," Lizzie muttered. She watched the doorknob, waiting for the slightest indication that she might be interrupted and relieved of this interrogation. The room was never a comfort to Lizzie. It felt suffocating, with its large chairs taking up too much space, and its small windows, making it difficult for Lizzie's eyes to escape the room. "My sister made me come here."

"Do you think she's wrong in bringing you? Do you feel that you don't need to be here?" The doctor's face remained cautious, but calm, her eyebrows almost touching as she scrunched her face trying to figure out the patient. She turned her head a little to the side, playing with the star-shaped stud in her earlobe, to seem less interrogative. She was the kind of doctor who wanted to make her patients feel like she was a friend and confidante, rather than a behavioral specialist, but after weeks of making circles with Lizzie, Dr. Stewart had grown frustrated with her delusional patient.

"It's not that. I just don't want to leave the house," Lizzie tried not to look at her. The more she looked at her, the tenser her body felt.

"Because you don't like to go outside?" They had had this conversation several times, but it seemed to be Lizzie's favorite topic. She spent many sessions complaining about how she didn't want to be there until at last she could leave.

"Right. If I go outside, he'll find me." Lizzie concentrated on her fingernails, picking them and then, after she was tired of that, she traced the lines on her hands.

"Do you feel safe with your sister?"

Day after day this incessant questioning went on and still nothing ever changed. Lizzie could feel the fatigue in her face and her heart felt frail, like it would burst if she had to live with another minute of this.

"He doesn't know where I am, but when he does, he'll come." Lizzie's wandering mind always put Dr. Stewart in an uneasy state. Lizzie noticed it by the way she shifted in her chair and cleared her throat as if she could cough the feeling out. It was not the first time this had happened, and it would not be the last. After Dr. Stewart had adjusted, she sat patiently waiting for Lizzie to regain control over her thoughts.

"Yes, but do you feel safe with your sister, Lizzie?"

"Of course I do. She protects me. I would already be dead if she hadn't found me," Lizzie said, biting her nails instead of picking at them.

"Well, she's right outside the door. Do you still think you're in danger here?" Dr. Stewart pointed to the door, and Lizzie could picture Jen behind it, ear gently pressed to the wood, listening intently for anything out of place, her red hair falling in her face.

"I guess not. It still won't help when he finds me," she said.

"Why don't we talk about that night, okay? I want you to tell me everything you remember."

Lizzie cradled herself in her arms, shivering. "I've already told you a thousand times, but you still don't believe me. Once he realizes I'm here, it'll all happen again."

"I know you've told me before, but I would like to hear it again. You've been suppressing some powerful memories. Once you unlock those memories, you will be able to move forward with your life and heal. Would you like to feel better, Lizzie?"

"No, I can't. I can't remember. It doesn't make sense in my head." Lizzie had held the memories back for so long that she had been able to keep them from herself. It was only in small glimpses that they would appear to her throughout her day, triggering a psychotic episode until she was able to push the image back down in her mind again.

"That's okay. You don't have to try to make sense of it yet. Just close your eyes and visualize the place. Try to gather as many details in your mind as possible. What did it look like? What did it smell like? Does that help?"

"I can't. I don't want to," Lizzie said, her mind beginning to form the image while she tried to push it back.

"Can you try for me? It will help you feel better. Don't let your fear overpower you. It's time for you to take charge of your life."

Lizzie bit her lip and closed her eyes, trying to focus in on the fuzzy image of the darkened room. She entered the back of her mind and latched on to the memory.

Dr. Stewart cleared her throat again. "Now, describe to me what you see."

"It's really dark. There's just gray. Gray floor, gray walls, and blue. Not blue." Lizzie could feel the tears begin to form.

"What's blue, Lizzie?" Nothing. "Lizzie, tell me what's blue?"

"Oh!" Lizzie cried, tears trickling down her cheek. "No, no, no."

"What's happening, Lizzie?"

"Pain. Everything's going black. I can't see. I think I'm dead, but I'm waking up under my bed with my sister Jen standing over me. I have to leave." Lizzie began to rise from her chair, but Dr. Stewart motioned for her to sit again.

"Is there anything else you can remember? Anything you might be leaving out?" Dr. Stewart said it so quietly Lizzie almost didn't hear her, but when she did, she opened her eyes again, the memory fading into the back of her mind.

"No. I've already told you there's nothing more. Why do you keep asking me that?" Lizzie rocked back and forth impatiently in her chair. "Can I go home now?"

"What about James? Can you tell me about him?" \

Lizzie burst into tears. James had always been the best big brother in the world. He still was in Lizzie's eyes, no matter what they said. "James is dead. What more do you want me to say?" she said, pulling on her hair.

"Lizzie, I need you to calm down, okay? It's important for you to try to unlock that memory. I know you're afraid, but it might help your flashbacks if you stop suppressing your memories. Can you tell me where James was?"

An image of her brother flashed before Lizzie's eyes, and she pulled her feet from the floor, climbing higher into her chair. Dr. Stewart tried to calm her by getting her to sit down before she fell off the chair's back, but Lizzie didn't even realize she was there. She saw blood, oozing out of a hole in James's head, darkening his brown hair. She remembered the sound of his body, smacking against the concrete and the splatter of blood on her feet.

"No," she shrieked, leaping out of her chair, and knocking the table over.

She threw all the papers on the floor and tore everything from the shelves. Jen, her big sister, rushed in through the doorway, and Lizzie could hear Dr. Stewart scolding her for interrupting. She still believed that she was in control of her patient, but Jen didn't care what she wanted. Jen grabbed Lizzie to stop her from thrashing, and she sank to the floor, realizing that James wasn't really there. They stayed there a moment, Jen rocking her in her arms while Lizzie kept yelling, "My brother loved my family, and he would never hurt me. He was protecting me, and that bastard killed him."

"Shhh…it's okay. Everything's going to be okay." Jen could always soothe her.

Lizzie knew how guilty her sister felt for allowing the therapy to go on, but she was running out of options. Lizzie sobbed loudly into Jen's blouse, the buttons bumping into her nose.

"Ms. Moore, can I please speak with you privately for a moment?" Dr. Stewart asked.

Jen nodded. She helped Lizzie, who was shaking, off the floor and pointed to the hallway. Lizzie shook her head, clinging to her sister's arm. She scrunched her body to make it as small as possible. She was taller than Jen, even though Jen was seven years older.

Any time Lizzie had a public breakdown, people would stare in bewilderment at this towering girl trying to nestle her body under the arm of someone at least five inches shorter than she.

"Lizzie, sweetheart, can you go wait out there for a second? I promise I'll be there very soon."

Jen gently pulled Lizzie off her arm, gathering Lizzie's hands together so she was left outside the doorway, hugging herself. They closed the door on her, leaving Lizzie sniffling on the other side, still shaking.

"Your sister is out of control. Her outbursts have gotten worse, and I'm worried she may become a danger to herself and others. I'm going to recommend a psychiatrist at one of the local centers. She may have to be hospitalized for a little while for some treatment." Dr. Stewart tried to whisper it to Jen, but Lizzie could still hear.

"No. Lizzie isn't going to stay at a hospital. She's too afraid to leave the house without me. How could I put her there? No. She was doing better before I brought her here. Maybe we could try an at-home treatment. Do you do house calls?"

"I'm sorry, but I think it would be better for Lizzie if she were put into a safer environment until her episodes subside. Your sister is extremely ill. She is a danger to herself and those around her, and I can't ignore my concern. I think she needs more intensive therapy and medication."

Lizzie bit her lip. She wasn't sure if she should stay and listen or run. She couldn't go to some hospital unprotected. He would find her there.

"Medication? Yes, that's all you quacks think about. Let's just hop her up on drugs and make her so high she can't remember her problems. No, we tried that in California and it just made her even more unstable. I won't let my sister become some lab experiment for the next medical cure. She doesn't need a pill, she needs comfort and love."

Lizzie had never heard Jen spit so much venom in her words before. It felt kind of good to know someone hadn't given up on her. Jen was the only reason Lizzie even tried at all. A wave of guilt hit her mind when she thought about how little she'd been trying lately.

"I have to disagree. I think your sister relies too much on your care and maybe that care isn't the best situation for her anymore. Lizzie needs to learn to become self-reliant and to know that the world is a safe place for her. I highly recommend that you find her better care, even if that means she doesn't stay with you." As Dr. Stewart finished her sentence, Jen was silent. Lizzie could almost sense the heat of her anger through the door.

When Jen finally spoke, she was surprisingly calm, but firm. "I'm taking her home where she feels safe. It has done her more good than your crack job methods of cure. All you're doing is reminding her every day and scaring her to death. My sister belongs with me. Thank you for your time, Dr. Stewart, but your services will no longer be required. I'm sorry I made this mistake."

"I'm afraid you're making a huge mistake now. Your sister needs proper care in an orderly place," she said as Jen was opening the door.

These words were a little louder with an intention to draw Lizzie in to them, as if understanding them would help Lizzie now.

"My sister needs the love and support of someone who's not going to accuse her of lying every time she wants to talk about it. We'll just have to figure out some other solution."

When Jen opened the outside door, Lizzie exhaled a small sigh of relief, but her relief was halted by the sight of Joel waiting for them downstairs in the lobby. Lizzie's smile turned into a scowl, and suddenly she felt the need to bite someone.

Jen and Joel had been dating ever since they had moved here about two months ago, and Lizzie wanted him gone. He looked normal enough: thick brown, spiky hair, brown eyes, and an athletic build from all those handyman jobs he had, but he was almost too perfect for her taste. Lizzie stared at his face again, trying to find something she didn't like, and decided that his ears were too big and ape-like to fit the rest of his image, and he almost never smiled a full smile. He would give her one of those slight smiles where the corners barely lifted, but never a full smile with shiny teeth and dimpled cheeks. Something about his smile bothered her.

"Hi, Lizzie. How are you feeling today?" He opened the front door for her as he gave that signature smile. Lizzie tried not to gag from disgust. Then he opened the car door for Jen. Lizzie couldn't help wondering why he was trying so hard.

"How do you think I'm feeling, Joe?" Lizzie called him Joe to annoy him. Lizzie hated when he was around because, truth was, she needed her sister, and he was a distraction. It was selfish, but she couldn't help the feeling. She kept hoping she could push him far enough to give up, but he took in whatever she threw at him with almost no reaction.

"Let's just get Lizzie home where she feels safe so she can rest. She's had a very strenuous day."

Jen had to play referee every time Lizzie got like this. Lizzie felt bad for treating her sister this way. Jen was there for her when everyone else abandoned her, but Lizzie couldn't help it. Somewhere deep inside her was that little voice that said her snarky attitude was undeserved, but it was hidden in a place she never seemed to reach. It was her defense mechanism.

"Of course—back to that dark, dismal basement where the ravenous pitbulls can gnaw at my legs while I starve to death in bloody oblivion." There it went again, Lizzie's infamous word vomit spilling out of her mouth before she could control it.

Joel never understood Lizzie's sour sarcasm. He just took it at face value, accepting that Lizzie, in her unstable mental state, believed all of these things. None of that was true. Lizzie didn't believe Jen would hurt her, but she knew someone out there would, and if she didn't pretend to sarcastically enjoy the thoughts, they would bubble out of her head in fear and she'd implode.

"You know your sister would never lock you up."

Joel always came to Jen's aid, but that only provoked Lizzie more. Her sister was a strong, independent woman. She didn't need someone like Joel defending her. The whole thing made Lizzie nauseous. She could just picture it now. A penny rolling along a sidewalk and as Joel went to pick it up a piano drops on top of his head like those crazy cartoons. Lizzie had a very vivid imagination lately. "Maybe one of these days when you feel better, we can all go out to dinner together. Doesn't that sound like fun?"

"Hmmm…go out to dinner with Jen and Joe, or stay home and rot? Personally, I think I'll take my chances with ravenous dogs gnawing on my head. At least they would be merciful and end the torture quickly."

"Lizzie, that's enough!" Jen said, but Lizzie was just getting started.

"What do you think of me now, JoJo, old boy? Huh? Do you think I'm crazy yet? Well…guess it's too late for me now, JoJo. I'm going round the bend. I've lost all my marbles. I flew over the cuckoo's nest. What do you think of that, JoJo chap? Well, I do believe, sir, that you have lost all your marbles. Now would you care for some tea and crumpets? Huh?"

He smiled at Lizzie again. "I don't think you're crazy. You must be suffering from some neurological breakdown, but soon you'll feel much better. Not to mention that your behavior's a reflection of your incessant need for attention."

Flames of hate slithered up her spine until they reached her face. They flickered over it just enough for her cheeks to boil and her brain to heat as the comment registered with it.

Jen gave them both a look that could have scared a soldier and, for the rest of the ride Lizzie was silent, lost in her thoughts of sheer loathing.

Chapter 5

Brian

February 2002:

It was Mom's birthday again and their father had decided to work late instead of face another memory of his wife. Having their father home only meant excessive drinking, yelling, and hitting, so the children didn't mind the absence. The first year had been hard without their father there to comfort them, but they had adjusted, pulling from the strength of each other to keep going.

"Let's make some cupcakes," Shelley said, pulling the flour from the cupboard.

"Why,?" Brian asked, watching his sister shuffling through drawers and setting stuff onto the kitchen counter.

"Because Mommy would've made some," she said, opening the pantry door. "I can't find a cookbook?"

"Mom's not here to eat them, Shelley," Brian said, trying to be reasonable.

"Well, so? She made cookies for my stuffed animals, and they couldn't eat them either," she said.

"Do you even know how to make cupcakes?"

Brian was getting frustrated. Mom was dead. What

was the point to all of this? Dad would be home in a few hours, and they would all go to bed without this day being any different than the other days in this month. Of course it was also Valentine's Day, but he really didn't care that much about girls yet. Sure, they weren't gross anymore, but they weren't that fun to deal with either, especially if they were as silly as his sister.

"I thought you could teach me," she said, face beginning to pucker, lip quivering. "I can't find the book."

"I'll go get it," he said, rolling his eyes.

She was always doing things like this, no plan whatsoever, just barreling through her impulses until she was satisfied. If she had planned, they would have a cake mix and some frosting, but whether or not they had the things they needed to make these awful cupcakes mattered little to Shelley. She would find a way, because it was what was important at the moment.

He pulled an old recipe box down from the shelf and picked out the recipe that looked the easiest. He gathered the ingredients together and step by step went through the process of showing her how to make the cupcakes. She squealed excitedly when he put the pan into the oven and he smiled, relieved that he had managed to at least keep her happy for the afternoon and take his mind off his mother. Of course, they didn't have any frosting for when they came out of the oven, but Michelle didn't seem to mind. She took a big bite, spilling bits of cupcake onto the floor. She laughed, kicking the crumbs away, and took another bite.

As Brian took a bite of his cupcake, he heard the slamming of the door. He scanned the messy table as the footsteps grew louder down the hallway.

"What the hell is this?" his father said, appearing in the doorway.

Brian set his cupcake on the counter, too nervous to

eat under the watchful suspicions of his father. "I was going to clean it up," he said, trying not to stare into his eyes.

"Oh, you were going to clean it up, were you? When was that exactly? When I beat into your head not to make a mess in my house?"

He balled his hand into a fist and Brian backed away from his father. He wasn't sure what would come next, but he knew the amount of pain it would bring. His brain began to unravel from itself as he tried to think of a way to escape, but there never was one.

He could feel the fear building and he just wanted to make it all stop.

"It's my fault too, Daddy, I made him make—"

"You, shut up! I don't want to hear another peep out of you, and don't you dare stick that finger in your mouth or I'll pull it off," his father yelled, pointing a finger at his sister. He hardly ever hit her. Usually he would send her to her room while he punished Brian. This used to annoy Brian because he was never given protection from his father, but he soon realized that she wouldn't have safety for long. "Get over here, boy."

Brian shook his head, planning out an escape route. He darted for the door, but his father caught his shirt. He tried to slide out of it and his father yanked him back with a laugh. He pulled him to the ground and kicked him in the stomach to get him to stay down.

"Did you really think you were going to outrun me? You're a stupid, lazy piece of shit that couldn't outrun a ladybug. Get up already, you wimp, and you quit whimpering right now, or so help me, I'm going to smack you 'til your head rolls off." He pulled Brian up from the floor and Michelle burst into tears. Their father turned on her, releasing his grip on his son.

He charged on his daughter, smacking her hard

across the face. She leaned back and fell to the ground, tears turning into hysterical sobs.

"I told you to shut up."

A flicker of anger burst forth from Brian's soul at the sight of his sister on the ground, and he charged at his father, slapping him across the back. The hit did nothing but anger him more.

He turned toward his son, picking up the cupcake pan and beating him on the head with it. Brian curled into a ball on the ground, hands covering his head as best they could. The pain stung across his fingers and his hands, but the throbbing in his head was far worse than anything he'd ever felt. He sobbed openly, not seeing any point in trying to hold it in. His father threw the pan across the room and picked up his son again. Brian tried to make it harder, throwing all his body weight into the ground, but he was a lean boy, so his father had no trouble with his flailing son. He opened the door to the pantry and stuffed the protesting boy in, locking the door behind him.

Brian pounded on the door, screaming, but his father wouldn't listen. Then he heard his sister's screams and his head started to spin. He had to protect her. It was his job to protect her and he couldn't. He settled onto the floor, tears in his eyes and covered his ears, trying desperately to block out the sound, but he couldn't.

His mind went black, a darkness entering his brain that Brian didn't know existed. It crept through the caverns of his brain like poison spreads through veins. Since his mother's death, his brain had tried to compartmentalize itself by transferring his painful memories to some other source, and in order to do that, it had to create something new, another essence to protect Brian from his frailties.

The noise suddenly stopped, and his father swung the door open.

"Brian, clean up this mess, and don't let me catch you making one again, you got it?" his father said, hand still balled into a fist.

"Yes, sir," he replied, staring into his father's gaze with unflinching eyes.

It never occurred to his father that there was something different about his son, but Brian had no desire to tell his father what it was either. After all, who would believe that anyone could be two people at once? When his father walked away, he smiled, whispering to himself, "It's Brian Matthew, Father."

Chapter 6

May 2002:

The weather was beginning to get too hot for long sleeves. While the other boys couldn't wait to throw on their T-shirts and shorts, Brian was running out of explanations for the bruises on his body.

He hated living with his father, but he couldn't lose Shelley. He'd heard bad things about foster care. They'd separate them, bouncing them around California until he had no idea how to find his sister again. He could endure a few more years to stay with her. He sat in study hall, drawing and thinking about what might be waiting for him when he got home. He was a quiet kid with few friends, but he didn't seem to mind. Even when he was by himself he never really felt alone anymore. Sometimes he would talk to himself as he drew.

"Needs more shading," he would say to himself and then wonder why he had suddenly noticed it.

Mrs. London, his study hall and history teacher, seemed to watch him while he drew. Brian tried to ignore her presence, but her interest scared him. If she found out the truth, he would be without his truest friend. She never said anything. Sometimes she would walk the aisles to see what the children were working on, but she went to her desk without a single whisper. When the bell rang, she signaled him to her desk.

"Your grades are starting to slip again, Brian," she said. "Is everything okay?"

"Yes ma'am," he said automatically. He had been hearing this ever since his mother died. He would be doing well in his classes then suddenly not remember the material they had been discussing. His grades would decline, and his father would be called in. The teachers suggested it was a lack of focus and some medication would fix it. His father thought it was laziness. "I just have trouble remembering things. It doesn't always stay in my head if I learn it."

"Well, then you're not really learning it properly, are you? Perhaps I could show you some ways to keep track of everything. Would you like that?"

Brian had heard and done it all before: the flashcards, the repetition, the acronyms and acrostics, but with little success. How could he remember something when he could barely remember learning it at all? He looked at Mrs. London, wondering if he should tell her this, but decided against it. He knew she wouldn't understand. He didn't understand it either. He nodded, agreeing to go over it with her next study hall. He hurried out of the room.

He wasn't used to running late for gym class. He usually ran to the locker room to change before the other boys arrived. They wouldn't understand his bruises, and he had no intention of explaining them to a bunch of childish boys. They already teased Brian for the way he spoke, acted, and thought. He really didn't need to give them more reasons for thinking he was a freak.

"What took you so long, loser?" Andrew, one of the most persistent kids, asked.

Brian didn't respond. He had hoped that ignoring

him would work better than all the failed responses of the past.

Andrew didn't find this reaction any better than the others. "I'm talking to you," he said as Brian tried to squish into a corner for more privacy while he changed. Andrew strode across the room and gave him a shove into the wall. "I'm talking to you. Jeez, when did you get so weird?"

"After his mother died. He's probably got brain damage," another boy said.

"Is that it? You miss your mommy, retard?"

Brian had been through this several times before. Usually, he waited it out until Andrew and his friends lost interest. It had given him satisfaction to know that it bothered them when he didn't react. Brian wasn't a fighter, but he was never alone. From within, Brian Matthew was there, always waiting for Brian to be at his weakest so that he could be.

He knew all about Brian, and realized that he couldn't exist without him. He wanted to learn. He'd slip in and out of his mind while Brian was studying. He knew that Columbus sailed in 1492 and FDR was president during World War II. At home, Brian Matthew was stronger. He took the pain long after he thought the body would break, and Brian's mind was in disarray. At Brian's weakest, Brian Matthew was at his strongest, and Brian was feeling weak now. He receded inside himself and blacked out, unknowingly letting Brian Matthew take over.

"What did you call me?" Brian Matthew shoved Andrew, and his friends seemed surprised.

"I called you a retard. I would say it's from your mother, but she's dead so I guess we'll never know." Andrew shoved Brian Matthew hard, and Brian Matthew lost control. He charged Andrew like a football player, knocking him to the ground. They rolled on the floor punching each other. One of the boys tried to interfere, and Brian Matthew kicked him in the knee. He beat at Andrew's face wildly until he heard a pop and his nose started to drip. Andrew squealed and tried to protect his face with his hands.

"Stop it. Stop it," one of the boys said, grabbing Brian Matthew's arm.

Brian Matthew found himself unable to stop. He could see his father's face and every punch gave him more satisfaction. Someone ran from the room and appeared a minute later with the gym teacher.

"Enough, Brian," he yelled, and Brian Matthew realized what he had done.

He looked down at the boy, fist still in the air, and receded back into the mind. Brian scanned the room to see what was happening, uncertain of how he got on the floor. He pulled himself back up and stared down at Andrew, nose bloodied.

"What happened?" Brian asked, feeling lost. Brian Matthew remained silent, watching the mess he had caused. "I don't—"

"You're both coming with me," the teacher said, helping Andrew to his feet. Brian followed behind them down the hall, still unsure of what had taken place.

Chapter 7

Lizzie

August 2012:

Pulling into the driveway, Lizzie was relieved to see their old house again. The house was way out in what some would call "the boondocks." Jen felt it best that Lizzie stay out of the city for now, or at least what the Mainers would consider the city. It was really a small town built on a lake and surrounding rivers.

Her house was wedged on the top of a hill in the middle of a wooded area where the neighbors were a twenty minute walk away. There were a few trees in the backyard and then a large strip of open field filled with dandelions and wildflowers, where the road stretched on for miles. The road swerved on to a dirt path that circled around to their house.

As Jen pulled into the driveway, Lizzie noticed that the house was a dark gray with black shades, three stories, and a slanted roof that had black tiles on it. Lizzie hadn't really paid attention to much since she got here. She would try to focus on something, but then it would morph into something else, fading like a splash of watercolors on her eyes until there was nothing at all.

The front yard consisted of a bunch of dead leaves and weeds. There was one random tree in the front yard that had been struck by lightning many years ago. It was already late afternoon, and the limited streak of sun glowed against the tree's cracked and blackened trunk.

Lizzie was surprised when a boy was waiting on the front steps. He was hunched over, half asleep, listening to his neon green iPod. His face looked somewhat familiar. Lizzie tried to focus her thoughts enough to wander back in time to a place where she had known him: his light gray eyes contrasting with his thick chestnut hair. All her memories were beginning to fade. She couldn't even remember the last time she felt happy. As they approached the boy, Lizzie noticed a lump on the bridge of his nose. She feebly recalled her hitting a baseball into his face.

"Hey, how've you been? I haven't seen you in months." He greeted Lizzie so warmly that she was immediately repulsed by him. What reason could he possibly have to be so cheerful? A few images flashed quickly through her mind, but they were so jumbled together that she had a hard time piecing them together to come up with a name for this boy.

"Who are you supposed to be? The magical fairy of happiness?" Her attitude made him feel awkward, and he kicked his feet together as he spoke.

"Well, I got kicked out of school, so my parents sent me here to live with my grandma. They say that she'll keep me in line. I had heard you moved out here, so Grandma dropped me off to visit with you. I figured you wouldn't mind." When he spoke, the slight fogginess in her brain subsided, and she remembered it was Nick.

His grandmother had been the one to suggest that they move here in the first place. Lizzie couldn't believe she hadn't recognized him. It had only been about three months, and he hadn't really changed much—a little taller and muscular maybe, but nothing too out of the ordinary. He had been an important part of her California life, but he'd also been the last person she saw before—no, she didn't want to think about the accident right now.

"Whatever." Lizzie ushered him through the doorway.

"It's good to see you again. A friendly face is exactly what Ms. Grumpy Pants needs," Jen said warmly as she brought the groceries in. Apparently Jen thought that this pathetic, overly happy lump would be therapeutic for her.

In the front hall was the staircase. It wound around in a circle, and at the tippy top of the stairs was the entrance to the tower. This was where Lizzie prowled in her domain. It was the only place she felt safe anymore, and the place she couldn't wait to return to. It had a darkness to it that she loved, even though she was afraid of the darkness. She knew that eventually he would pull her back down in it to die, so she prepared herself, embracing the fear that kept her up at night. She stomped up the stairs to her domain and he followed along like a little lost puppy, unsure of what he was supposed to do.

"Whoa…" he said, entering her room. It was painted black with dark purple streaks along the top of the walls. It only had one tiny window that Lizzie kept thick black lace curtains over. Everything in the room was dark. Not a single light or bright color could be found, except for her hot pink bedspread. "Nobody back home is going to believe that the cheer queen has transformed into the queen of the night."

Cheer queen? Images flooded back to Lizzie's head. A series of lines of fifteen girls all dressed in blue and silver uniforms. Fifteen girls dancing to the rhythm of the songs, and one girl in the middle becoming the center of the universe.

Lizzie was captain of her cheer squad and voted best dressed in her freshman class.

Nick had been her best friend, a member of the soccer team and president of his class. Everything had been boys and make up, dances and dates. Her whole life revolved around her friends, and she was the center peg in their social circle or at least, she was in her mind. They had quickly forgotten her after she was pulled from school when she had her first flashback. Regardless, she had had a beautiful life. Her grades were remarkable, at least pretty good for her standards, and she was well loved. She was the only daughter of the wealthiest couple in wine country and was lavished with gifts every day. She also had the greatest big brother in the world, who loved her like a sister, even though he knew she didn't belong to them. What more could she have asked for?

Apparently Jen thought she needed a sister, because the minute Jen turned eighteen, she came back for Lizzie and, after three years of searching, she showed up on her parent's doorstep. Jen hadn't received the luxuries that Lizzie had. From what she had told Lizzie, she was bounced from one foster home to another until she was old enough to take care of herself. All that meant to Lizzie was that she didn't know what a family was and wanted to invade Lizzie's.

Lizzie didn't want her sister. She didn't need to know her "real" family. The whole concept was absurd—stuck in some stupid apartment with her idiotic sister who insisted on "getting to know" her, as if Jen was going to be a big part of her life after almost ten years. So what if Jen was her blood sister? Lizzie had been adopted when she was a baby, and that gave her parents and a great big brother. They didn't need some girl coming in and breaking up their happy family, but Jen had argued her case well to Lizzie's parents.

"But you and I can really get to know each other again. I want to see how great my little sister has turned out, and your adoptive parents are okay with me being around," Jen said.

Adoptive parents? They had never been anything but Mom and Dad. They were the only family she knew, and the only family she wanted. No matter how much she pleaded with them, they insisted she get to know her sister. Families shouldn't fall apart, they told her. If this woman wanted to get to know her then she would, begrudgingly, make an attempt and if the nights she slept over at her sister's house turned out bad, Lizzie had friends just around the corner.

Nick had always been the closest to her. He comforted her over the phone until she fell asleep the whole first night at Jen's. That was the hardest day there. Eventually Lizzie adjusted and the two grew closer—until the night Lizzie stormed out.

Thinking about it now made Lizzie's head flood with images again, images she'd been pushing back. Lizzie shook her head, trying to shake the memory from her brain. She didn't want to think about this right now. She just wanted to be a normal girl, normal Lizzie, back home living her perfect life when her parents still loved her and her brother, James, had still been alive.

"Lizzie? Are you okay?" Nick grabbed for her arm but she yanked it away. Her head was throbbing as she tried to pull away from her memories. They were sucking out her energy. A loud ringing pierced her ear canals. Around her, the world started spinning. She saw a flash of glitter from her pink laptop, sitting on her desk. She saw a flash of stripes from across her walls. She even saw the glow of Nick's neon iPod spinning and swirling in front of her, and the whole time the ringing kept beating in her ears.

"No," she shrieked, knocking her nightstand to the floor, tipping over a cup of water from the night before. "Make it stop."

"Lizzie." Jen was running up the stairs. Nick, frightened, ran out the door. Lizzie was glad he did, because her anger was mounting and she didn't want to hurt him. The ringing grew louder and louder, pounding into her brain. It hurt so bad she thought her ears would bleed. Jen grabbed her in her arms. Lizzie pulled on them and tried to scratch herself with her nails. Jen made sure Lizzie's nails never grew long after Lizzie started scratching herself in her sleep. Jen closed her hands over Lizzie's to stop her. "Shh…it's okay. What's the matter?"

"Make it all stop. Make the ringing go away. I can't take it anymore." Tears streamed down her cheeks.

"It's okay—everything is going to be okay. There's nothing here that will hurt you. The ringing will stop soon. Take a deep breath and relax. It'll go away, I promise. Nothing's going to happen again."

Lizzie did as she was told and the ringing stopped. Her memories sank to the back of her thoughts and all was at peace again.

Jen brought Lizzie to her bed and helped her under the covers. It always made her feel like an even bigger child than she already was, but having her sister tuck her in always made her feel protected.

"It's just a bad flashback, but now it's over and everything is all right. Get some rest, okay. Maybe later, we can talk if you want. What your mind needs right now is some uninterrupted sleep. I'll be right downstairs if you need me."

Lizzie snuggled into her cocoon of blankets for a few moments but she couldn't sleep. She heard Jen downstairs walking to the door. Sneakily, Lizzie crept out of bed and opened the door just enough to peek, but she couldn't see much. She eased herself a few steps down the winding staircase. Nick was getting ready to leave, confused and shaken. Jen was trying to scoot him out the door while answering as little questions as possible.

"Is she okay? Does she need me to stay with her? Because I can totally do that if—" Nick said, still unsure what had happened.

"My sister isn't well. I'll call your grandma sometime when I feel it's best for you to visit. Please don't come unexpectedly again. Lizzie needs her rest. Your grandma should be here soon. Why don't you just wait outside?" Jen did everything she could, except for physically throwing him out, to get Nick on the porch. He reluctantly left, still troubled and bewildered. A few minutes later, Lizzie heard the gravel of the dirt sputter under the tires of a car as it came and went.

Lizzie got back into bed. She snuggled farther into her blankets, but instead of getting comfortable, she felt more and more restless. She tossed and turned for several minutes, switching directions until she felt that she had covered every inch of the bed. Knowing that sleep wasn't in her near future, she arose from her bed again.

She scanned her room, taking small steps to keep herself alert, but nobody was there. She slowly turned the knob on her door and peered down her staircase. Her sister's bedroom was the first door by the stairs, and the curving steps provided the perfect carrier for sound. She wasn't sure if she was saying anything, but she knew Jen was in her room. Lizzie crept down her winding stairs and leaned against her sister's door, where she thought she heard whispering. She peeked in through a crack and spotted Jen sitting cross-legged on her bed, speaking to Joel as he sprawled out behind her. A moment of fear hit Lizzie when she realized they were talking about her.

"What am I going to do with her, Joel? I don't know

what else there is. I can't put her in a hospital." She massaged her temples. Stress had given Jen headaches that made her irritable, but she tried to restrain it around Lizzie.

"Putting her in a hospital would be the last thing she needs right now. You can't keep her locked away from the world forever. School will be starting soon, and I think the best thing for Lizzie is to put her back into her normal routine. She can never face reality if you continue to let her live on the outskirts of it." He rose from his position and scooped Jen in his arms lovingly, trying to comfort her and be firm at the same time.

"I know I've sheltered her too much, but I don't think she's ready yet. What if she can't handle it? What if she never goes back to herself?"

Her sister worried so much about her, but the truth was that Jen was right. Lizzie wasn't ready to face all those new people. She could tell already that Joel was going to make sure that happened whether she liked it or not. He didn't care about her. He just wanted some "alone time" with Jen. There wasn't any evidence to support her thoughts, but she still felt them. She didn't really hate Joel. She hated the idea of sharing Jen. Lizzie would be dead soon and Jen would be able to move on with her life then. Why couldn't he just leave them alone so her sister wouldn't get distracted? Lizzie knew the whole thing was unfair, but every time she promised herself she would try harder, something would happen and she'd have to start all over again.

"I know, but sometimes you just have to take the risk. The longer she's isolated, the harder it'll be to integrate her back into her normal life. She'll become too used to having that security all the time. She has to learn that bad things happen and you've got to deal with them in a calmer manner. I don't mean to be harsh because I worry about her too, and I know she has been through a traumatic ordeal but too much compassion will only hurt her in the end. She's not a baby anymore." There was a strange glint in his eye that Lizzie noticed every once in a while when he looked at Jen. He smiled big and kissed her on the cheek. "Besides, she's a tough cookie, like her sister."

"I guess that's pretty true," Jen said. "I am pretty awesome, aren't I?"

"The best," Joel said, giving her a full kiss on the lips.

Lizzie gagged a little and snuck back up the stairs. She shut the door gently, and shuffled back to her bed, pulling the covers back over her head. The argument was definitely over, and Joel had won. She would be attending school soon.

She buried her face in her pillow and hoped that sleep would come, but it had been elusive. It was impossible to drift to sleep with so many crazy thoughts running in her head. Images would dance around in her mind, changing mechanically from one to the next, never in any particular order. How would Lizzie be able to focus her mind for school when she couldn't even focus it to rest? Her head was always spinning.

She tried counting sheep, but then a thousand questions would pop into her mind. Why count sheep? Why not count fish? What color were the sheep? Why would the sheep jump over the fence? What if they were gobbled up by the wolf? She felt her body sliding into slumber and she gave in to it. Before she could realize it, she had been pulled into a dream.

Lizzie arose from her bed suddenly. The thunder boomed in the background and she could hear the hard pounding of the raindrops on the roof. She glided across the room in her fuzzy pajamas. Among the flashes of lightning she could see her door slightly ajar. When she opened it, she was in her adoptive parents' second home, a house on the shore for summer break.

Was that how I left it? Lizzie wondered. Every step she took the floor creaked loudly. Each sound became a series of words: *no, stop, don't go*. When she eased open the door it screamed with fright.

It's just a dream, she thought. Her brother, James, lay dead on the floor. His auburn hair was matted against the floor, blood was running from his temple and his hazel eyes were glazed over, staring out into space. *It's just a dream. It's just a dream.* Then his body jolted upward and hit the ground hard again. Blood rippled out of his body, covering the hallway. She could feel the sticky liquid between her toes and the smell of copper drifted into her nostrils, causing her stomach to churn.

I have to get to Jen. Lizzie headed toward her sister's door, but something smashed against it. Then the most terrifying shrill echoed through the house followed by a small, wheezing gasp. Someone fumbled for the doorknob and the floorboards shrieked again as Lizzie backed up slowly. *Get out now.* The door flew open as Lizzie sprinted down the stairs. She could hear the heavy footsteps clumping down the steps after her. He was a big man. That was something Lizzie vaguely remembered. But when she tried to escape before, he had turned into a nimble tiger ready to pounce, quick and steady in every motion. This time his movements seemed more painful. *Jen must have given him a run for his money*, she thought.

Lizzie sprinted out into the rain. Her old house didn't have stairs to the back door because her parents were remodeling. She forgot that and tumbled down the edge to the ground. Rain poured all over her, soaking her in a muddy haze. She dashed for the woods. *Woods? We live by the beach.* There was no way he could find her in complete darkness and shelter. Lizzie found a nice spot behind some blackberry bushes. The thorns stung at first, but she became numb to them. The key was survival, and a little pain could be endured if that gave her a greater chance.

Muddy footsteps sloshed by her. Her heart pounded in her chest. Her breathing was virtually non-existent. One small sound and he would be slashing right into her. A few feet away he stopped and turned around. The booming got louder, ringing through her entire body, screeching in her ears. Step...step...step...he slowly moved back toward her. He peeled back the bushes, and Lizzie's green eyes met those burning blue ones piercing her face.

"We see you." He smiled and, as he did, he lifted something out of his pocket, a veined eye. He twiddled it between his thumb and pointer finger like a marble. The coloring was very distinct, exotic looking. It resembled a reddish brown with flecks of gold, like the color of autumn leaves. *Jen.* Lizzie screamed while the sinister laugh ricocheted through the forest.

"Lizzie. Lizzie, wake up," a voice shouted to her. Hands tried to grab her, but she kicked and shrieked as hard as she could. The hands pinned her down and she tried to wriggle away. "Lizzie, it's okay. It's just me."

Lizzie shot awake to find Jen gently rocking her in her arms. She could feel the sweat pouring off her face. Those feverish eyes were stamped into her mind. Lizzie got up and went to the bathroom. The cool water on her face felt soothing, relieving that burning sensation all over her. She gazed at herself in the mirror. Her hair was all amiss and her skin was paler than usual. Her eyes were dark and sunken.

Could all that have really been a dream? It was so

vivid that it seemed unlikely. But there Jen was, completely unharmed, trying again to help comfort her. Lizzie was tired of this pain and fear. She was tired of Jen taking care of her, of her throwing away her life to watch Lizzie. Of course, Lizzie complained about Joel from time to time, but the truth was Joel was the only thing Jen had left.

She had quit her job, moved from her home, and left all her friends behind. Here, she didn't have time to make new ones and, for the first few months, didn't step out of the house unless she had to take Lizzie to her appointments. Lizzie didn't want it to have to be that way for her. So Lizzie did what she had to do. She shut down entirely, finding a way to become numb to her feelings. If she could fake it long enough, her sister might believe she had moved on and be able to move on as well.

Her sister tucked her back in and kissed her good night, and Lizzie did nothing. She watched the ceiling for a little while until her eyes grew heavy and her vision blurry with sleep.

Chapter 8

Brian Matthew

January 2005:

Brian Matthew had come home late again, and his father decided to beat the time into his head. The pain became insignificant over the years. With the help of another, a second other existing in Brian's body, Brian Matthew learned to embrace the pain and use it for a later purpose. When he was finished with Brian, his father screamed at his sister, "You get your ass in here and make me something to eat!"

"I have to do homework."

"Homework, my ass." He wobbled into the next room. Over the years, he had developed a system to his drunken balance. He grabbed her by the hair, dragging her into the kitchen. She fought him, biting down hard when she got hold of his hand. He knocked her into the wall. "You stupid bitch! You're as bad as your mother!"

Brian Matthew could hear Francis growl in the back of his brain. A faint image appeared in his mind and he heard his mother's voice, singing Mockingbird to him. "Hush little baby, don't say a word. Mama's going to buy you a mockingbird." The sound was sweet, like the fluttering of a hummingbird in his ears and, for a moment, he expected to see her heavenly presence beside him. It faded into the background and left him with the other's voice.

Brian, as always, hadn't reacted to the comment. He was as vacant in his own mind now as he had ever been when this other, who called himself Francis, and Brian Matthew were talking. Francis was shouting in his head, voice booming over and over like the pounding of a bongo drum, *Kill him! Kill him!*

Brian Matthew ignored him, humming the song, trying to replicate the sense of her presence. "If that mockingbird don't sing, I'll buy you a diamond ring." Instead, it distorted into a warrior cry in his head.

You have to protect her. Protect her, Francis yelled over and over until he thought his head would burst.

Brian Matthew charged into his father, putting him into the wall. His father slid to the ground and knocked him over at the knees. He caught Brian's neck and started to squeeze, saying, "You think you can take me, boy?"

Then Brian Matthew saw Michelle jump onto his father's back, biting his ear and digging her nails into his shoulders. Their father jumped up, releasing his grip around Brian Matthew's throat. He pulled at her fingers, bending them back, and she crumpled to the ground. Brian Matthew gasped and choked, trying to suck in enough air to keep going. Their father picked his sister up, shaking her out like a dusty welcome mat. Regaining his breath, Brian Matthew rose to his feet.

Kill him! Protect her! This time it was him, echoing the voice's chant. He pulled a knife from the drawer. Looking back, he saw Michelle impale his father's arm with her teeth and he released her, dropping her to the floor.

Brian Matthew ran at him and plunged his knife into

his back with enough force to smack him against the wall. He held him there with his opposite arm as he tried to press the knife as far as it would go. He released his father, pulling the knife from his back. His father hit the floor, gasping for air. His mouth moved angrily, rapidly, but only choking wheezes could escape. The veins on his neck pulsed and enlarged as his skin tinted a sickly white. Brian Matthew leaned in to see the wound. Blood, a foamy pink, bubbled out of it. He was mesmerized by the way it was colored like a trickling, foaming bubble bath. For a moment, he considered doing something to help. Instead, he stood there, holding the knife and looking down at the body as he watched his father go still and pale.

He'll never touch her again, Brian Matthew thought.

Feels good, don't it, Francis said with smug satisfaction.

Michelle, recovering from her own shock, pulled the knife from his hand and dragged him from the scene, but the metallic smell lingered in his nostrils and Brian Matthew realized he didn't hate it.

They cleaned themselves up and left the apartment. He traced the lines on his hands, as she pulled him along, trying to see the red in the creases, but his sister had been thorough in helping remove it. Outside, the afternoon still had its warm light. They took the bus downtown and sat in the park. For a while they were silent. He watched an older woman at a bench farther down from them feeding the pigeons, their bellies fat from her daily service. On the path, a dark-haired woman was jogging along, curly hair bouncing and dog trailing behind her.

"They're going to take you away," his sister said, breaking the silence.

"I know," Brian Matthew said, his mind already far away.

"What should we do?"

"Go to the station and tell the police what happened. They'll find you a place to stay."

"You won't come with me?" she asked, her bottom lip beginning to protrude and quiver.

"I can't."

"But where will you go?"

"Kids disappear all the time in the city." He turned away for a moment, feeling a knot of guilt in his chest.

"And I can't change your mind?"

He could see how much she wanted to. "No."

"I love you, Bubba," she said, reaching to give him a hug, but he pulled away, afraid that he might cry if she did.

"I know."

It's easier not to tell her, Francis said.

But I do love her. I want her to know that, Brian Matthew said.

She knows.

He didn't know when he'd see his sister again, but he refused to drag her down with him. After they had sat some time together in silence, he got up from the bench and started walking down the sidewalk towards some place unknown. As he walked, he started to bite his upper lip and scrunch his face to prevent himself from crying.

Stop being such a weakling, Francis said. *You're strong, remember? You don't need anybody.*

He glanced back at his sister, who was still sitting on the bench. Her head was between her knees with her ponytail flipped down to one side of her cheek. He paused in his movements.

I do need somebody, he told Francis.

He quickly walked back to the bench and stood in front of his sister. She lifted her head when he shifted his feet beside her. Her face was red and wet, with one tear still nestled at the corner of her eye. Brian could feel his own tears choke in his throat, but he couldn't let them free.

Not here, he thought. *Not in front of Shelley.*

He bent down over her and, as gently as he could, wiped the escaping tear from her cheek. Michelle stood up and hugged him around the waist. She was quite tall for her age, but he had recently gone through a growth spurt and managed to tower above her great height. As they hugged, he wondered if they would ever find each other again, but he decided he wasn't certain of anything anymore. He released her and sped forward, making sure not to look back this time.

He took a bus back to the house and gathered as much as his backpack would carry: food, drinks, a change of clothes, and a flashlight. As he hustled down the stairs again, he noticed the door in the kitchen was open a little. A terrified thought flooded into his head that maybe his father was still alive.

Yes, 'cause a knife through his chest wasn't enough to kill him or anything, Francis said.

I need to see it for real, Brian Matthew told him, entering the kitchen. His father was still on the ground by the wall, eyes open, mouth in an accusatory frown. As Brian Matthew stared at the man he used to idolize, the man who used to dance around the house with his children, the man who had once loved his family, he felt nothing. He backed out of the room, down the hallway, and out the door, stuffing his father's wallet into his bag on the way out.

Where are we going now, Francis asked him as he turned the corner and ran down the next few blocks. He needed to get back on a bus and into a city before the cops started poking around the suburbs.

I hear Seattle's big, Brian Matthew said, not quite

sure how he'd get all the way through two states with what little he had, but too determined to worry about technicalities. They would find a way like they always had.

Chapter 9

Brian

November 2005:

Brian awoke one morning on a park bench. He couldn't remember how he'd gotten there, but he knew he wasn't in his hometown anymore. His park had flowerbeds and a large oak tree where kids played frisbee with their dogs. He had always wanted a dog, but his father hated pets, especially ones that shredded shoes and peed on the floor. This park was designed for children, complete with a yellow swirly slide and red, squeaky swings. Next to the swings, a blue merry- go-round spun slightly in the breeze. He pulled his jacket tighter when the wind blew through. He was relieved that there was no snow on the ground yet.

He should've been afraid, but he wasn't. Instead, he was relieved to be aware of the surroundings again. Ever since his mother's death, his days had gotten fuzzier, starting with a week of third grade where he had learned cursive, but didn't remember learning it. His teacher showed him all of his work to remind him, but he was never able to get the hang of it. After a while, his teacher became frustrated with his inability to duplicate the beautiful, flowy lettering that his homework had produced and sent a note home to his father requesting that he didn't do his son's homework anymore. His father, enjoying one of his sober nights, was as confused as his son. He had seen Brian do the homework, but neither of them realized it had been someone else, another essence lying beneath Brian's surface, one who was very sad and very alone.

Brian sat up on the bench, stretching his limbs and neck, and pulled the bag he had been using for a pillow across his lap. It was a ragged, red backpack with a hole in the left side pocket. He opened it up to find it filled with his clothes and some food.

I've finally done it, he thought. *I really ran away. Shelley has always wanted to.*

But where was Shelley? Did he really leave without her? It didn't make any sense. Shelley had wanted to run away not him. He had never understood this urge, but when she cried she always got her way, and she cried a lot when she talked about leaving. Brian knew his father hit her. He had seen it once when she came home with a C on her science test, but Brian didn't think it happened often enough to run. Still, he knew it had been one of his sister's strongest desires and sitting on this bench alone brought him more confusion than any blackout ever had.

He looked around, but there was only one small group of teenagers huddled together in a circle. One boy with purple hair was pointing toward him and talking to the others. They nodded and the group walked toward Brian. Uncertain what to do, he zipped his backpack up and flung it onto his back, preparing to run if he needed to. He had never been in a fight before and had no idea how to defend himself. He tried to maintain composure, but the fear made his hands shaky on the straps. He hoped that he'd be able to outrun the group, but he had always felt himself to be average in life. He probably could outrun a couple of people, but an entire group gave him little confidence. Inside, Brian Matthew and Francis were preparing to fight.

"You lost or somethin'?" the boy with the purple hair asked.

"No," Brian said. "I'll figure it out myself."

"Well, where ya headed?" he asked, ignoring Brian's caution.

"I don't know. I'll know when I get there."

"It's not safe out here alone," the boy said. His face softened, causing a rippling effect of softened faces in the group, and Brian's body released tension.

"I thought my sister was with me, but I can't find her," Brian said, looking around again, but no new faces had entered the park.

"Why don't you come with us and we'll help you find her? We're kind of a family," a blonde girl said. She had big green eyes that took up most of her face, giving her a small, pouty mouth and a tiny button nose.

"I…ummm…" Brian thought about his options. He could go home, but his stomach hurt when he thought about it. If Shelley was out here somewhere, he couldn't just return home without her. He could look around on his own, but he wasn't familiar with the area and, as much as he hated to admit it, that made him nervous. "I suppose that would be okay."

"I'm Liam," the boy said, holding out his hand for Brian to shake. "This is Phoebe."

"My friends call me, Honey," the girl said, smiling as they walked out of the park and down the unfamiliar street.

Days later, Brian had been welcomed into the family as if he had always been an integral part, and Honey was right about calling it a family. All the children were runaways, but they bonded together as tight as siblings, sharing food and blankets at the shelter, or huddling together under a bridge on rainy nights when the shelters grew too full for them.

Brian had never traveled outside of California before, and Seattle was chilly and rainy this time of year, but he didn't mind that much. He bonded with his new family and, though they didn't have the luxuries that home once had, he didn't miss his father in the least. He found that to be a bit odd, but he couldn't find a place within himself that thought of him and the others had no intention of telling him why. They knew that their existence depended on secrecy. As long as Brian didn't know what they had been up to, they could continue without him realizing that something unusual was going on inside of him.

His one distress was that his sister still wasn't with him. He didn't know what had happened to Shelley and that scared him more than any of the confusion of the past few months. He was supposed to be the older brother, the protector, and now she was out there somewhere without him. Honey had helped ease his mind a little. She reminded him of Shelley and together they spent most of their days searching the city for her, but the people who did reply hadn't seen her or thought the description too vague to even know if they had. Brian wasn't sure how many blue-eyed blondes there were in Seattle, but he realized quickly how most teenage girls that past him could be Michelle from behind.

One day he had enough. He flung his backpack onto a bus bench and sat down, shaking his head as if he could fling it off. He felt his search was beginning to feel hopeless, and that hopelessness caused him to turn inside of himself, reaching for support in a place he didn't know existed. Brian Matthew and Francis waited with anticipation for him to break down the barrier that prevented them from escaping again, and as his mind filled with distress, the wall slowly chipped away from itself.

"Don't worry," Honey said, patting him on the arm. "We'll find her soon enough. It's just that the city's so big. We still have plenty of places to look. Why don't you have something to eat?"

"Okay," he said, but he was slipping into the dark, and Brian Matthew stepped forward, prepared to take his place.

Honey pulled out a sandwich and tried to hand half to Brian Matthew. He took it reluctantly, nibbling a little at the corners to try to relieve some of the hunger. Brian Matthew hated stealing. Francis thought his feeling was illogical. They were hungry so they should take what they wanted to eat, but it bothered Brian Matthew. So far, they had managed to survive off the supplies he'd packed and his new friends had stolen food for Brian, but it still felt wrong. Beside them, a man discarded a newspaper into the trash can. Brian Matthew glanced over it and noticed something strange in the bottom corner. One of the articles read, *California Man's Death Still Unsolved and One Teenager Still Missing*. Below the caption was a picture of Brian. Brian Matthew's eyes widened and his breaths became shallow.

Throw it away, Francis yelled.

"That looks like you," Honey said, leaning over his shoulder. "Let me see."

"No," Brian Matthew said, but she snatched the paper from his hand and began to read.

"I thought you said you ran away from home?"

"I did," he said.

"But you didn't tell me your father was murdered. Why didn't you say any—hey, wait up. Where are you going?" He was running down the street. He had to get out of there before she put all the pieces together. He couldn't risk her turning him in to the police. He ducked into an alley, hoping to lose her, but she was right on his trail. "Why are you running? I thought we were friends."

"We are," he said, trying to think of where to go next. He needed to get away from her questions before something bad happened.

"Then why are you running from me? Did you do something bad?" She shifted back and forth to block him from leaving again.

Get rid of her, Francis said. He was starting to panic and Brian Matthew could feel the pain of his voice in his head. *Get rid of her now. We can't have her telling. Get rid of her.*

"Shut up, just shut up, already," Brian Matthew said. He hadn't intended to say it out loud, but Francis was driving him crazy.

"No, not until you tell me the truth," Honey said, getting closer. "You'd better tell me right now or I'm going to the police."

Get rid of her. Get rid of her! I'm not going to jail!

"Stop," he said, swinging his fist in the air and connecting with Honey's mouth. He hadn't intended to hit her, but he couldn't take the shouting in his head anymore.

She pressed her hand to her cheek for a minute, too stunned to move, but then he saw the fear slip into her eyes, and she tried to run. He grabbed her from behind, lifting her off the ground and pulling her back into the alley before anyone could see. She kicked her feet into the air with little success and tried to let out a scream. He covered her mouth with his hand so that all he could hear was a few squeals.

"Shh," he said, but she squealed louder, trying to wriggle from his grasp. He squeezed harder and she gasped for air. "Just keep quiet."

He didn't realize how tight he had been squeezing her until she dropped to the ground. He looked at the limp body with bewilderment, not sure what he had done. He tried to find a pulse, but there was none. Images flashed through his head of his sister being flung around by their father. Honey couldn't be more than Michelle's age and he had killed her.

You did what you had to, Francis said, unfazed by Brian Matthew's display of emotion.

Then why does it hurt so much?

Because you're not as strong as me, Francis said. *But you will be.*

Brian Matthew wasn't sure what that meant, but he didn't like the sound of it. He glanced down at Honey one last time and hurried out of the alley, wondering where they would travel next.

Chapter 10

Lizzie

August 2012:

The next day Jen went down to the school and enlisted Lizzie immediately. School would be starting in two days, but Lizzie didn't care. All the feeling was drained from her body still. She had slipped her brain into a fog, creating blurry images of her memories and the events of the day. Who cared if she went to school or not? She ate heartily, not feeling the cloud of death hanging over her. She felt little pleasure in her daily routine, but things felt less scary than they had been before. Jen was excited about Lizzie's newfound appetite.

"Wow, keep it up, girly, and you won't be able to fit into them skinny jeans of yours anymore," Jen said, watching Lizzie shovel another spoonful of eggs into her mouth.

Her autopilot brain gave her sister a wide smile. Jen didn't even know the difference.

"Since Lizzie is in such high spirits today, how about we all go out to dinner tonight? My treat," Joel suggested.

Why sit at home doing nothing? Lizzie thought. It was better than sitting in the dark alone. Lizzie had cast off her emotions in the darkness and was afraid if she was left alone for too long they would float back to her. She spent the morning watching cartoons in the living room while Jen ran errands and Joel went to work.

Jen slid into the house, bags of groceries in her hands and mail in her mouth. "Lizzie, you'll never guess what happened."

Jen always had to go back to the store at least twice a week to get things she forgot the first time. On top of the grocery bags was a manila envelope marked *Lizzie* in big black letters.

"What? The fruit was on sale at the supermarket?" Lizzie helped her with the bags and picked the envelope out from the top. "Where did you get this package?"

"It was on the porch. There doesn't seem to be any return address. Maybe Nick dropped something off and decided not to come in. But that's not what I wanted to tell you. It's about Dr. Stewart. She's dead. Apparently, they found her in her room with one of her ears missing. The killer must have cut it right off. Isn't that unbelievable? There really are a lot of sickos out there nowadays—" Jen looked up, still holding a can of chicken noodle soup.

As she was speaking, Lizzie had reached into the envelope. Something squishy hit her fingers and then she felt skin on her skin. She tore open the package and an ear fell into her open palm. It had dried blood along its edges and a purple stud still in its lobe. When it rolled in her palm, she saw the star shape of the earring and any thought she had had of it being a prank turned to ash in her brain. She stared at it with mouth wide, and behind her she could hear the can in Jen's hand drop to the floor. Lizzie dropped the ear to the ground, shock flooding her. How could she be numb when it was happening again? Jen rushed to the phone and dialed nine-one-one.

"Don't pick that up," Jen ordered, noticing Lizzie inching her way back over to the object.

Lizzie's mind was half locked in the surreal fog she had been in all morning. She remembered the strange texture of the ear and, for some reason even she couldn't understand, wanted that feeling again. She looked at her sister, trying to obey her even in her strained state of mind.

Jen shook her head at her. "That's evidence. You destroy evidence and they'll put you in jail in a heartbeat."

"What's happening?"

A startled scream emanating from Jen's small frame as his sneaker crunched against the ear announced Joel's arrival.

His eyes looked somewhat unnerved but the rest of him stayed composed. He looked down at the broken splotch on the floor. "What on earth is that?"

"Someone left it for me," Lizzie said, feeling the sound escape her in an airy whisper. She swallowed several times, hoping to push back down whatever was blocking her voice. She spotted a piece of paper sticking out from the envelope. She pulled it out and read *Nobody's Listening*. The paper fluttered to the ground next to Joel's foot. Lizzie raced up the stairs and dove into her covers.

Even if she was wrong, she still felt safe in her room. It was her own little sanctuary to protect her from the world. She knew Jen would be up to check on her soon so Lizzie tried to compose herself. If she could just hold things together like Joel did when Jen was around, then Lizzie wouldn't worry her anymore. She practiced making faces in the mirror, but none of them looked right on her. She started with a half-smile, but that looked more pained than happy. Then she tried a full smile without teeth, but that was zombie Lizzie not happy Lizzie, and her full smile, big and bright, just made her look more crazy than they already thought she was. Eventually, she settled for her slight frown. It was okay to freak out once in a while, especially if you had just held a human ear.

Lizzie went into her bathroom to scrub the gunk away. She could feel shock rising in her body. It curdled down deep into her stomach and forced its way up, suffocating her. She could feel it in her throat, cutting off her air supply, but it wasn't just panic. She vomited into the sink, taking in gasps of air when she could. Her body shook uncontrollably as she held the soap in her fingers, trying to get the feeling of skin against skin off her fingertips. She scrubbed until her skin was blotched red all over, but it still didn't seem like enough. She heard doors open and slam again a few minutes later.

"Lizzie, the police are here. They need you to come downstairs," Jen hollered up to her.

When Lizzie didn't move, she heard footsteps on the stairs, and Jen knocked on the door.

"Lizzie, can we please come in? They're not going to hurt you. They just need to ask a few questions."

"Hi, Lizzie, I'm Officer Perry. I was hoping I could speak with you for a second," he said.

"Okay," Lizzie said, wanting to get the whole thing over with.

The two entered and Officer Perry scanned the room, jotting down a few observations. Lizzie was surprised at how young he was, only a few years older than Jen. While he looked young, his demeanor was composed and prepared, as if he had been working cases far longer than his few years.

"You were one of Dr. Stewart's patients, correct," he said, looking over her books on her desk.

"Yes, Lizzie was having behavioral problems," Jen said and Officer Perry held up his hand, signaling for Lizzie to respond.

"Yes, for about three months. She was helping me overcome some personal fears," Lizzie said.

"But you had an altercation with her at your last appointment. The secretary said she heard a commotion in the room and then you and your sister were seen leaving. Is that right?"

"Yes it is. Dr. Stewart's methods weren't very helpful, so Jen told her that we wouldn't be back again," Lizzie said, not liking where these questions were headed. She looked at Jen, who was biting her lip so hard that Lizzie thought she was going to make it bleed.

"I see. And where was everyone this morning during the incident?" He had scribbled down a few more things while she spoke and was now observing some drawings she had hung on the walls.

"I had been watching cartoons when Jen came in from the grocery store. Joel didn't get here from work until a few minutes later."

"And where was the envelope found?"

"I found it on the porch when I arrived home," Jen said flatly. Her face had hardened and her eyes were starting to flicker with that quick temper she had when she felt attacked.

"All right. I just have one last question, for Lizzie," Officer Perry said, eyeing Jen. "Can you think of anyone who would want to do this to you?"

"I…ummm…" Lizzie looked at Jen for help, not sure if she should say anything. "Have you ever heard of the Boogeyman?"

"Like the imaginary monster?" Officer Perry raised his eyebrow, hearing something that caught his interest.

"No, you—" Jen cleared her throat and Lizzie caught her insult on her tongue before it spilled out of her mouth. "No, not the imaginary one. I mean the real one, the one from California."

"I see. Ms. Moore, there are a few more things I would like to discuss with you downstairs, if that's all right. Thank you for your time, Lizzie, and don't worry, we'll catch whoever's responsible." He tipped his hat to her and left the room with Jen following close behind him.

Lizzie felt sick again. She shuffled in the bathroom and vomited, trying to expel all the disgust from her body. She wasn't sure what Officer Perry thought of her answers, but she didn't have the energy to go downstairs and find out. She flopped onto her bed, pulling her pillow over her head and crying into her sheets. She was so tired of all of this. When she had run out of tears, she wiped her face, trying to recompose herself before Jen came back up. At last she heard the cars drive away and the tension in her body relaxed a little.

"Lizzie, come downstairs. We're still going to dinner. It's time you get some fresh air."

This was Lizzie's chance to prove she was going to be all right. She dragged herself from her room and went with them. The police had come and gone all day, collecting evidence with what little they had. There were no traces left of fingerprints so they just cleaned up the remains and took them back to the lab to identify.

Dinner was very somber and unappetizing. Lizzie still felt nauseated from the events earlier, making the sight of food almost impossible to stand. She sat quietly, picking at her food, little chunks of chicken covered in spaghetti sauce and parmesan cheese. Thoughts were bursting like little explosions all through her head. Her mind wandered back to her dream last night: those cold eyes. It was almost too much of a coincidence. There was no way Jen could ignore the truth now. He was still out there, and he knew where she was.

With everything going on all around her, Lizzie felt

almost calm just knowing that she wasn't wrong. She really wasn't crazy.

"Try to eat something, kiddo. You'll want to keep up your strength," Joel encouraged.

He wasn't about to let Lizzie's depression ruin his precious date with Jen. Lizzie knew he was just trying to impress her by being "helpful." He was so plastic that if he had stood next to a fireplace, he probably would have melted. Lizzie didn't want his help. She wanted him to leave her and Jen alone.

"Call me a kid again and I'll drive this fork through your throat," Lizzie snarled.

"Lizzie, you won't talk to him that way. There's no need to take your emotions out on him. We're just worried about you. You don't eat or sleep. You lash out and do irrational, unexplained things. This has got to stop. Whatever it is that's bothering you, you have to tell us. I can't do this anymore. I'm not a mind reader. I know you're in pain, and you won't talk to me about it. If you'd just let it out, you would feel better, but you're so stubborn that you won't let me in."

Lizzie had even reached Jen's breaking point and she felt so completely alone. But that didn't stop her anger. "You know what's wrong with me. I've told you a thousand times. He's going to kill me."

Jen yanked Lizzie away from the table while Joel was hastily paying the waiter who had noticed the scene they were making.

Lizzie yelled all the way home. "You know it's true. We've got to do something. He's found me, and we have to leave. But you're too busy with your boyfriend to see that."

"James is dead, Lizzie. They found his body not far from the house, and all those bodies in that house linked to him. What on earth would make you think you're not safe now? This thing with Dr. Stewart—there has to be a better explanation."

"It wasn't James. That's the explanation. James tried to save me and that bastard pinned the murders on him. He made James kill himself. He had him blow his brains out, and then he attacked me. I'm not crazy. I was there, and I know what I saw. The guy had these crazy blue eyes and he was humming. He started choking me with his bare hands, and then he picked up the knife and sliced me through the gut. And now he is coming here to finish me off."

Frustration and panic started to flood over Lizzie. They weren't listening to her. Nobody ever listened to her. Just like he had said.

"Lizzie, I took this psychology course this summer and you have a transferring problem. Your mind doesn't want to remember things the way it was because you care about your brother, so you imagine things to be different. You've convinced yourself that your alternate reality is the truth. I know it's hard for you, but you'll never heal until you let your brother's memory go. Your sister and I want to help you with that, but we can't if you're not willing to cooperate," Joel said, trying what Lizzie believed to be his attempt at helping.

"Are you retarded? What do you think, I whipped this guy out of my ass? Like he's just some crazy imaginary enemy that I made up out of thin air? I don't have an overactive imagination. Stop being an idiot and listen to me. This guy was real." Lizzie wanted so badly to gouge his eyes out and the indignity of it all was that Jen sat there quietly listening to what he had to say. She cared more about him than Lizzie.

"I don't think you made him up at all. I think he was another victim that you witnessed and pretended that it was really your brother who was the victim. It's a very common rationalization that teenagers do when things don't make sense to them," Joel said.

"Would you stop acting like you know the inside of my head? You don't know what you're talking about. Some stupid ass summer class didn't just turn you into some psychological expert. You're an idiot who is trying to impress my sister, nothing more. You probably didn't even take that class. There probably wasn't any said class to begin with," Lizzie said, folding her arms.

"Lizzie enough. That has to be the stupidest thing I've ever heard. Out of all the things Joel could choose to lie about, why on earth would he choose to lie about a class?" Jen's nose twitched and her eyes narrowed, giving Lizzie a warning.

"Because he's a moron. What else?" Lizzie ignored her sister and Jen glared at her again.

"If you really don't believe me, then look it up. I swear it's all true. I'm even certified to be a counselor, although I'd prefer something more fulfilling. Most teenagers today just don't want to be helped," Joel said, developing a small twinge in his voice that Lizzie always sensed when he seemed annoyed with her.

"That's right, I don't. Why should I need help for speaking the truth? I mean, if I'm lying then how do you explain the little gift I got this morning?"

"She does have a point," Joel said, looking at Jen intently. "Maybe she's not safe here right now. Perhaps if we moved her some place more remote—"

"No. Lizzie is just fine here with me. I can take good care of her. I can," The words caught in Jen's throat, and Lizzie could see in the mirror that her eyes were starting to water. She pursed her lips a couple of times and cleared her throat. "The Boogeyman—James had a lot of national publicity, and the police believe he might have developed a few fans. They think it's a copycat." Jen waited for Lizzie to respond, but when she didn't, Joel spoke instead.

"They did suggest another option," he said, looking at Jen who shook her head with disagreement. "She has the right to know."

"You mean they believe me?" Lizzie looked at Jen, eyes bright and attentive, but Jen was still staring at Joel, her right cheek sucked in as if she were biting on its inner side.

"There's nothing to tell her," she said firmly, but he didn't listen.

"The police have suggested that perhaps your confrontation with Dr. Stewart earlier may have something to do with her death," Joel said.

"They think I'm a murderer? That's ridiculous, how could I murder someone? I was home all night and all morning."

"That's what I told them," Jen said, "which is why this discussion is unnecessary." She tensed her hand around his, trying to signal him to stop.

"Get mad all you want, Lizzie has the right to know they think she's a nutcase."

"I didn't kill anyone," Lizzie snapped.

They were starting to talk to each other like she wasn't there.

"I know that. I'm not suggesting you did, but the police are looking into it. So if you can remember anything—" Joel looked at her through the rearview mirror. She noticed that his eyes were more than just brown. They were a deep brown, unblemished with flecks of other colors. There was a pure quality to them that made Lizzie want to believe his sincerity in that moment.

"I don't know anything, Joel. I've already said everything I remember, but you guys don't believe me." Her words that time were softer, less biting, but still just as sad and frustrated as her anger had been only a few minutes earlier.

"We're just trying to help you," Jen said and suddenly Lizzie could see her turning back around on her. This released another fit of anger. She felt caged, cornered, like they were trying to get a blackbird to hum a robin's song.

"The only help I need is a bodyguard to make sure this bastard doesn't break me open like a piñata. So stop trying to comfort me. As soon as this guy is found then I'll be fine again. But how can I be fine while a maniac is on the loose, and I'm written at the top of his shit list in bold print?"

Jen bit her lip, face stone, brow furrowed. Then it softened and she released the hold on her lip. "You know I'll always protect you. If you really believe in this, then we can do some research about the case and see what we find. Maybe there'll be information in the old newspapers or something. Perhaps we can find out who the copycat is. If we don't find anything within the next three months, then you have to stop this madness—understood?"

"You can't really be indulging in her fantasy? Your encouragement will only prolong her recovery. Do you think delving into more of this awful stuff will make her feel better?"

Jen was listening intently to Joel, a thoughtful crease in her brow, but Lizzie could tell that Jen had already made up her mind. A smile crept across Lizzie's face. Jen was finally taking her side. Nothing had ever brought her more satisfaction before. It was like savoring a little piece of chocolate when you know it won't last, so incredibly sweet and victorious.

"I don't think it's exactly a fantasy. You saw what happened today. Someone is trying to frighten her and we need to know why. The police think it's a copycat of the

Boogey—James. If we learn the details of those cases, then maybe we can discover who it is that is trying to replicate him. Clearly, they know Lizzie is connected to him, so there may be a good reason to be afraid and, besides, it will keep her mind busy so she can be calmer for school," Jen said decidedly, but Joel wasn't giving up so easily.

"I really don't think you'll find anything, and even if you do, the police will never reveal enough details for you to figure out what your clues mean. It sounds like a wild goose chase to me." His face turned into a full frown, souring the almost symmetrical beauty of it.

"Well, nobody asked you." This day kept getting better and better for Lizzie. "I agree. If nothing's found, then there'll be no more craziness."

For some reason Lizzie felt completely exhausted when she got home. It seemed like she could never get enough sleep. Some nights she would lie in bed for hours, staring up at the ceiling, while others she was tormented with restless nightmares that she was never able to piece together to make sense. Jen came upstairs with her to make sure everything was alright. Then she tucked Lizzie in and turned out the light.

"Try to get some rest, kiddo. Think of pleasant things, like going to the beach or watching a funny movie." Jen closed the door behind her and Lizzie listened to the tapping of her feet on the stairs.

Lizzie stared at the ceiling for a minute, knowing that no funny movie would ever give her peaceful sleep. Lizzie crept from her bed again. They always talked when they thought she was asleep. Now would be the perfect time to enjoy a really good fight. She hoped Jen would get so mad that she threw him out of the house forever. Maybe he did care about her a little bit, but he wasn't helping.

The only thing Joel was good at was causing Lizzie

more stress, and she didn't need more of that in her life.

Jen sat on his lap in the chair. "Are you angry with me? 'Cause I still think I'm doing the right thing."

His face looked concerned but not really angry. There was a slight curl in the bottom of his lip that detected remnants of his annoyance, but nothing indicating an impending fight. "No, nothing you do ever makes me angry. I just worry that this may make things worse for Lizzie. Although I suppose screaming at her really isn't helping either. I guess we can try all the possibilities until one works for her. If you feel comfortable with this, then I'm on board."

"Why is it that you're always so calm? You're stuck in a crazy house with me all day long and you always know what to say to clear my head. How come you never lose your marbles?"

"I do, but I'm better at hiding it. Besides, you keep me sane. I don't know what I'd do without you."

Oh brother, how sickening. Lizzie couldn't believe how fake this guy was, but something about him seemed different. The way he looked at her. Maybe, even if Lizzie didn't like him, he was good for Jen. Lizzie saw real love for her in his eyes. He would never hurt her. Like it or not, Joel was going to be there for a long time, and for some reason, that didn't bother Lizzie as much as she thought it would. He might not be much to her, but he was a lot to Jen, and that meant something to Lizzie. It was in that moment of watching his face that Lizzie realized her anger had been misplaced. Truth was, she didn't really know Joel well enough to make her quick judgments about him.

She slumped back into her bed. Tonight she didn't feel like counting sheep, so she counted fish instead. Each little fish jumped over the bridge to the other side of the pond.

Her mind wandered, and eventually the fish started baaing and so she went back to sheep.

Lizzie wondered what was so special about sheep. She remembered watching Lambchop as a kid. How ironic for a lamb to be named after the food it produced. Would she ever name a pig Bacon? Likely. But what about naming a chicken Egg, or a cow Milk? It just didn't seem to fit. It sounded sort of silly to her, but then again all her thoughts were silly lately. Lizzie's eyes drooped and she felt herself being pulled into a deep slumber.

Baa! Baa! A strange sound was heard in the distance. Lizzie crawled from her bed and the cold air swept through her pajamas. Her bed was placed in the middle of a large field. It was still dark out and the cool air kissed the tips of her ears and cheeks. Fog rolled in like waves and filled the meadow with haze.

How did I get here? Lizzie heard the soft pounding of feet and the fog evanesced. A line of sheep stretched across the field. Each one was a unique color. One after another, they hobbled up to the fence and leaped over then disappeared. At the end of the line was a very tiny one, quivering in the cold with the purest white wool Lizzie had ever seen. It stood there impatiently, rocking to and fro, waiting for its chance to make the jump.

Out of the darkness, a pair of scarlet eyes crept up behind the poor little lamb. Lizzie tried to scream to it but the sound wouldn't come. A wolf leapt out of nowhere, teeth sharp and dripping with spit, and tore the sheep to bits, pulling on its flesh with rapid precision. Horrified, Lizzie turned away and started to run, but a few feet away from her she hit something really hard with a thud. Rubbing her sore butt, she went to gather herself up until she saw them, those blue demon eyes piercing through the shadows. Lizzie sprinted forward but an arm shot out toward her, pulling her back down. She dug her nails into the earth until they bled, but he only tugged harder. Slowly he managed to drag her to him.

"Finally we can end this. You won't be a bratty burden to anyone anymore." He grabbed Lizzie's throat and clasped down as hard as he could.

She choked and sputtered, feeling her lungs shrivel up and begin to collapse. She stared into his blue eyes and noticed the irises begin to come in and out of focus. She clawed at his arms, pulling and ripping the skin. At every painful scratch he laughed, until the laughter turned into hysterics. She felt the air coming out of her and she slowly drifted into oblivion. She floated along in what seemed like space until she landed in the middle of town.

Where am I? She wandered along the road for a long time to her house where Jen was sitting. Her head was covered with her scarlet hair and sobs would sometimes escape her lips. A little blue and pink stuffed bunny lay on the table: Lizzie's bunny. *Am I Dead?* Then Jen rose, turning to look at Lizzie who gasped, sucking in air but having difficulty exhaling. Her arms were sliced all the way down from the elbows, with blood dripping off them. Her sockets were two endless black holes. She rubbed her arms affectionately and played with the blood in her hands.

"I should have listened to you. You were right. We're all bad and must be punished for what we've done. He punishes us all, and you can't run away. He always finds you. You can't escape the Boogeyman."

Lizzie screamed until she felt blood gurgle up into her mouth and she thought she would drown in it, but she couldn't because she was already dead.

Seconds later she jolted awake. She waited for a little while for Jen to come in, but she didn't. Apparently Lizzie wasn't as loud as she thought she had been. Inside her head, she was still screaming, but outside she was calm and Jen didn't even realize there had been any disturbance. Lizzie went to the window and peered out into obscurity. She watched carefully, looking for the wolf to come out of the darkness, but no one came. Lizzie rocked herself back to sleep, hoping that her next dream wouldn't be her last.

Chapter 11

Brian Matthew

January 2006:

B rian Matthew wasn't a thief. Sure, he had crossed a lot of fine lines in his life, but theft hadn't been one of them. He stared at the bag of Doritos in his hand, cursing his stomach for not being more durable. He had lasted twenty-four hours, but that wasn't enough time to come up with a more sensible plan.

This isn't very nutritional, Brian Matthew told Francis, who was watching from within.

That's not the point. It's food, and we need food. Francis was a bit more agitated than usual. *Just grab it so we can get the hell out of here.*

I don't think I can do this. It feels wrong. Brian Matthew put the Doritos back on the shelf. He looked around to see if anyone was watching him, but the girl at the counter was too engrossed in her *Cosmopolitan* to notice.

Are you kidding me? You just killed old what's-her-face like yesterday and now you draw a line. Stop being a baby and take the damn Doritos.

I'm not really that hungry. We can wait another day. Brian Matthew walked toward the door, but something unusual happened. He lost control of the body for a second and his leg jerked back.

I'm hungry, so if you won't do it, I will, Francis said.

Brian Matthew let out a small growl. He looked up and the cashier girl was staring at him. He gave her a nod hello and she went back to her magazine. He walked back over to the aisle, pulled the Doritos from the shelf, and bolted for the door, not bothering to see if the cashier had looked up.

A few days later, in another city somewhere in Oregon, hunger took over his mind again and still Brian Matthew struggled with his conscience.

Let's at least get something of substance this time, he said. *We can't live off of Doritos and junk food forever.*

Yes, mother dear, Francis said, *I don't care what you get, just get something.*

Brian Matthew grabbed a sandwich out of the cooler. He looked up at the register and was met by the cashier's gaze. The guy was about his height with a larger build and a thick red beard that he would stroke every so often out of habit. Brian Matthew wasn't sure what to do with him. He was clearly keeping an eye on him and that made him nervous, but he had a natural charisma that seemed to reassure most people. He gave him a nod, giving a slight smirk that came naturally to his face. He stared at the sandwich in his hand, feeling at a standstill.

What do we do? Francis asked and Brian Matthew could feel his agitated paranoia beginning to build.

I'm going to look at the chips. Relax. I'll take care of this, he said, trying to reassure his companion.

He's looking right at us, Francis said.

Calm down, Brian Matthew said and, as he reached for a bag of chips, several people entered the store. When they got to the counter, he shuffled in between them out the door. The cashier hollered after him, but he was running at this point and nobody could get ahold of him. After a few blocks he noticed nobody was following him and slowed his pace. *Told you it'd be fine.*

We have to go back, Francis said voice steady but hollow.

What? Why would we do that? Brian Matthew asked.

We have to kill him, he said.

What? No, we don't.

You don't understand. He saw us. Now all he has to do is report us to the police and it's the end for you and me. We need to keep going. We need to live.

Brian Matthew didn't want to admit it, but Francis had a point. If anyone ever found out about them they would be eradicated like pests and Brian Matthew didn't want to die.

He wouldn't really report us, would he? he asked, unsure what to do.

Of course he would. We mean nothing to him. He doesn't care if it ruins our lives. We have the knife already in our bag. We have to go back.

Brian Matthew opened the backpack and dug through its contents. When he found it, he stared with disbelief. It looked like the kitchen knife from the house. He hadn't dumped out the bag in so long that he hadn't noticed it was in there.

I didn't put this in here, Brian Matthew said, terrified that something had happened without his knowledge. For once, he caught a small glimpse of what Brian felt when he awoke to gaps in his memory.

I did. You were so busy with your own thoughts that you didn't see me grab it, Francis said, feeling satisfied that he had done something without Brian Matthew.

Is there anything else I should know about? Brian Matthew asked, feeling a vile taste that lingered down to the pit of his stomach.

Nope. My conscience is clear, he said. *So what are we going to do?*

We're going back, Brian Matthew said, stuffing everything back into the backpack. *But just one more time. I'm not a murderer.*

Of course you're not. Francis laughed.

He already decided what Brian Matthew was and he planned to see that his destiny was fulfilled whether he liked it or not.

Chapter 12

July 2007:

It was so easy for Brian Matthew to get around. After all, he was young, charming, and looked trustworthy. Who wouldn't want to help a young fella get a lift? He had traveled a lot this year, finding minimal work when he had the opportunity, and hitchhiking to a new place when he grew restless.

The last place he had worked was in a little town near the border of Oregon. His last job was washing dishes at an old fifties diner where the waitresses still wore roller skates and checkered uniforms. It gave him enough money for a cheap motel when he grew weary of sleeping in the local park. The bedding had cigarette burns in it and the black and white television only had one channel, but it was home for the moment.

"My parents run the campground a few miles out. I'm back from school for summer vacation and wanted to surprise them. I'm a week early." He gave the older woman he was riding with a smile. He knew how to make it just perfect enough to be adored. The elderly always liked that. He had always looked older than he was. He was tall like his father with early developed masculine features that made people believe he was already eighteen or nineteen, even though his seventeenth birthday wasn't for several months.

"Oh, isn't that sweet. I bet your mother will be so excited to see you. What are you studying?"

He turned away from her to hide his frown. *She mentioned her*, he told Francis as his teeth clenched and his face tightened.

Keep your cool. We don't need to be so conspicuous. You'll have your chance when we get to the secluded campgrounds.

But she said Moth—

Stop being so weak, Francis growled. *It's your own fault for saying parents and not father. Of course, she'd assume you have a mother.*

"History," Brian Matthew answered, ignoring the grumbling voice inside.

"Oh, that's nice." She pulled into a little U-turn spot next to two off-roads with wooden signs. The one on the left read, *Bear Lake Campgrounds, Main Entrance, a 1/4 mile. Check in here.*" The other read, *Private Campgrounds.*

"Thank you very much," he said, shutting the car door, deciding his interest in her had faded.

"You're welcome, dear. You take care." She pulled away from the entrances and drove away.

When he was sure she was out of sight, he took the path to the right. He strolled down the road, trying to determine the perfect spot to relax, but after a little while, he got hungry.

I'm getting impatient, Francis growled.

Shut up. I'm trying to pick the right one. It has to be an odd number. Brian Matthew had always liked numbers. Francis was more of a letter person, making up lyrics and humming them inside.

It always annoyed Brian Matthew, but then again, most things Francis did annoyed him.

Jeez, what a nut you are, Francis said.

Shut up, Brian Matthew said, feeling the irritation in his brain. *At least I'm not the one that wants to kill everyone.*

Oh, but you do. You and I are the same.

Brian Matthew hated when Francis said that. He was wrong, and as soon as he had quenched the last thirst of blood from Francis's thoughts, Brian Matthew would have him out of this body forever.

Each camp was separate from the other, having its own road wedged deep into the woods. "The perfect wildlife experience," the brochure that he had found in the nightstand next to the motel Bible had said. Being a city boy, he had never been camping outside of his living room, but it couldn't be that hard. Besides, it was perfectly secluded.

By the time he reached the fifth off-road, he had decided that that was his choice.

Five is a good number, he thought.

He slid off the road a bit into the trees, but kept it in sight so he wouldn't get lost. He had developed the habit of easing his way through places so he wouldn't spook anyone, but he hadn't anticipated nature's noisiness. Fallen branches and twigs snapped beneath his feet while others rustled when he pulled them back and released.

This is ridiculous! How much noise can you make? Francis snapped irritably. *It's like trying to get a baby to shut up in the middle of a crowded supermarket.*

As Brian Matthew grew impatient with all the noise, he heard the sounds of unrestrained laughter. He stopped short behind the trees, listening to giggles and waiting for night's shadow to conceal him.

He could tell from the girls' laughter that they were

incredibly drunk. They danced around the fire, lighting it before the sun had completely set. They both had dyed hair, one neon orange and the other streaked with fluorescent pink. As the orange girl spun around the fire, he thought he saw her eyes connect with him—an impossibility that his mind insisted could and did happen. He leaned out of the bushes slightly to get a closer look.

Her eyes were a crystal blue, surrounded by the red glow of the flames. For a second, her hair shone a golden color, the kind his sister must have and his mother had, but he shook the image away. When the girl's appearance cleared from his desired delusion, he realized how he couldn't see her eyes using only the fire's glow.

She lied to me, he thought, withdrawing into the bushes again before the girls saw him. He felt his nose twitch uncontrollably as his frown traveled from his mouth to his cheeks and then to his eyes.

In her hand, she had a large poker stick that appeared to be more of a lower branch than a twig. He watched it shift between them, thick and long with a sharpened end from where the orange girl had scraped it down with a pocketknife. The pink girl danced around, raising it in the air like a warrior as she made battle cries, laughing as she did, while the orange girl smoked a cigarette, twirling her purple lighter in her fingers. It was almost too easy.

You're too hungry to be picky, Francis told him.

But he still had to wait, just a little bit longer. He could see the sun beginning to set.

At nightfall, the girls went in the tent, laughing off their drunken stupor as they each grabbed another bottle of Budweiser. He watched them disappear into the tent without making his initial move.

I should go now, Brian Matthew told Francis.

Oh, don't be foolish, you don't want to jump up all crazy and give them an advantage.

Brian Matthew had grown tired of this game. *I don't know if this is a good idea.*

What? Of course it is. She lied to us. Besides, this is what we were born to do. The way Francis said it made Brian Matthew's stomach queasy.

I don't want to be, Brian Matthew said.

Be what? Francis shouted, hurting his head. *A monster? A freak? Well, you are. Put them out of their misery.*

Okay, Brian Matthew told him reluctantly. *Just one more time.*

He arose from his hiding place and grabbed the largest stick from the fire, the poker stick, its end glowing orange from the embers of the flame. The last thing the girls heard was the soft whisper of Mockingbird, the lullaby that Brian Matthew had never forgotten.

Hours later, Brian Matthew watched the lake, a peaceful blue, rippling in the wind, turning gray as it hit the shore. He watched the expanse of trees and mountains, stretching along for miles on the horizon. He observed the contrast between the blades of grass and the red of the dirt as the blood flowed in rivulets back into the earth.

In the end, everyone goes back into the earth, he thought.

He had watched his mother as they lowered her into the ground and remembered seeing her body, frozen in beauty and glistening pale, in the casket. He felt the rush of satisfaction knowing that somewhere his father had been put into the ground or maybe not even that, maybe he had just been turned to ash when no one showed up to claim him. Maybe his sister had claimed him, but what thirteen-year-old could plan her father's funeral?

She wouldn't waste her time and tears on him, Francis said. He had been in this body with him for almost half of Brian's life. He used to come and go, but Francis's frequent appearances the past five years had led Brian Matthew on his journey to here, to a place where he could watch blood in the dirt without flinching. As he watched the rest of the blood drip from inside the tent into the surrounding dirt, he recalled the slight pang in his chest, telling him that this was wrong, but it was shrouded by the icy indifference of his distorted mind.

Staring at the dirt, he wiggled his toes inside his worn out shoes. The shoes pressed into the reddened dirt beneath him. He thought about the girls in the tent. Did they have sisters? Did their mothers used to sing them to sleep? He had slept fine last night, curled into the growth like a bear without his cave. It didn't even bother him that a few feet away corpses were being drained.

You have a taste for it, Francis said, his tone slithering through Brian Matthew's brain. As the early morning hours approached, he arose from his slumber to watch the rest of the blood drip away.

Like the rain, nurturing the earth, he thought. He wondered what things grew out of blood.

Hate, Francis answered. *It shouldn't matter now. They are nothing now because in the end everyone goes back into the earth.*

Even us, he told Francis, but Francis didn't like that idea.

Not true. When we are done the entire country will know our names.

Brian Matthew shook Francis's idea out of his mind. *No.* Brian Matthew sighed deeply, letting out a gust of unsure air, and grabbed the lighter from the tent. He walked over to the tree line and grabbed branches from the ground, feeling the rough texture of the bark against his fingers. He set them down in the metal ring the campground owners had provided and looked around for a piece of paper. He had read somewhere that paper helps a fire start, but he couldn't remember where he had seen it. He pulled the brochure from his pocket. An elderly couple was waving on the cover, eyes bright and optimistic.

The perfect wildlife experience, he thought. He lit it, watching it slowly burn down in his fingers. He liked the way the edges burned red when the flame touched them. He threw it into the fire pit and settled into a fold-out chair to watch it die again.

Chapter 13

Francis

October 2007:

Francis had had enough of Brian Matthew's insolence. He thought they were different. He thought Francis was an impulsive animal, but Francis would teach him. *We're more alike than you think,* he told Brian Matthew once as they had stood over the dead man in the alley. *You crave this bloodshed as much as I do.*

He had said nothing then, but Brian Matthew had started doing less for Francis and then he scared Francis.

"Maybe it would be better if we gave Brian back his body," Brian Matthew had said one night. Anyone walking by would have thought he was talking to himself, but Francis knew what he was really doing. He was trying to get rid of him. Well, Francis wasn't about to let that happen, so he did the one thing he was good at in life: he got angry.

Now, he had spent two hours spotting possible candidates for his next adventure, but no one had caught his attention. It had become fairly dark and the anger was building from within his stomach. He stopped outside of a small neighborhood home, the kind of house that settled into a block of other tiny houses, each one distinguished by its color and choice of lawn ornaments. This one had those ugly gnomes arranged around the tree, like they were having some happy little gathering. Francis scrunched up his lip with disgust and gave the gnome closest to him a swift kick. It rolled onto its side and he smiled at his victory.

The house was already dark when he peered inside through the glass doors. A sliver of moonlight cast shadows of large furniture and decorations on the walls. The light also cast his reflection in the glass. He ran his fingers through his newly black hair. Francis had liked the change. It made him different from the two Brians.

"Hello," he said to the image, trying out his voice for the first time. It was rough and raspy in a way that he didn't like. It reminded him too much of the Brians' father. Francis had always known that the man that had beaten him every day hadn't been his father, but someone had to endure the punishment when Brian couldn't and Brian Matthew had fallen into tears. And Francis was strong. Without him, Brian Matthew wouldn't have faced his father, and Brian's sister Michelle wouldn't have survived her twelfth birthday, but nobody would ever know what he had done. No matter how many times as a child he had explained to the people he was Francis not Brian, they still couldn't see him. He tried in his music classes when Brian was thirteen and couldn't remember how to read music. Francis knew how to, but his teacher wouldn't listen. They'd just see Brian, but not anymore. He would make the world recognize him.

Infuriated, he picked up the toppled gnome from the grass and slammed it against the door, shattering the glass. He reached his arm through the hole and flipped the lock open, stepping inside of the house. He stubbed his toe against a chair, knocking over a lamp in the process. The smashing sound as it hit the floor caused a flurry of movement above him, confirming his realization that his outing wasn't going well. For once, he missed Brian Matthew's stealthy and patient movements, but he had been silent ever since Francis took over.

"Who's down there," a male voice called as a light illuminated a staircase on the other side of the room. "If you don't get out of here right now, I'm going to call the police."

Francis could've turned around like Brian Matthew would've, but he wasn't done yet. Smirking to himself, and feeling the anticipation of adrenaline rush to his stomach, he bounded up the stairs, three steps at a time. A man was at the top, baseball bat in hand, but it wasn't enough. He barreled into the man, knocking him onto the carpet. The bat rolled from his grasp and Francis picked it up.

The man punched him in the back of his head and Francis jammed the handle of the bat into his throat. He coughed and grasped his throat, trying to regain his air, but Francis wouldn't give him enough time for recovery. He tightened his grip around the handle and smashed the bat against the man's face. His head bounced a little as he hit the carpet, creating a gash on the side of it. The sight of the blood fed his adrenaline, and Francis hit him repeatedly, watching the gash turn into a pool. He smiled, admiring the work he had done. It seemed easier to him than when Brian Matthew did it. Pride swelled inside of him because he could finally claim something as his own.

A scream behind him drew his attention from his creation. A woman was standing in the doorway, arms wrapped around her flannelled body. Francis gave her his best Cheshire Cat smile and charged for the door. She screamed again, slamming the door shut. He could hear her fiddling with the lock, but her reaction time was too slow. He rammed the door with his shoulder and it burst open. He grabbed her by the throat, choking the scream from her breath. Her eyes met his and he watched as all recognition drained from them before tossing her limp body to the floor. He laughed joyfully.

"You see this," he said out loud to Brian Matthew. "I don't need you anyway."

"Mommy," a tiny voice said behind him.

Francis's heart began to thump and he thought he was going to vomit as he turned to face the child. She had wavy, raven hair like her mother's and a gap in her teeth where one tooth was missing, seen as she widely yawned at him. She cradled a doll in one hand and sleepily rubbed her eyes with the other. He wasn't sure what to do. He wished he could blend into the wallpaper and disappear when the child left or press rewind so that he could pick another house, any house besides this one with its sweet-looking little girl.

"Mommy," the child said again a little softer as she noticed the towering man in the doorway.

Take her to the neighbor's house and leave her at the door, Brian Matthew said. It was good to hear his voice for a change, especially when he could be calm enough for the both of them.

"Mommy's very tired right now," he said, inching toward her. "Why don't we go down stairs and let her rest?"

"Mommy said not to talk to strangers," she said, backing away from him.

Get her out of here, Brian Matthew growled in his brain.

I'm trying to, Francis told him. He smiled at the girl. "You're a very smart little girl, but I know your mommy, and she would think it's okay."

He reached his arms toward her. If he could just get a grip on her, he could carry her out of here, kicking and screaming if he had to, but his rough voice and large frame made him less than inviting to a small child. She kept backing up until she felt something wet on the bottom of her foot. She screamed, bursting into tears as she came across her father's body, and ran for the stairs.

"No, wait," Francis yelled as he ran toward her. He was almost there and reached out to grab her arm when he saw her feet tangle underneath her. He tried to catch her, but she toppled head first down the stairs. When he got to the bottom, her body was still. His heart was racing and his memory was flashing back to Michelle and the fear in her eyes when that man beat her. *I'm not like him.*

He turned his head to listen for breathing and a small gasp escaped her lips. He scooped her up, carrying her through the open door and started running. He wasn't sure how far the hospital was, but he'd remembered seeing one by the park he had passed earlier that day. When he finally managed to retrace his steps, he spotted a nurse outside the building, smoking a cigarette.

"Oh, thank you," he said to the air, not really sure who or what he believed he was thanking. "Please, you've gotta help me. My little girl fell and hit her head."

Francis knew that he looked too young to be the child's father. He was, after all, only seventeen, but who was she to judge him. She spent all day taking care of sickly patients who were probably dying of lung diseases and she still sucked in the chemicals of that cigarette. She didn't pay much attention to his youth as she ushered him into the lobby.

"I need a gurney here. I've got a female approximately five years old with head trauma."

The entire staff sprang into action, whisking the child away through the double doors.

Francis slid around them to the front door and snuck out before the secretary could notice. He burst into a run the minute his feet hit sidewalk, and he didn't stop until his legs gave out, hitting his knees against the grass. It was still early morning and the area was deserted, so he did something he had never done before; he cried. He cradled his head in his hands, trying to stifle the tears, but they kept coming.

This is why you need me. You never think about the consequences, Brian Matthew said.

She was just a baby, Francis sobbed. *And I took her mother away.*

What about those other people? Don't you think they had families? Brian Matthew said gruffly. He cared little for Francis's pain.

She was innocent, he yelled. *Like we were before Mom died.*

Only because Mom protected us from Dad's abuse.

Don't say that, Francis snapped. *That thing wasn't my father. He might've been yours, but he wasn't mine.*

Whatever you say. Brian Matthew sighed. *So what do we do now?*

I don't want to be out here anymore. Will you look for a place to stay? Francis was too afraid to stay out any longer. He had found something in himself he didn't like. It made him weak and vulnerable.

What about Brian?

I don't think he could handle this right now, Francis said, not trusting Brian enough to release his body. If Brian was out, he'd go looking for answers and answers would lead to them and that would lead to no more Francis or Brian Matthew. *We know what's best for him.*

Fine. I guess that seems fair for now, Brian Matthew said, but he was as concerned for his preservation as Francis was.

Chapter 14

Lizzie

Lizzie, breakfast."

Lizzie hadn't felt this hungry in a long time. She sprinted down the stairwell into the kitchen, where a stack of raspberry pancakes the size of tennis rackets were sprawled onto the table. Lizzie remembered the first breakfast Jen had ever made her. It was extra burnt toast with a side of rubbery eggs. After that, Lizzie demanded that Jen take cooking classes. It turned out that once she received a few lessons, she was a natural.

"What's the occasion?" Lizzie asked suspiciously. This had to be a bribe for something.

"Why do you assume there has to be an occasion? It's Sunday morning and I want to share a big breakfast with my favorite little—" Jen flipped another pancake on the stove as Lizzie interrupted her explanation.

"Cut the crap and get to the point." Lizzie took a humongous bite of the pancakes. The fruitiness melted in her mouth. She hadn't eaten pancakes in so long. She scarfed them down greedily, trying not to forget that her sister wanted something.

"Well, it's just such a lovely day. I was thinking that maybe you and I could paint the guest room." She held a bucket of light blue paint.

Why was everything so blue in this house? Lizzie was so sick of that color. When she was in the mood, she was going to run down to the store and buy fifty different colors to paint the house with. Hopefully Jen wouldn't get too mad.

"Cool, I guess. All this just to paint the guest room— oh no. Who's coming to stay with us? It better not be that idiot Nick. I swear if he runs his mouth, I'm throwing him all the way back to his grandmother's."

It wasn't that Lizzie didn't like Nick. Actually, it might have been nice to have a real friend again, but she was afraid of what he would think. She already felt like a big nut job as it was. She didn't need him to tell her.

"I'm not sure about Nick coming over yet. I've got to figure out if it will be better for everyone to wait until we straighten the situation out."

Lizzie knew exactly what she meant, until she stopped being crazy and got in a happier mood. But Lizzie wasn't crazy and when she proved it, Joel and Jen would be down at her feet begging her forgiveness. "Actually, I decided to convert the room into a full time bedroom so that Joel can stay with us."

"What? Are you crazy? Why would you want that inbred to move in with us? He's so boring. I'm not kidding. Every time I look at him, I have a seizure and go into instant coma. The guy is so dull. He'll ruin all our fun. Not to mention the fact that he hates me." Lizzie was beyond disgust. She was on the verge of a psychotic tirade.

"He's not boring. We have lots of fun together. You're the one who's boring, sulking in your room all day. Oh woe is me, woe is me, oh, look a butterfly. You know I heard you baaing in your sleep last night when I came up to check on you. Do you dream that you're a sheep or something?"

Lizzie choked on her orange juice. "Oh, yeah, I dream I'm animals all the time. The other day I was a kangaroo. I woke up with my hands in my sweatshirt pocket in mid-hop."

Jen looked at her out the corners of her eyes. "Jeez, you're such a strange child. One of these days, I'm going to save up money to get you a CAT scan. And Joel doesn't hate you. Why would you think that?"

"He's so twitchy. He always gives me funny looks and when he thinks I'm not looking, his eye twitches. And I'll bet he growls at me in his head too. He hates me so much. He only pretends to like me because he wants to impress you so he can get some. Don't give me that shocked look. I'm not an idiot. If he moves in then, I'll move out." She crossed her arms and raised an eyebrow at her sister.

"No you won't, because you have no place to go. It won't be that bad. I'm sure you'll get used to him. He doesn't hate you. You're just being weird. If you help me paint the room, then we can do some research on the internet and I'll even take you to the library to check out old newspapers."

"Hmmm...I probably could do all of that without you. Of course, leaving the house by myself would be hard. Then again, you are taking me to school tomorrow. Fine, it's a deal. But I still don't like him. Twitch, twitch." Lizzie jolted repeatedly for effect before strolling out of the kitchen.

A few minutes later, the girls had their old jeans on and were painting the guest room another shade of blue that Lizzie hated as much as the rest of them. They worked along in silence for a little while, until Jen decided that Lizzie needed something more. It started out as some harmless fun, Jen placing a blue dot on her sister's nose. Then it turned into a battle. Blue paint buckets splashing all over the room dyeing the white sheets all over the floor. By the time Joel arrived with his stuff, two little blue aliens greeted him. Joel brought Lizzie a can of neon orange spray paint and she sprayed her name on her room wall. Then she gave Joel's hair an orange spritz while Jen dumped the rest of the blue paint down his back. Then the battle ensued with the girls attacking Joel from both sides. Two blue piles shuffled into the bathrooms while Joel sat drying, waiting for one to be free.

After everything was cleaned up, they all had tacos for lunch and Lizzie invited Nick over because Jen felt she was in a well enough mood. Nick was thrilled to see her in higher spirits.

She had forgotten how much of a glutton Nick was, so they decided to race. Lizzie devoured her four tacos in ten minutes, half as much time as it took Nick. Joel and Jen sat there cheering her on.

"It's not fair. You have a whole pep squad cheering for you. Competitors feed off of that energy. Besides, you cheated anyway. Next time I say we have hotdogs instead." Nick always beat Lizzie at hotdogs. It amazed her how easily her memories of him returned.

"Next time I'll be your cheering section," Joel joked waving imaginary pompoms. "Ra-ra- siskboom-ba."

"Wow, babe, you're a better cheerleader than I was," Jen said, admiring her large boyfriend, waving his arms in the most girly fashion he could think of and shaking his butt.

"Damn straight," he said, giving Jen a kiss on the lips.

Lizzie laughed so hard that her sides hurt. So he wasn't such an old stiff, after all. Who knew? "We should do stuff like this more often. How about later we have a football game?"

"I'm down. I'm pretty tough." Nick flexed his muscles, but it was more like flexing a limp noodle. Nick had always been pretty skinny and wimpy. Lizzie noticed that he had gained some definition since she had seen him last, but nothing like the football players she used to know.

"I can still take you," Lizzie growled, flexing her own biceps. "I have more muscle than you."

"I have to agree with her, Nick." Jen teased.

For the first time in a while, Lizzie felt at home. Granted, they weren't her perfect specimens of family and friends, but it was what it was and she felt content. Lizzie wondered how long this fuzzy feeling would last. She kind of enjoyed it, but at the same time felt very exposed. Still, she decided to embrace the emotion while it lasted. Even Joel was immersing himself in the fun, and Lizzie seemed to enjoy his presence there as much as Jen's. It was like having a brother again. Her chest felt a little tight at the thought of replacing James, but she pushed the feeling back down, not wanting it to ruin their fun.

"I can top that." Joel flexed his muscles and his whole body rippled. Lizzie never really noticed how incredibly large he was. He was so gentle with Jen that she didn't realize how easily he could break her. Jen was pretty average height, for a woman, with a toned frame. Jen always used to joke with Lizzie about getting more muscle. When she got mad at her, Jen would call Lizzie "Barbie" because of her thin, model-like frame. Lizzie called Jen "Shamu." Joel looked like a giant in comparison. He was over six feet tall, and tremendously muscular. He could break both girls at the same time without even working up a sweat.

Lizzie was beginning to get lightheaded. It was a sudden rush of flashbacks. She was at Jen's old house on the beach. It wasn't much, just a little two bedroom on the boardwalk, but it was all Jen had, so Lizzie adjusted. She had gone to the movies with a group of friends, and it was already almost midnight. Nick walked her home after the movie that night, and just as she was starting to go inside, he pulled her to him in one quick kiss. It was short but sweet, and the taste lingered on her lips hours after he was gone. She remembered how happy she had felt. She danced around her room for hours, wondering if her feet would ever hit the ground. Nick had always been a good friend, but he never really showed any affection beyond that. Then she remembered the next day, when she had visited Jen and the fight they had.

"Why do you make me stay with you so much? I have a happy life with designer clothes and my own bathroom. I can hang out with my friends all night long and my parents don't question where I am or hound me about schoolwork. I was fine until you came along. Now I'm stuck in this shithole with you," Lizzie said.

"I'm doing the best I can, but that's not good enough for you. You're a pampered little brat. Why don't you want to stay here once in a while instead of traipsing all over town with your shallow friends? Sure, it's not the Hilton, but it's not a cardboard box either. I'm sorry if it doesn't live up to Miss Princess's standards, but it's my home and you'll like it. "

"I don't have to like anything of yours. I don't even have to like you," Lizzie said.

"Oh, and I suppose you're so great? You're a spoiled, little rich kid who doesn't know the meaning of hard work, of blood, sweat, and tears. Maybe that doesn't mean much to you, but it does to me. Like it or not, we're the only real family each other has, so we're stuck together and, right now, you really suck at the whole little sister thing," Jen said, narrowing her eyes at her sister.

"I wish you had died too so I wouldn't have to visit you. I like my real family, the ones who would give me what I want, the ones who trust me," Lizzie said, not caring if she sounded like a brat or not. She was used to having her way.

"If you like it so damn much, then leave. You're more trouble than you're worth anyway. I don't need some prissy ass spoiled teenager complaining about every detail. 'But at my house we have our own bathrooms. And we never use the public beach, and every day someone carries my lazy, fat ass to school.'" Jen flailed her arms around her head and strutted around in imitation as she spoke.

Lizzie had stormed out of the house after that. She was going to go home where she belonged. She wanted her real family back with their comfy living and the freedom they gave her. She had been visiting with Jen for over two years and Jen still didn't trust her. Then she had the nerve to ask her to move in with her after yelling at her for wanting to spend time with her friends. This was ridiculous. It was supposed to be an amazing night— Valentine's Day, the day of love, ruined by Jen's idiocy. Her foster brother, James had called her cellphone after Jen called him at work. Lizzie flipped the phone open and placed it against her ear, but he spoke before she had a chance to say anything.

"She doesn't mean the things she says. Why don't you go back inside and I'll come get you in the morning? I'm sure once you guys calm down, you'll be able to work everything out." Lizzie pictured his stern face, trying to be the voice of reason, and she rolled her eyes. Of course, he knew her too well for her to get away with anything. "I'm serious, Lizzie. No eye rolling."

"I don't need to work it out. I'm leaving. I'll just walk home." She flipped the phone shut, not wanting to even hear his response. It was already getting dark again. She needed to find her way out of here soon or she'd be late for dinner with her friends. They were supposed to go out for pizza, but no, that was too much for Jen to comprehend.

"Stay home with me, Lizzie," Lizzie mumbled, creating a whiny voice to imitate her sister's. "We would have fun, Lizzie. Well, no wonder you don't have any friends."

Seconds later, she felt a snap as her heel broke off. She took the shoe off and examined it before throwing it across the sidewalk. Lizzie staggered along the streets trying to find anything that looked familiar. She really wished she had her dad's Porsche now. Nothing looked even remotely recognizable. It was pitch black outside and the wind nipped at her nose. This area of town was completely different from Lizzie's. She could still taste the saltiness in the breeze. She must have still been close to the ocean. She decided to back track and leave in the morning. But she couldn't seem to find the house. They all looked the same. Tiny white houses close to the seashore, there was no definition as to which house was Jen's. Suddenly, she heard a quiet sound, a soft humming. It sounded like a nursery rhyme.

"Hush little baby, don't say a word. I'm going to buy you a mockingbird. And if that mockingbird don't sing, I'm going to buy you a diamond ring. And if that diamond ring don't shine…"

Lizzie hadn't thought much of it at first, but then she heard the footsteps behind her and panic rushed through her as she darted into the street. She had been so clumsy that she tripped over herself and hit the pavement. She remembered a shadowy figure standing over her, and then everything went black.

Lizzie shrieked. These images were too much—flashes of pain, voices arguing amongst themselves, and singing. She hated that horrible singing. She couldn't handle them all at once. Nick tried to grab her and she knocked him to the ground, pushing aside the dining table. Jen wrapped her arms around her and Lizzie wriggled with fright. She punched Jen in the stomach and ran for the door. Nick had sprinted ahead of her and was blocking her way. She grabbed a knife from the sideboard and pointed it at Nick. "I have to get out of here. He's coming for me. He knows where I am. I have to leave."

Joel grabbed her from behind. His arms were so massive that she couldn't wiggle free. She dropped the knife on the floor and he carried her up the stairs. Jen followed behind him, trying to soothe her with her words. He plopped her into bed and they wrapped her into a cocoon. Jen held her down, patting her hair and whispering in her ear.

"It's okay. Nobody's coming for you. You're safe here. I won't let anyone hurt you, I promise. Why don't you get some rest? School starts in the morning, so maybe it's best if you just relax for the rest of the day. We can do stuff some other day."

"But he's coming for me—he is—I know it," Lizzie mumbled, feeling a little dejected and easily dismissed. "Will you stay in here until I fall asleep? Joel can stay too...I guess."

"Whatever's best for you," Jen said. Joel still wasn't Lizzie's favorite person, but he was big, incredibly big. If anyone could protect her, it would be him. Jen sat on the edge of her bed and stroked her hair. Lizzie slid as far into the covers as she could and tried to relax.

"I probably should take Nick home." Joel uncomfortably tried to dismiss himself. But Lizzie started to sing and he couldn't help stopping to listen. He walked back over to Lizzie's bed, but hesitated at the thought of calming her. Instead, he made his way back to the doorway, hoping that Jen wouldn't need his help.

"Hush, little baby, don't say a word. I'm going to buy you a mockingbird. And if that mockingbird don't sing, I'm going to buy you a diamond ring. And if that diamond ring don't shine—"

Jen tried to hush her sister—who was starting to work herself into a psychotic frenzy—but with little success.

"Good night, Lizzie," Joel called from the doorway. "Try to get some sleep."

"Where did you hear that from? I don't think I've heard that since I was a little girl. Why don't you sing something more relaxing like…um…I don't know. Lizzie? Are you okay? Lizzie?"

Lizzie appeared blank, her expressions numb, dead to the world. Jen knew not to shake her out of it because last time she'd tried, Lizzie flew into a tempered fit. Best to leave her to herself, lost in her thoughts.

Immediately after Jen's pitter-patter on the stairs was heard, Lizzie buried herself in her blankets. She hadn't blanked out like Jen had thought, but she didn't feel like answering questions right now either. She knew that her sister wouldn't bother her as long as she kept quiet, and she needed quiet more than anything. She peered out from under her covers, making sure no one had snuck into her room, but it was dark, except for the glow from her laptop. She sat like that for several minutes, trying to concentrate on the glow to prevent her head from spinning. She wasn't sure how long she sat like that, but it was enough time to hear Joel return from taking Nick home. The window in her room was covered by her curtain, so Lizzie didn't even know if it was light out.

Eventually, she got up from her bed, sat down at her desk, and flipped open the laptop. Her mind was still on high alert, but she decided to push that aside to do something useful. She knew Jen would be up later to make sure she had returned from her stupor, but now was the time for research. She typed in the *Sunny Gazette* and then the word she feared the most, Boogeyman. Newspaper articles flooded the screen.

The first one that popped up was an article that Lizzie had remembered at least a month before her own abduction, *Beware the Boogeyman*. It talked about a pattern emerging of people being stabbed to death and stuffed under their beds. There had been no leads and none of the victims were connected, unless you count them all living in California, which wasn't much of anything.

Lizzie stared, puzzling over the article. All her friends at school had talked about it. Nick even stood behind the tree and did a kidnapping imitation. It had been a joke then. Who cared what had happened, as long as it wasn't them? Lizzie had been so focused on picking a dress for the prom that she demanded that everyone stop talking about the stupid article and help her. She had no idea what a difference a few months could make.

The next article caught Lizzie by the stomach. It wasn't connected to the Boogeyman, but was published in the same paper as the first article, *Unsolved Mass Murder Five Years Later*. The article was about an officer's determination to solve a case that had haunted his career for five years. A four-year-old was orphaned after her parents were murdered in her home. The little girl was spending the night at a friend's house and when her parents didn't come to get her the next day, the mother of the friend brought the child home. The father was found in the hallway, head bashed in, and the mother had been strangled. The thing that caught Lizzie's attention was the little girl, Braiden had a twin sister, Erika, who had been home sick that night and later reported as a Jane Doe in the local hospital. Police were contacted the night before by one of the doctors to try to identify the child, but little had been discovered until they were contacted the next day by the family friend. According to one of the nurses on duty, the child had been rushed into the emergency room by a young adult in his early twenties.

The child had suffered from a severe brain injury after falling down and later died of a seizure during the night. In a brief moment of consciousness, the child told her nurse that a dark angel had rescued her after she fell down the stairs. Descriptions of this "dark angel" had varied among the staff, and police seemed to be running out of leads before they could progress. All suspects had checked out and the case grew cold. Now nine years old, Braiden was staying with her grandparents and struggling to recover.

Lizzie stared with horror at the pictures of the family. The little girl, Braiden's, eyes stared like two dark coals in the snow. Her face was numb like Lizzie's. She could feel the pain of that child within her own soul. A picture of Erika's little face was gleaming next to the picture of Braiden. She probably had once been that happy, just like Lizzie was once that happy before. Erika's light might have been the one who was doused, but Braiden was the one with the face of death. Erika's was forever frozen in her joy while Braiden's would forever be locked in its pain. Lizzie couldn't bear to look at it any longer. It reminded her too much of that day she had woken up in the hospital. The image of that day flashed across the front of her mind.

Her eyelids had felt heavy as she slowly lifted them open. Jen had been standing over her, tear stains on her cheeks, eyes reddened and swollen. Her foster parents had been sitting in a chair a few feet away, looking as worn as her sister. Lizzie had tried to sit up, but pain shot across her stomach and it lurched, churning up all that was left inside of it. Her arm had throbbed as if the pounding of her heartbeat had been placed inside of it.

"Don't move," Jen had said, gently settling her back on her pillows. "You don't want to hurt yourself more."

"I heard our witness was awake." A gruff voice had said and a man walked in with a badge on his shirt pocket and a thick, brown mustache that seemed to curl down to his chin instead of up to his nose.

"I don't think she's ready," Jen had said, shifting to the end of the bed and obstructing Lizzie's view of him.

"Ready for what?" Lizzie had asked, but was ignored.

"I'm sorry, but we need to ask her now while it's fresh in her mind." He had looked to her father who nodded in agreement.

"Ask me what?"

"Lizzie, I'm Officer Miraz. I'd like to ask you a few questions about your ordeal? Do you remember your brother attacking you?"

Jen had dropped into the chair beside her bed. Lizzie's mother let out a small sound and had openly wept on her father's shoulder. The officer had looked at her with a small twinge of sadness in his eyes. Lizzie's heart had thumped loudly, connecting with the ticking of the clock, making her aware of every second. She had parted her lips twice before the word had come out.

"What?"

Lizzie shook the memory away again. She didn't want to think about that day, or any other day before it. She turned away from the computer and her own memory, but a sudden bleep caught her attention. An article appeared with today's date, *California Native Arrested in Maine*. A woman was found wandering the streets in a dazed state. When a police officer tried to assist her, she screamed at him that she had to stop the Boogeyman. The police officer tried to take the woman into custody for her own safety, and she attacked him. The woman was later identified as Michelle Smith of California and police were trying to contact the family. Police were going to keep Ms. Smith in their custody until the family was notified.

Lizzie jotted down the address and placed it in her backpack. After school tomorrow, she was going to see this woman. Maybe she was a survivor too. Maybe she was a lunatic. What if she were dangerous? Lizzie wasn't sure, but she had to find something that could give her a clue. If this woman was who she really claimed to be, then she could tell Lizzie who to look for.

Her heart tightened in her chest. What if it was just another dead end? What if everyone was right? What if she was crazy? Lizzie often wondered about her sanity. She had been this way for so long that sometimes she couldn't even remember what life had been like before. She was so used to her own irrational behavior that she assumed it was justified. But what if it wasn't? What if she was so lost in her own illusion that she had even convinced herself of something that wasn't real? Whatever this woman had to tell her, Lizzie would soon discover what was lying within herself.

She yawned. Her mind gave in so easily lately. She didn't want to sleep. She feared what she would see, but nothing could keep her mind from drifting into dreamland. All she could do was hope for enough rest for tomorrow. Lately, it felt like she was always resting and yet never truly at peace...

Lizzie heard someone crying and she tried to follow

the sound. It was a faint whimper, like the soft coo of a dove. Before she saw her, she heard the sound.

"Hush, little baby, don't say a word, I'm going to buy you a mockingbird. And if that mockingbird don't sing, I'm going to break that stupid thing, and you will scream and you will cry 'cause you'll know you're going to die."

The tiny blonde figure stood in the corner of the room facing the wall, rocking back and forth. She looked older than Lizzie, but with the same pale skin and frail frame—a frame that Lizzie recognized though she couldn't remember why. Little strands of hair fell along the sides of her back. She turned around and Lizzie gasped with surprise. She held one of her eyeballs in one hand, the blood dripping down the side of her cheek with the optic nerve still attached to its socket, and a switch blade in the other. She laughed, sounding like a shrieking cat before she spoke the words, "We see you."

Then she evanesced into the gloom. Lizzie wandered around in obscurity, waiting for the next image to come, but nothing came. She was left in desolation all night long, pondering what she had seen and learned. Could this woman truly be the answer she was looking for? The night faded into a wasteland and soon the school day arrived before Lizzie could figure out why that image was so familiar.

"Lizzie, hurry it up in there. You're going to be late."

Lizzie shuffled into the bathroom. Physically she felt refreshed for the day, emotionally she already felt exhausted. She slumped over the bathroom sink, scrubbing her teeth fiercely. Lately she had become more mechanical. Each stroke was perfectly planned to move back and forth twenty times in each section of the mouth. Then three swooshes of mouth wash and then on to her hair. Lizzie twirled some of the delicate strands around her finger. She glared at her reflection in the mirror. The girl peered out at her mockingly, sneering at what she had become, a shadow of a person. She tried to make herself look more cheerful. She grabbed a hot pink elastic from the drawer and put her hair in a ponytail. She gave the mirror a little smile, but it felt too unnatural. Jen called to her again.

"You won't have time to eat."

Lizzie raced down the winding stairs to the kitchen. If there was one thing she was ready for today, it was breakfast. She munched through an enormous stack of chocolate chip pancakes, with butter melting in globs in the center, and proceeded to some extra crispy bacon. At least she would be well fed in case the cafeteria food stunk. After downing a glass of orange juice and grabbing a donut hole for the car ride, she headed off to school.

All the way there, Jen gave this big lecture about "turning over a new leaf," and Lizzie nodded and smiled, pretending to listen. Then Joel started up about "being yourself," and Lizzie didn't even seem to mind his presence. Granted, he was at times boring and annoying, but he would suffice. She kind of preferred him to those other guys Jen had dated, who insisted on feeling her up all the time. Joel was a gentleman and kept their relationship mostly private which was absolutely fine for Lizzie. Who wants to see their older sister making out with some guy all the time?

"Hey, Lizzie." Arms waved around frantically from the parking lot.

Lizzie shrank about ten inches into the seat. Nick was waiting for her. The last person she really wanted to see right now was shouting across the parking lot for her. Lizzie still didn't know what Nick thought of her freak outs, and she preferred not to embarrass herself in front of him anymore. But there was no avoiding him. Nick was everywhere. Reluctantly, she stepped out from the car and he rushed to her side wrapping his arm around her shoulders.

"Guess it's you and me from now on, huh?" he said. "Isn't it great that you already have someone here you know? You should be thankful I'm a nuisance."

"It's a great joy," she remarked, rolling her eyes.

"Hey, we have almost all the same classes." Nick said, reading Lizzie's schedule. "Gotta love small schools."

"Whoopee. That's just swell." This was going to be the longest day of her life.

Nick wasn't kidding when he said it was a small school. Lizzie couldn't remember seeing a school that had only one building before. It only had two floors. Lizzie was used to thousands of kids, not hundreds. She would stick out like a peacock in a chicken coop. Nick noticed her hesitance at the door and gave her arm a little squeeze, pulling her along inside as they searched for the right room.

They found the classroom just as the bell rang. The teacher hadn't arrived yet, but all the kids were chattering away, until their eyes fell on Lizzie. Lizzie didn't understand the ways of a town. In the city, there are so many people that not everyone could focus on one individual. In a small town, news traveled fast, and every eye in the room stared so intently at her they could've pierced through her skin. She felt her body heat and knew that her appearance was more telling than she would have liked it to be. Silence filled the room as the two proceeded to the back of the tiny classroom. As they moved, a chorus of whispers burst out in a round throughout the room, but Lizzie could only catch faint sentences of it.

"She lives in that creepy old house."

"She's a freak."

"I heard she murdered her parents."

"I heard she's a Satan worshipper."

Lizzie turned and stared down the curly-cue redhead that she heard make the comment. The girl recoiled in what Lizzie thought was either embarrassment or fear, but she couldn't make up her mind which.

"Hey. What the hell are you all looking at? I don't want to stare at your ugly-ass mugs all class. Turn around before I make you." Nick's attitude stunned the teens into looking away.

Lizzie muffled laughter in her sweatshirt. Nick smiled at her and whispered in her ear. "You'd think they've never seen an emo kid before. Don't they have televisions? Maybe they're all Amish."

Lizzie giggled quietly until she suddenly had an epiphany. She looked down at her clothes. She had a baggy black sweatshirt on, with black and white plaid pants, and black Converse. How did this happen? She had become the kid in school that her friends used to make fun of. She used to make fun of them, too.

She remembered Nick hissing at this one girl back in California who used to growl at people when they walked by. She looked over at Nick's attire. It was Abercrombie and Fitch right down to the socks. She could only imagine what people must think of his friendship with her. It seemed like two extremes of the spectrum, a daughter of the devil and her best friend, the Abercrombie model. But he didn't seem to care. He smiled at her, as big as she thought his face could manage without ripping, giving her the thumbs up once in a while.

"All right, class, settle down, settle down." A nasally voice came through the doorway. A little, round man with big black-rimmed glasses entered the room. "I am Mr. O' Hare and I will be your mathematics teacher this semester. Since we have new students, why don't you tell us a little something about yourselves?"

Lizzie wobbled out of her chair, the attention flooding back to her face. She gulped hard and thought of what to say but, "My name is Lizzie and I'm from California," was all that came out as she looked down at her hands and twiddled her thumbs.

"That's wonderful. I'm sure it must be very sunny out there."

Lizzie rolled her eyes with disbelief.

"Now your turn please."

"Well, my name is Putzi and I am from Iceland, Alaska. My three favorite things are women, football, and beer."

"Iceland?" Mr. O'Hare frowned. "I've never heard of such a place. Is it a very small town?"

Lizzie snorted with laughter along with half the class. Mr. O'Hare glared at them, attempting what seemed to be a technique of ignoring Nick's silliness to somehow punish him, but Lizzie knew it would fail.

Nick winked at Lizzie. "No, actually it's considered huge in Alaska. Three families, six Eskimos, five polar bears, four seals, and one lost penguin named Earl. Everyday my family and I went out whaling and we made blubber cakes for midnight snacks."

Finished with his story, Nick abruptly sat down as Mr. O'Hare's face turned a deepened shade of red. He shook his head and proceeded with his class with no acknowledgment of either Lizzie or Nick for the rest of the time until the bell rang.

"This is for you, Mr. Hardy," the teacher said as he handed him a detention slip.

"Great," Nick said, biting his lip. He looked at Lizzie, shaking his head. "Genevieve is going to kill me."

The next few classes were much like the first, more

peculiar looking teachers with funny voices. Lizzie was so bored that she got a detention for falling asleep in chemistry class. Jen wouldn't be impressed when she heard about this. Nick's behavior improved as the day went on. Later, he explained that he just didn't like Mr. O'Hare.

"The guy seemed like a real moron and that stupid voice was aggravating. 'Would you please turn to page one-hundred-fifty-five so I can pretend that you're learning something from me?'" Nick plugged his nose for improvement of his interpretation.

Lizzie got more comfortable as the day went on, although people still stared at her. It was nice to have Nick around, after all. He already knew a bunch of the kids from all the summers spent here with his grandmother before his parents made it a permanent arrangement. If Nick was okay with Lizzie, then his friends were too.

"Are you walking to my house after school? Genevieve said that you're welcome to stay there until Jen gets out of work," Nick said.

Jen didn't need the money, but she hated living off of the money Lizzie's parents sent her to take care of their lost child, so she waitressed four nights a week, mostly while Lizzie slept.

"Yeah. I have to talk to the cheering coach this afternoon to see about maybe trying out like Jen wants me to, but I'll meet up with you afterward. Can I have the directions to the house?" At least she would have some place to go. Lizzie remembered that she had met Nick's grandmother once when they were younger, but all she could recall of her was that she was an amazing cook.

"Sure, if you think it'll take too long for me to wait. It's right down town next to the post office. It's a tiny purple house with white trim and a basketball hoop in the driveway. Old Granny can really slam dunk. Oh, but don't tell her I called her that. It's Genevieve or nothing, as far as she's concerned."

Lizzie sat down for her next class, art. It was the only class she didn't have with Nick. The one thing she could clearly remember about him was that he had absolutely no artistic ability. In third grade, Lizzie received an A for a self-portrait, while Nick drew a distorted line that was supposed to be a cobra. Needless to say, he was thrilled when he realized that this school didn't require art class.

Ms. Fisher was fresh out of college and all the guys knew it. She had round rosy cheeks and voluptuous curves decorated with a rope-twisted leather belt. When she turned to address the class, all eyes were fixated on her hazel irises and the curly brown hair dipping below her shoulder blades.

"Good morning, class. For those of you who haven't had me before, my rules are simple. I demand nothing but the utmost respect and participation in my class. Those of you who expect to pass by drawing a dot on the paper are going to be sadly mistaken. Other than that, I want your creativity to have absolute freedom. Any questions?" The class remained completely silent, so she continued to her next thought. "Today we're going to start on your first project. You'll only have a week to work on it, so it does not have to be perfect, but I'll be expecting a dedicated effort. Our first semester, we're going to spend time on conveying emotions in images. The first emotion I want you to play with is fear. Paint or draw what you portray as the most terrifying thing in the world. You won't have to present them, but I'm looking for volunteers to display them in the lobby. I want you to begin now. Take at least ten minutes to come up with your concept, and give me a rough draft by the end of the class. This is just a small sketch of what you wish your final piece to look like. You may begin."

Lizzie watched as all the others immediately started sketching. Spiders and snakes and all other creepy crawlies spread out among the pages. They had no idea. Lizzie stared down numbly at her empty piece of paper. They didn't know the meaning of fear. Lizzie could still feel the sting of the blade ripping through her chest. She could still hear the cynical laughter echoing through the dark room. She could taste the sweat and blood pouring like raindrops around her lips and that voice echoing in her head, '*If that mockingbird don't sing, Mama's going to buy you…*'

His singing seemed like a dream and Lizzie sometimes wondered if she had imagined it entirely. It seemed so unnatural and yet something about it felt true. She didn't want to begin to capture this horrible memory on the page. She sighed, watching the others draw with little hesitation.

Finally she picked up her pencil and began to sketch. At first, she wasn't sure what exactly she would draw. Instead, she let her fingers take the lead and they guided her along the paper. She sketched a tiny room with shades all around it and, in the center, coming out of the darkness, she put those evil eyes.

Ms. Fisher came around to examine all the student's sketches. When she got to Lizzie's, she stopped and focused for a second, taking her time to examine the work. Then she looked at Lizzie, who felt kind of embarrassed and gave her a smile. "If this is what you can do with a sketch," Ms. Fisher said, "then I can't wait to see your painting. Excellent work."

Lizzie was relieved that she didn't ask questions. The other teens gawked at the drawing as Ms. Fisher still held it in her hand. They seemed somewhat disturbed by their classmate's interpretation, but Ms. Fisher didn't comment any further. She seemed to ignore any stereotypes about people, and Lizzie knew she would like her a lot. Ms. Fisher was the only one who didn't try to be your friend and ask personal questions. She just accepted things as they were.

As the day rushed to a close, Lizzie became more and more anxious. She wasn't sure what awaited her at the police station, but she had to find out. She had to prove to Jen, once and for all, that she wasn't crazy. Deep down, she knew more than anything she had to prove it to herself. When that final bell rang, she bolted for the downtown bus. She was in such a hurry, she fell into another student, knocking them both to the ground.

"Watch where you're going, loser," the girl said.

Lizzie peered up at her. She had scarlet hair cut to shoulder length, and big emerald eyes. Her ruby lips were turned down in a frown and she was clearly wearing too much make up. Two girls, one blonde and one brunette, scrambled over to help her up. They kind of looked like Barbie's version of Charlie's Angels.

"I swear if you damaged my new heels, you're going to be dead."

"It was only an accident," Lizzie mumbled timidly. Her nerves were too racked right now to pick a fight with a queen bee.

"Well if it happens again, then what I do to you won't be."

"Hey, Fiona, did your ass get wider from this morning, or is it just me?"

Fiona glared over her shoulder before she noticed it was Nick. For some reason Nick had always had a magnetic personality, especially for mean girls. She tried to feign a smile, but Lizzie could tell how agitated she was. Nick oinked at her until she decided to leave. She snapped her fingers, and the two girls followed along after her.

Then Nick turned to Lizzie and winked. "I'll see you later."

Lizzie was so distracted that she barely made the bus. The bus rattled on its old tires and Lizzie could see some of the paint chipped off the sides of the other buses as they left the school parking lot. The driver was an elderly woman who seemed to pay no attention to the new student riding her bus. So many children surrounded her that Lizzie realized it didn't really matter to her who was on or not. In the first few seats, the elementary school children shrieked with laughter, shouting across the aisles at their friends next to them. In the back, teenagers set their bags in the seats so they wouldn't have to share, feet propped up on the back of the seat in front of them, staring out the window. She coached herself the entire ride, reassuring that everything would go according to plan. Once she knew the truth, she could move on with her life and forget the whole thing. When she got to the police station, she realized she was still unsure if her plan would work, but she knew she had to try. She pushed aside that crawling feeling of failure and walked into the front lobby.

"Excuse me. I'm here to see my cousin, Michelle Smith. She's been missing for a while and I heard that the police might have found her. She's very ill."

"Your cousin? And you are?" He looked up from his pile of paperwork. "How old are you, kid?"

"I'm her cousin Janet." Lizzie pulled her fake I.D. from her pocket. *Thank you, Nick.* It was the one thing she had remembered to keep from her wild adventures in California.

"Janet...Jackson?" *I'm going to kill him.* She had forgotten how incredibly stupid the name had been.

"Yup, that's me: Ms. Jackson." Lizzie's brain was about to explode. She happened to be the worst liar on the planet. She pulled her face back in a tight smile, hoping it would somehow charm him. But the officer seemed to give her the benefit of the doubt.

"Look, I really can't allow you to see her until I check into this. You look younger, kid. Now I'm going to make a couple of phone calls, and then you're going to tell me what you're really doing here. So sit tight for a few minutes, and I'll be right back."

He walked away, and Lizzie tried to think of what she would say to Jen when he finally figured out who she was and called home.

A voice caught her attention as a suspect broke loose of his handler. The officer ran at him, chasing him down as two more came up behind to assist. While everyone was assessing the situation, Lizzie rose from her chair and slid into the back room. *I love small towns*, she thought, smiling with simple victory.

Chapter 15

Francis

December 2007:

It took him two months to get back to California, but Francis decided it was worth it. He didn't want to travel anymore. He didn't want to talk to Brian Matthew. He didn't want to hurt anyone else. He just wanted to go home and, without Brian Matthew's approval, he set out with what little they had to return to find the one person that had loved him, Michelle. He knew that Michelle wasn't his sister, but she was the closest thing he had left to family, and she never knew the difference between them.

As far as she was concerned, they were all Brian and she loved her brother more than anything.

Francis didn't know what to do when he got there. He had no idea where Michelle was or if she were even staying in this area anymore. Brian Matthew felt the same urgency to see his sister as Francis did, but he was trying to be more realistic.

We shouldn't go back there. What if someone recognizes us? Brian Matthew told Francis.

Who would recognize us? A lot's changed now. Do

you think I should dye my hair back though, so Michelle will think I'm Brian? Francis asked.

She's not going to be there anyway. She probably went to a foster parent in who knows where. How do you expect to find her then?

I'll have to steal some more dye. It might be easier for me to trick her that way, Francis said, ignoring Brian Matthew's objections.

That was the first thing he did when they arrived downtown. It was so much easier for Francis than Brian Matthew. His impulsive, guiltless nature gave him slick movements ideal for theft. It happened so fast that sometimes even Brian Matthew didn't notice until he revealed the object outside the store.

A few hours later, in a public restroom at the bus station, he admired his newly blond hair. He hadn't realized how much he'd missed the color until he saw it in the mirror. It felt more like him, though he wouldn't admit it to Brian Matthew that he enjoyed having the same hair color. He had done other things to change his looks, like going to public gyms to build muscle. He always felt the Brians were far too puny looking, and he couldn't stand anything that made him appear weak.

We still don't know where she is, Brian Matthew said.

We'll check the school and see if she's there, but there's something I need to do first, Francis said, pushing stray hair out of his face.

What's that?

We're going home. He stepped out of the bathroom and, rather than wait for a bus, hailed a taxi. He had the driver stop a block from the old house and he walked the rest of the way, heart racing. He wasn't sure what he'd find, but he felt something pulling him toward this place, and he couldn't ignore his feelings the way Brian Matthew did. Francis had been born out of feelings, and it was that impulsiveness that always guided his path, despite its potential consequences.

Arriving at his childhood home proved to be more difficult than he had imagined. He remembered the house number, but when he got to the mailbox, the house was so changed that he were unsure if he'd come to the right place. The house had been painted blue, with gray shutters and a gray door. Rose bushes were added to the lawn, as well as a swing set and a pair of lawn gnomes.

Is this the right number? Francis asked.

That's the one, 315. Did you think she'd just be sitting on the porch waiting for us?

A car pulled into the driveway, revealing a couple with a young boy and girl. Francis watched them for several minutes as they unloaded their car of groceries. It reminded him of Michelle and of the little girl at the house, so sweet and innocent like these children, now tainted with blood. It seemed so unfair to him that things had gotten so far off track, but then he remembered that pain was the only reason he existed, and his heart felt sick. He had arisen from Brian's pain, and, since he came into this body, he had brought nothing but pain. It had never really bothered him until he'd seen the pain in that little girl's eyes and, now, watching the happy family in his old home, he found himself almost reduced to tears.

Do you want me to come out? It's not a good time to fall apart, Brian Matthew said, already knowing what Francis was starting to understand. *We're not meant for anything more, you know? We're not even supposed to be here, so whatever is the matter, you can't fix it. We're not real.*

It feels real. Why do I feel like this?

Francis wasn't sure what he wanted exactly, but he could feel something missing inside him, and it caused him a deeper ache than anything had ever given him.

"Excuse me, can I help you?" The mother had noticed him standing next to the mailbox and approached him, not sure why a man his age was staring at her house.

"Oh, I'm sorry. I used to know someone who lived here," he told her.

She nodded, going back to her family, and Francis strolled down the street, looking back a couple times to see the family duck into the house.

A week later, a girl caught Francis's eye at the high school. He had hung around as teenagers left the school, hoping to find one that looked even slightly similar to Michelle and, after several possible candidates, he had narrowed it down to one girl with golden blonde hair who happened to play sports. He cornered her one day after basketball practice, pulling her into a broom closet and covering her mouth with his fingers. She squealed and tried to wiggle away from him.

"Please be quiet, Shelley. I'm not going to hurt you. I just need to talk to you." He spun her around so she could see his face. She stared at him for a moment, putting her hand on his cheek. His eyes grew watery and he sniffled, trying to stop the tears. "Do you know who I am?"

"Brian? Is that you?" She seemed uncertain as she studied his face with her eyes. "Nobody calls me Shelley anymore."

"I do," he said and he started to cry, hugging her to him. She started crying too.

"Why did you leave me behind?"

"I'm sorry, Shelley. I should've taken you with me," he said and, for once, he knew he wouldn't have to be alone.

Chapter 16

Brian Matthew

May 2008:

Today was a struggle for Brian Matthew. He had grown used to lurking in the shadows, away from public eyes. He had stayed near Michelle for months now by sleeping on benches, and under trees when it rained. Some days he managed to get a little money for motels by helping little old ladies with yard work or delivering groceries. It wasn't anything fancy, but it was better than outside on the colder, harsher days.

Michelle had blossomed with the support of her new parents. She was an honors student. She played basketball and was on the tennis team. When they were alone, Brian Matthew could sense the scars that she held from the past but she never let them show. Now he was risking suspicion to see his sister's tennis match. He hadn't any intentions of going to anything that would leave him exposed, but the dejected look on Michelle's face made it impossible for him to refuse her.

What if somebody thinks we look familiar? Francis asked. *What if a police officer is there?*

Who's going to notice us? We don't even look the

*same and that was years ago. Shelley said that most peo-
ple thought we died,* Brian Matthew said. *Besides, I'm
just going to hang out in the back anyway.*

He had been walking toward the court as they argued, disregarding Francis's paranoia. Michelle's first
match had already started, but they hadn't missed much.
He kept to the back of the crowd like he'd promised
Francis he would, watching Michelle as she prepared for
the lobby. The other girl was running Michelle all over
the court. She bounced from side to side like one of those
pinball machines. Then the tide turned as Michelle hit the
ball to the other side, sending her opponent on the run.
The girl tried to keep up, but she miscalculated a hit and
the ball got away from her. They announced the point for
Michelle, and Brian Matthew got excited.

She's got this, he thought.

One point doesn't make the whole game, Francis
said. He was right. A second later the girl sent Michelle
running again, but this time she couldn't bounce back.

Damn. Why did you have to jinx it? Brian Matthew
said.

Three matches kept them on edge, waiting with anticipation to see if she would be victorious. When the final match ended and they announced her win, he cheered
loudly. Michelle shook hands with her opponent and left
the court. After stopping to speak with her coach, she
headed over to a couple that Brian Matthew assumed
were her new parents. He tried to ignore the jealousy that
was building, but he couldn't push it back down.

She's my sister not their daughter, he thought.

How do you like that? Francis said. *She didn't even
wave, and we're family.*

She has a new family now. She has to stay with them,
Brian Matthew said. *You don't want her to draw attention to us.*

I guess not. But still... Francis sounded sulky, but Brian Matthew wouldn't indulge him.

We'll just go visit her later, after her parents go to bed. I'm going to walk a bit. Brian Matthew shifted his eyes away from Michelle's happiness. He didn't really care about being cautious. Francis was paranoid anyway, and Brian Matthew wanted to be out in the open for a change. He passed a brunette girl on the street, hair slicked back in a high ponytail. She looked him over and nodded at him, lips curled into a smile. He gave her a nod back, curling up one of his lips in a similar motion. It felt good to be noticed. Several other girls nodded as well when they passed him on the street.

Why are they all looking at you? Francis asked. *They never pay attention to me.*

That's because you walk around like you're Frankenstein, Brian Matthew said, trying to give the girl that passed him his savviest smile.

What do you mean? Francis hated it when he didn't understand something. And he didn't understand women. It hadn't been a problem before. Francis didn't like people and had no desire for interaction. Watching Brian Matthew fit in so easily, he couldn't help being jealous and Brian Matthew could sense it.

I guess I could help you if you want, he said.

I don't need your help, Francis scoffed. *I don't need anybody. I was just wondering what's so different about you.*

Uh-huh. We'll see, Brian Matthew said, knowing that something was changing Francis, but not wanting to discourage it.

Chapter 17

Francis

April 2009:

After graduation, Michelle moved in to a place of her own, keeping in contact with her foster parents, but never revealing that she had been reunited with her brother. After years of street life, the boys were thrilled to be sleeping on a couch again.

Michelle had wanted to get him a bed, but Francis didn't want her charity. He often went out at night then came back to visit several times a week, but when he grew weary of gypsy life, he would curl up on the couch, knowing that someone in this world cared that he was in it.

Brian Matthew didn't mind the support of his sister. They had always leaned on each other, and he never felt stronger, but he still knew what Francis soon forgot. She didn't belong to them. They were intruders in her brother's body, and she would never know the difference. Michelle didn't question his mood swings. He had been through a lot and she was left with scars too.

If he raised his voice at all, she would start to rock, singing "Mockingbird" until he quieted, and at night, she would scream into the darkness until the nightmares went away. At first this startled the boys, but nothing they did relieved her of her distress.

Then one day, the boys felt themselves being pushed back into the mind without their control and Brian appeared, bursting into confused and relieved tears when he saw his sister. Michelle didn't know what was happening, but she patted his shoulder, singing to him.

"Where am I," he asked, examining some of the details of the room.

Michelle had stopped singing, unsure of what was going on. She sat on the edge of her bed next to him and felt his forehead.

"Are you feeling okay, Bubba?"

"It's really you, Shelley? Isn't it?" he asked.

"Of course it's me. Who else would it be?"

"You grew," he said.

You should stop this before he scares her, Francis said.

I can't. He's in control, Brian Matthew said, annoyed with the trapped feelings he had.

"Maybe you should lie down for a minute. I knew sleeping outside would get you sick." She tucked him into her bed, feeling his forehead again. "Now if I can remember where I keep the thermometer…"

"I'm sorry," he said. "I didn't realize I'd found you. Everything is kind of fuzzy."

"Did you hit your head?" She rubbed the top of his head, feeling for a bump. "Do you need to see a doctor?"

"I'm fine, Shelley. Really. I'm not even tired. A doctor will tell you the same," he said. Michelle seemed uncertain, and Brian's head was still spinning. "After we left, did you ever go back to see Dad? I mean, is he still around here?"

Shelley froze in her movements, turning around to

look at him. Her pale skin looked gray, and she was struggling to take deep breaths. Brian watched her and tried to put everything together, but there were too many blanks in his head. Shelley opened her mouth and closed it several times before composing herself.

"Perhaps some rest will help your memory," she said.

"No, no, I'm fine," he said, to the boys' relief. "I just forget things sometimes. I think it's probably a side effect from the accident. I'm sorry for startling you."

"I'm fine, Bubba. I just want to make sure you're okay." She gave him a hug, and the day continued as if nothing had happened. But after a few days, Francis broke free again, taking back what he thought rightfully belonged to him. He was, after all, the one who kept them alive.

Francis had been content with living his life as Shelley's big brother, doing odd jobs for money, and staying in one place for a while. But once again, he found himself searching for something he hadn't realized he was missing until he saw her. Glowing smile, light, wispy laugh: there was no other girl in his mind before or after he met her. He had developed aliases while he traveled and decided for his safety he would continue using them, not allowing even Michelle to call him Brian in public.

At the time of their meeting, he had been the overly dramatic punk kid, Adam Tyler. His dark make-up made him an easy target for any pretty boy that passed him on the sidewalk. Francis was almost twenty-one, but his mind maintained that naïve, teenage mentality, where he considered anyone who eyed him a threat to himself. With Brian Matthew's help these past few months, he had grown more controlled when given his freedom.

That family was to be his only kill if he had any decision in the matter. Michelle had been helpful too. He didn't tell her what happened, but she could sense something was different. Sometimes he had nightmares of the little girl screaming, and Michelle would hug him until everything was okay. He was so reassured by her that he didn't have the heart to tell her he wasn't either of her brothers, but Brian Matthew didn't seem to mind him taking over the brother role for a bit. \

He had even tried to be a normal adult, approaching people to strike up conversations, but he was big and awkward, unintentionally intimidating people. He didn't possess the proper social etiquettes like Brian Matthew did. Brian Matthew could blend into any situation, but Francis stuck out.

One day he had wandered into a youth center that he had heard about from fliers, where kids and young adults could go for after school activities like sports and music classes. He was astonished by the massive group playing on the basketball court. He thought about going to talk to them, but then he got nervous, hanging back to observe them instead.

Brian Matthew laughed, enjoying his friend's discomfort. *And you say I'm defective.*

Shut up, Francis said. *I'm working on it.*

He looked around for a smaller group to try to approach, but all of them seemed as large as the first to him. Just inside the lobby, he spotted a small piano that was still vacant. He remembered how much Brian's mother loved his piano playing when he was a child. She was an elementary school music teacher and gave lessons out of their home while his father was at work, but Brian couldn't play the piano anymore. He'd forgotten when he'd pushed the pain of his mother's death back too far in his brain, but the memory had stuck with Brian Matthew, and when Francis was awakened, he was a natural musician. He sat down on the bench and brushed his fingers against the keys. Francis had never experienced the feel of his fingertips pressed to ivory. He hadn't been out often enough to really get the full effect, but he knew which keys to press and so he did, enjoying the beautiful sound he was creating.

I still play it better, Brian Matthew said.

Whatever, Francis said, ignoring his constant companion.

"You're pretty good," a voice beside him said.

He stopped, hitting his hand against a key that made a sour note, and his eyes locked with a pair of amber ones. She was curvy and petite, her body accentuated by the pair of yoga pants and tight tank top she had on. Nobody had ever approached Francis before, not like Brian or Brian Matthew.

Whoa, Brian Matthew said, but Francis couldn't respond. His heart was thumping loud in his chest and his face felt warm.

"Sorry, I didn't mean to interrupt you. I just always admired someone who could play an instrument. I wasn't ever able to take lessons." As she talked, he watched the fullness of her lips, wondering what her lip gloss tasted like.

Don't be such a creep. Look at her eyes and listen to her, Brian Matthew said. He could feel that tingling sensation that Francis felt, and the last thing he wanted was for him to screw it up. When Francis messed up, people usually died.

"It's pretty easy actually. I just let my fingers tell me where to go," he said, not sure if what he said made any sense, or if his gravelly voice would frighten her away.

"That's wonderful." She smiled. "Maybe you can teach me some time. Do you come in here very often? I don't think I've seen you before."

"No. I'm new in the area. My name is Francis."

Francis could almost feel the mental smack Brian Matthew gave him.

You gave her your real name, he said, feeling very unimpressed.

"It's nice to meet you. I'm—"

A child came over in a tutu, tapping the woman on her shoulder. Her blonde curls flashed the boys back to images of shattered glass and blood on Michelle's clothes, but neither of them wanted to remember that. It was Brian's memory, not theirs.

"Ms. Martin, do you like my new ballet slippers? Mommy found them for me." The little girl twisted her feet around, modeling her new sparkly pink shoes.

"Those are pretty, Lexi. Tell the girls to start warming up and I'll be right in." The girl walked off, and the woman turned back to Francis. "It was nice to meet you, Francis. I hope we see each other again soon."

He nodded and kept watching her until she had disappeared behind the studio door.

I like her, Brian Matthew said.

Me too, Francis said, and he smiled.

Chapter 18

Lizzie

August 2012:

Lizzie crept in and the door creaked shut behind her. The room was dimly lit with a table and chair in the center. On the table was a glass, half full of water, and a pale hand twirling her finger inside of it. Her head was face down, resting on the table, and matted blonde hair moved back and forth as her little form rocked. Then she started to hum and spoke in a rhythmic whisper.

"I love little pussy, her coat is so warm, and if I don't hurt her, she'll do me no harm. Mademoiselle went down to the well, combed her hair, and brushed it well, then picked up her basket and vanished! One for sorrow, two for joy, three for a girl, four for a boy, five for silver, six for gold, seven for a secret never to be told…"

"Michelle, my name is Lizzie. I was hoping maybe you could help me." Lizzie kept her hand on the doorknob as she spoke, wondering if maybe she should just leave now.

"All the pretty ponies are gone. What happened to the piggy? I cut him for supper. Where are all my dolls, brother? They're dead. I've ripped them apart. Big girls don't need to play with dolls." When she said this her voice grew raspy and frantic, as if she were driving her thoughts into frenzy.

"I think I might know the man you are looking for. Could you tell me about him?" Lizzie slowly moved towards the table, left foot, right foot, but stopped again when she spoke.

"Mary, Mary, quite contrary, how does your garden grow? From the blood of innocent children, all lying in a row..." Michelle's head bobbed loosely on the table, but still didn't rise to address her visitor.

Lizzie moved back toward the door. This woman was beyond lunacy. *She's going to make me crazy*, she thought, realizing how out of her league she was.

"Jen doesn't know you're here, does she? Of course not, she would not approve, oh no—he will not be pleased either."

Lizzie froze, the mere mention of her sister registering with her mind. "How do you know about Jen?"

"Very pretty girl, Michelle, oh yes, both very pretty girls but so ungrateful. Oh, this will not do, this will not do. Lizzie must be taught a lesson. She must learn to appreciate such a wonderful sister. I never had anyone like her. I was stuck with you, devil girl. Can't take care of yourself. Always a burden. And after all I've done for you, you wouldn't help me because you're such an ungrateful little brat. That's what happened to Mommy. She left to get rid of you. She hated you. But things didn't go according to plan. He was not pleased, not at all. He came home in a fury. It wasn't supposed to be that way, but I was a bad girl. I didn't listen to him. I put you back." Her voice was frantic at first, but slowing to an end. She didn't even look at Lizzie, and Lizzie wondered if Michelle even knew she was there anymore. Suddenly, she started to sniffle and her voice turned into a soft whisper. "He took him from me. He was such a sweet boy, a good brother. He loved me and now he's gone. Why did he leave me behind?"

Lizzie shuffled her way to the table, trying not to make any sudden movements. Her heart was throbbing in her chest, beating loudly at her ribcage, as if it wanted to rip itself from her body and run away. She stopped at the edge of the table. Standing across from Michelle, Lizzie reached down and stroked Michelle's hair. It felt surprisingly soft, as if it had been the one thing she took time on, although it appeared as disheveled as the rest of her. Lizzie lowered her mouth as close to her ear as possible and asked her what she had been waiting for. "Who took your brother?"

The sniffles stopped and Michelle lifted her head from the table, rising from her seat as she did it. She leaned forward, the blue of her eyes expanding until it was all Lizzie could think about on her face, a blue that she couldn't help recognizing.

Suddenly, the August heat had grown icy in Lizzie's limbs and she shivered, wrapping her arms around herself to contain them. They were so close now that she could feel Michelle's breath on her face, hot and sticky against her chin. She waited a moment for Michelle to gather what was left of her thoughts to speak, but she just stood there, staring into Lizzie's face, her own ghostly pale and troubled. Lizzie looked around for any signs of someone coming. She wouldn't have much time left before they came looking for her so Lizzie asked Michelle again.

"Who took your brother? Please, I've got to know."

Michelle lurched out, grabbing Lizzie by the shoulders, unintentionally shaking her as her own body quivered uncontrollably.

Her eyes softened as a tear streaked the side of her

face. "Hell," she whispered, releasing Lizzie from her grasp.

Instead of settling into the chair at the table, she slid into the corner, cradling her legs with her arms and singing again, "Ring around the rosie, pocket full posies, ashes, ashes, all fall down."

Lizzie closed the door quietly behind her, overwhelmed with the possible explanations for everything that just happened.

She raced out of the doors before she realized she didn't know where she was going. Her head was already full of questions connected to small flashes of memory that she couldn't seem to sort out. She pulled an address from her pants pocket. Eleven Cherry Street. Hopefully, an afternoon with Nick's grandmother could clear her mind of the madness.

Chapter 19

Lizzie

February 2012:

Sixteen was supposed to be Lizzie's favorite number. She could drive, after she took lessons, and have the best sweet-sixteen party ever. Her mother had already started planning it when she was fourteen, with a little bit of nudging from Lizzie.

Peacock hues of blues, greens, purples, and gold covered the banquet hall her parents had rented in decorations. Delicate blue vases with blue, green, and purple feathers intertwined with peacock feathers settled on all of the ornate tables in the reserved hall.

White covered cake with gold borders encircling the lower and upper strips of each tier. Peacock feathers painted on in a climbing pattern up the cake. Inside was a rich white chocolate, with sweet raspberry filling.

Her dress had cost her mother hundreds of dollars. It was peacock green with spaghetti straps and a pleated bodice that reminded Lizzie of the flow of flower petals and feathers. A delicate band was bow-tied in the waist, and the skirt layered diagonally, like the rippling of waves. After much persuasion on her part, she had con-

vinced her mother that it was a necessity to buy a matching hat and earrings with feathers and lace. She was their
only little girl, so naturally, since money was never a
problem, she got whatever she wanted.

"I thought you wanted a pretty pink party," her father
said when she returned to the house with her new dress.
Pink had always been her favorite color.

"Dad, I had that when I was six," she said, rolling
her eyes with disbelief.

Jen had called her "spoiled" that day. She didn't like
that Lizzie always got what she wanted. It wasn't healthy
for a young girl to live a life without some disappointment. "Someday, you're going to learn that your whole
life can't be bought in neat little packages. You don't always get your way." She had been so right.

Instead, Lizzie spent her birthday in the hospital,
hooked up to an IV, bandages wrapped tightly around her
arm and abdomen. Her fingers were rough, and her nails
were cracked and broken. She should have scratched him,
she realized later, but she hadn't. She had wasted her energy and nails on the door, trying to escape her cold prison. She had noticed how he was constantly talking.

"Do you know how neurotic you sound? Why must
you be so compulsive?" His voice was hoarse and raspy,
as if he were intentionally concealing it, aware of the girl
just steps and one door away from him. A softer voice
whispered something she couldn't understand, and something smashed to the floor. "We can't let her go. We've
worked hard to pick her."

Lizzie wasn't sure what was happening to her. She
didn't know why she was being punished, forever tortured with nightmares and fragmented memories of icy
demon eyes, but she did know two things. She wasn't
crazy and her brother, James, was not a murderer. He had
been framed, somehow coerced into cooperation, which

led to his death. She had to cling to that, because if she didn't, she would be lost.

Meanwhile, Lizzie was left to pick up the pieces with hours of therapy and a sister who thought she was delusional. Even her own parents hadn't believed her. Lizzie thought about the night before she had cut all ties with them. She had crept from her bed, her hand hesitating around the doorknob. She had been too afraid to leave her room all day. When her father had entered earlier, she charged him, using her long fingernails to scratch his arms. He had picked her up and set her on her bed before bolting for the door. She kicked him, shouting. "No. No. Go away. You're going to let him in. Don't you understand? He'll kill me. Go."

In that moment in her California home, standing by the door, she could hear someone entering the house from the hallway, and she knew that things had to change. She could feel how wrong everything was, deep inside her gut, but had no way of stopping it. Lizzie listened, hand still on the knob, too afraid to open it.

"How is she?"

The voice was soft, but Lizzie knew it was Jen. She hadn't seen her since her parents brought her home from the hospital for the second time: This time hadn't been for her body. Her body would heal, but her mind...her parents weren't so sure.

"Not well," her mother said, in a way that sounded almost like she was struggling with self-control.

"She attacked me today. Look."

Lizzie imagined her father showing Jen all the tiny, catlike scratches.

"She has been here two weeks and is already beyond our control," her father said.

"We haven't gotten a good night's sleep in days. She just stays up all night, huddled in her bed, and when she sleeps, she cries out and wriggles with fear." Her mother's voice choked a little, and Lizzie could hear her stifle a sob. "We think that maybe she would do better if she stayed with you."

Lizzie's heart felt as if someone had dropped an anvil on her chest, but there wasn't anyone there to help pull it off.

"But she's your daughter," Jen said, not understanding any of this.

"We've just lost our son. My wife can't give Lizzie what she needs right now, and I can't stay home all day. I have people who depend on me." Her father sounded tired and distant. "Can't she just stay with you during the week? She's going back to school soon, so that will take up most of her day anyway. Let's just get her back into a normal routine, and when she feels better, she can come home."

Lizzie had slammed the door loudly so they knew she was listening, but no one came up to check on her. It had been the beginning of the destruction of her family.

Chapter 20

Lizzie

August 2012:

Lizzie looked up at the street signs. The town was so tiny that hardly anyone was around. On the next road over, she found Cherry Street. It was a small dead end, with only eleven tiny houses all standing in a row. Each house was painted a faded color like blue, white, or yellow, with white or gray shutters.

In the back yard each had a garden with blooming, orange flowers. Lilies were what she thought they were. They spread themselves around all the houses like a disease. *Herpes flowers*, she thought, chuckling to herself. It looked like something out of the Stepford Wives.

Outside one of the homes, a woman was hanging laundry. She had on a knee-length floral dress and plastic pearls dangling from her neck. She was humming to herself, and her smile seemed to be surgically implanted on her face. A toddler sat at her feet, dressed in what looked like to be his Sunday best even though it was Monday. He had curly brown hair that accented his round, chubby face. He sat beside the basket busying himself with his rattle. He grinned up at Lizzie as she entered the yard.

"Excuse me, but could you tell me which house is number eleven?" Lizzie gave her best voice trying to be as polite as possible.

"Why would you want to go to that devil woman's house? That's no place for a sweet girl like…" The woman caught a glimpse of Lizzie and looked startled. She grabbed the child and ran for the house, muttering something about the gospel. When she got inside, she screamed out at Lizzie. "You get away from my property. I want nothing to do with Satan's children. Be gone, evil spirit."

Lizzie was completely dumbfounded about the whole situation. She took her compact out of her purse. She looked incredibly pale and her eyes were weary. Her hair seemed to be getting darker, more like the shade of rope-soaked in formaldehyde instead of a golden cupcake, which accentuated her black attire. She realized that maybe she didn't look like the most approachable person right then.

Looking around, Lizzie noticed at the end of the road there was an old Victorian house. It was painted a deep royal purple, with white trim. Out in the front yard was an array of brightly colored flowers, and out in the backyard she could see a small glimpse of what looked to be some sort of animal cage, peering out from the row of bushes. The basketball hoop looked slightly out of place in the driveway and, as Lizzie reached the porch, she noticed the post office on the left. Lizzie hit the doorbell, which played the funeral march. She tried hard not to burst with laughter. She would hate to offend his grandmother before she even got into the house.

"You must be Lizzie. I'm Genevieve, Nick's grandmother. Come on in." Lizzie remembered meeting Genevieve once when she came to California for Nick's thirteenth birthday, but she had forgotten most of the details about her. She had aged gracefully, each wrinkle representing some sort of wisdom in her face. Her eyes had a violet tinge and had a youthful quality to them.

She dressed eccentrically, with long flowing skirts and colorful bangle earrings like a modern gypsy, come home after all her years of wandering. Her long, silver hair streamed down her back in a beautiful, intricate braid.

She scooped Lizzie up in her arms the minute Lizzie got through the door. Genevieve smelled of the ocean breeze and coconuts which made Lizzie feel at home again like all the summers she spent on the shore. "We're so glad to have you. My, have you grown. Nick didn't tell me what a beautiful girl you've become."

"Thank you. That's very sweet of you to say." Lizzie didn't feel particularly beautiful, but it was good to hear regardless.

Genevieve smiled with excitement. "Wait until you see what I have for you."

She escorted Lizzie through the living room and ducked out of the room for her surprise. The room was no stranger to color. It had a navy blue couch with orange pillows that felt smooth like silk. Each pillow had ornate flowers sewn on the top, with leaves traced along the sides. On the recliner, next to the couch, a blanket with the same color and pattern as the pillows was flung across the top. Sunflowers and pink asters decorated all of the stands and tables. On the golden brown coffee table, there were two red candles lit that contained the scent of raspberries. Everywhere one looked, there was something bright to tantalize the senses which kept Lizzie occupied until Nick's grandmother came back in. Four freshly baked cookies and milk were brought out on a tray.

"Nick told me you had an appetite as big as his so I made several batches of cookies. I hope you like pumpkin, chocolate chip. He went down to the store for me, but he should be back soon. In the meantime make yourself at home. I just need to tend to my garden for a moment." She glided from the room as if her feet were on a puffy cloud.

Lizzie took a huge bite of one of the cookies. Chips melted into her mouth like a chocolaty explosion, each morsel settling on her tongue, and erupting again with satisfaction in her stomach. These were by far the best cookies she had ever had.

"Honey, I'm home," Nick said from the doorway.

Lizzie shoved as many cookies in her mouth as she could get.

Nick peered down at the plate with only one cookie left. "What happened to the cookies?"

"What cookies?" Little bits of cookie flew out Lizzie's mouth, her chubby cheeks protruded out from the bulk of them. They burst into laughter. Nick dashed for the last one and Lizzie wrestled him to the ground. Nick tried to peel her fingers away from the plate, but she cried out. "Oww…oh, that hurts."

"Oh, I'm sorry. I didn't mean to—" Nick said as Lizzie punched him in the gut and popped part of the cookie in her mouth. "Hey, you cheated."

"It's not my fault you're so gullible." Lizzie stuck her tongue out at him playfully and tore off a small piece for Nick. "Here you go."

"Oh gee, you're so generous. Come here, you." Nick chased her around the room. He scooped her petite body in his arms and tipped her upside down. "Hmm…maybe I can get a cookie out of you, or maybe I'll just make you into cookies."

"Honestly, Nick, I've told you a million times that girls make terrible cookies. They're too sour." Genevieve walked in with a beautiful bouquet of freshly cut flowers.

"Here's some advice for you, honey. Never come between a man and his food."

"Or Lizzie and food, for that matter. She'd gnaw my hand off for a taco," Nick said, smile as wide as the horizon.

"Not true…I'd only gnaw off your fingers. It would take too long to gnaw off the wrist. By the time it would take me to eat your hands, I could just make my own tacos," Lizzie said smugly, wondering if maybe her morbid sense of humor had offended Genevieve.

"I would loan you my hacksaw if you were that hungry," Genevieve said, grinning affectionately at her grandson.

Who knew Nick's grandmother had as twisted a sense of humor as me, Lizzie thought.

"Grandma, you're supposed to be on my side."

Genevieve gasped for air holding her chest with one hand and fanning herself with the other.

"How dare you use that language with me, young man? You're going to give me an aneurysm with all that talk. I'm much too young and beautiful to be called such a foul word."

They all snickered with laughter. Lizzie was having so much fun, she had almost completely forgotten what happened at the police station, but sitting there with them, it came back to mind.

"Do you think I'm crazy," Lizzie asked, turning to look at Nick directly.

He bit his lip and looked at Genevieve. Lizzie could tell he was concentrating hard on what he should say.

"All the best people are," Genevieve said, giving Lizzie a gleaming smile that reminded her of Nick's. Lizzie smiled back, feeling better about their friendship.

"Hey, you want to get your future told?" Nick asked. "Can we, Genevieve?"

"If Lizzie is open to it, then I would be glad to," Genevieve said. "I'm a tarot reader."

"She's really good at it, too," Nick said. "None of that fake crap like the people on TV do."

"Ummm, okay," Lizzie said, not really sure if she believed in it, but not wanting to offend her hostess. Genevieve pulled out a deck of playing cards and shuffled them, breaking them up into three decks. "You don't use actual tarot cards?"

"That's complete poppycock. A person's truest essences are revealed in the ordinary things of life, like these playing cards. Cut the deck twice, then put it back together and shuffle it until you feel you've done it enough. Let the energy guide you to the right stopping point."

"I'll try," Lizzie said, doing as she was told. She didn't feel any energy like Genevieve described, but when she felt tired of them watching her she set the cards down again. "Now what?"

"Now I lay the top three cards on the table face down. The left is the past, the middle is the present, and the right is your future. Let's start with the past." She flipped over the card and Lizzie looked on with building curiosity. "Aww…the four of clubs. The four represents the foundation your life was built on. You grew up in a stable home where you were able to flourish. The clubs shows that you were a friendly, ambitious, and stubborn child, probably used to getting her way. Are you ready for the next one?"

"I guess so," Lizzie said, not feeling that impressed. Genevieve already knew a lot about Lizzie's life, so nothing she said was all that surprising that she knew, but she indulged them anyway.

"Let's see," Genevieve said, flipping over the next card, the present card. "Seven of hearts. The seven represents mystery in your life. There are secrets that you may be hiding, or secrets that you are trying to uncover in your life. Your life is also going through a period of change and transformation, which is causing your personality to change to hearts. Heart personalities are emotionally high strung, often moody, but also compassionate and protective of the people that matter the most to them."

"All right," Lizzie said, thinking of Jen. She would do anything to help her sister, if she could just keep her insanity in check. She thought for a minute about what Genevieve said about the secrets and considered telling Nick everything that was happening, but decided against it.

He doesn't need to know how obsessive I'm becoming. He probably wouldn't understand, she thought. "Okay, what did I get for my future?"

Genevieve flipped the card over, and instead of going right into her description, her mouth turned down in a frown. Her face grew heavy, sinking into itself, making some of her wrinkles more prominent. She looked at Nick and he shook his head, displeased with what he saw as well.

"What's the matter?" Lizzie asked, looking at the card. It was a three of hearts. She knew now what the hearts was and felt a little disappointed that her moodiness might not change, but she didn't know what the three meant. She picked up the card to further examine it and noticed that a star was drawn on the top of it. She looked at the other two cards and noticed that they also had stars drawn on them, but they were at the bottom of the card. She looked at the other two, but they were giving her a sympathetic look that she didn't understand. "Would one of you please tell me what this means already?"

"The three represents connections and the bond created from sharing a common goal," Genevieve began, hesitating to move forward.

"Yeah? And?"

"The stars represent the energy around a card. When the star is at the bottom, the energy is balanced, but when it's at the top, the energy is reversed, creating a negative energy around the card. A three represents close bonds that will develop, but a reverse three represents the loss of them, either in someone close to you or to yourself," Genevieve and Nick eyed each other as Nick bit his lip.

"It could be figuratively though, right, Genevieve," Nick said. "Like you're not the same person anymore, so you lose yourself."

"Well, yes, that's quite possible," Genevieve said, giving the two a nod.

"Or it could mean I'm going to die," Lizzie said flatly.

Of course this had to be as morbid as everything else was in her life. Why couldn't she say that she was going to the moon or becoming a princess or something? Why did she have to be so morbid? Lizzie still didn't believe it, but her own terrors were making it easier for her to entertain the idea that she might be right.

"You're going to be fine, Lizzie," Nick said, resting his hand against hers. "I would never let anyone hurt you. Pull a clarity card."

"A what," Lizzie asked, not sure if she wanted to hear anymore.

Genevieve handed Lizzie the deck again. "A clarity card. It's an extra card that can be taken from the deck to answer one of the recipients' questions. Reshuffle the deck, then ask a question to yourself and the card on top will have your answer."

Lizzie shuffled quickly, hands shaking as she closed

her eyes to think of her question. She had too many questions. How could she ever pick one? She thought of Jen and wondered if the future card was meant for her, but she couldn't ask that. She was too afraid of what she would find. She asked the one thing she'd wanted to know for a while, the one thing that preyed on her mind endlessly until she was exhausted with sleep and drenched in sweat.

Who is going to kill me? she thought, handing the cards back to Genevieve.

"The king of spades," Genevieve said, looking at the man on top of the other three cards. "The man is burdened with a deep past. He is aggressive, impulsive, and ill-tempered, but also charming and intelligent. Whoever he is, he will be an important link in answering your question, but you mustn't tell anyone what you asked. It might bring you bad luck."

"Thank you," Lizzie said politely, staring at the king. Something about that card made her stomach churn. She looked away, trying to think of something else to talk about. "Do you do a lot of readings here, Genevieve?"

"Not recently," Genevieve said, seeming to be in her own head as well. "I stopped them this summer after I had some difficulties."

"Oh? What happened?"

"A young man came to me seeking guidance, but he didn't like his reading. He was a very troubled young man and those eyes, so much pain in such a young face." Genevieve shook her head as if to stir the memory away.

Lizzie's body tensed at the mention of eyes. "What color were they?" she asked, feeling her stomach shift in a nervous swirl.

"It doesn't matter now. I'd rather not discuss it further," Genevieve said, twisting a ring on her finger that Lizzie thought was made of garnet.

Lizzie wanted desperately to push her. She had to know what he said, what he looked like, but the look in Genevieve's eye told her that she wouldn't get anywhere, and she left it alone.

"Cool, isn't she," Nick said as he escorted Lizzie to Jen's car an hour later. He had this goofy, little grin on his face that Lizzie couldn't quite figure out. What did he have to be happy about? Maybe he was on something.

"It was…interesting, to say the least," Lizzie said. "Maybe I can come over more often."

Genevieve ran out after them. Her silver hair swayed in the autumn breeze. She carried a silver tin with a blue ribbon on the top. "One more thing, here's some more cookies. I know Nick probably ate most of the other ones. You take care of yourself, hon. Not everything is always what it appears to be."

"Umm…thanks. I'll keep that in mind. It was nice meeting you."

Lizzie slammed the door behind her. She was startled to discover that Joel was driving. "Where's Jen?"

"She had to work late, so she told me to come and get you. I just brought over the last of my stuff. Did you have a good time?" He looked at her out the corner of his eye and Lizzie couldn't help thinking of her adopted father or even her brother, James. He always gave her this watching look when he was about to ask her a serious question, but couldn't decide how to go about it.

"Yeah. His grandmother seemed cool. She even gave me cookies." Lizzie smiled, holding the little silver tin in her lap. It was a good thing she had a fast metabolism.

"So, she was there. You weren't like…alone or anything?"

"Seriously? I'm not running around having sex with guys. Jeez, I mean it's Nick, for cryin' out loud." Lizzie could feel the heat rising to her face. She really didn't want to discuss what feelings may or may not be there with Joel. "Besides, it's not like you and Jen are saints either. I know what you're doing while I'm in school."

"Working like normal adults. Your sister and my relationship isn't being called into question, and neither of us are a teenage girl."

"I told you nothing is happening, so don't bug me about it," Lizzie said, not wanting to hear more.

"Chill out. This isn't an interrogation. It's okay if you like the guy. He seems like an all right kid, and it's not like you've been hiding it well. It's pretty obvious you—"Joel didn't even have time to finish his thought.

"Whoa! Back it up there, JoJo. There's nothing going on between Nick and me. We're just friends."

Another thought came into her head. Lizzie didn't really know much about Joel at all. Looking at him then, he seemed fairly normal. She tried to remember what exactly was annoying about him. He spoke his mind, maybe that was the problem. She didn't want to hear what he had to say. She clung on so desperately to be right, but what if she should just...she didn't know anymore. There were just too many things going on in her head lately. "What's your family like?"

"I'm an only child, and my dad lives in Florida now. He got tired of the snow. He said it was unnatural to be living like a penguin, when he could be sipping coke on a sunbathed porch somewhere." He smiled big, and Lizzie could only imagine him picturing his father's home.

"What about your mother?" she asked, waiting for him to continue.

"She died a few years ago, cancer. She was an amazing lady, the best. Her smile could light up the whole house and man could she cook." He laughed half-heartedly, looking back out the window.

Lizzie wanted to say something, but she decided to just leave him to his thoughts for now.

Once they reached the house, she rushed up the winding staircase to her computer. Now that Nick was no longer around to distract her, Michelle's words became more prominent in her thoughts. She hadn't gathered the courage to mention it to Nick because he probably thought she was crazy, and she liked him. The last thing she wanted to do was scare him off.

Her fingers scrambled across the keyboard, typing furiously. As she skimmed through the articles, things became more and more disheartening. Nothing could give her the proof she needed to confirm her sanity. Victim after victim flooded onto the screen, their imprisoned faces frozen on the fronts of newspapers.

That could have been me on the front page, she thought as the hours ticked away. Lizzie had suffered to live, but lately she had begun to feel like they were the lucky ones. She was still trapped in the nightmare. Part of her was beginning to fade, but the other part was fighting just as hard to regain herself. Lizzie slammed her fist on the keyboard, frustration overwhelming her. Tears of doubt poured down her face. She hastily wiped her eyes as Jen walked in.

"How's the search coming?" Jen's face always held the weight of the world in it and this time was no exception. Her skin looked paler than Lizzie remembered, and there were shadows under her eyes. She often forgot how much pain this caused Jen. Her sister had been right—Lizzie was a bit self-centered.

"How did you know I wasn't doing my homework," Lizzie said, feigning disgust at the unfair judgment.

"Call it sisterly intuition. Besides, what school gives you homework on the first day? So, how's it going?"

"Everything seems to be going around in circles.

Maybe it really is just all in my mind." Lizzie moved away from her laptop, sitting next to Jen, who had settled onto the bed. She rested her head gently on Jen's shoulder.

Jen always had a motherly effect on her. Lizzie felt calm and loved when she was there. Jen patted her head, stroking her hair.

"I don't think you're crazy. I think you're confused and need some resolution. I have something for you." Jen pulled a tiny bracelet from her pocket and hooked it around Lizzie's wrist. "This was mine when I was a little older than you. A dear friend gave it to me for courage and safety. I want you to have it so you feel protected, too."

"Thanks, but I always feel safer with you here. What happened to our parents?" Lizzie asked, blurting out a question that had never come to mind before.

"After you were born, when I was about six, Dad left us. Mom kept telling me it wasn't our fault, but I was never sure. I don't really remember much about him, except that he always smelled of Doublemint gum. He never came back." She paused for a second, as though she were searching her memory.

"And Mom?" Lizzie could feel the ripple of her sister's body as she took a deep breath in and slowly exhaled.

"Mom had a rough time finding work and a babysitter. She did her best, I suppose, but she had no family, and soon we couldn't afford our apartment. I remember the night we slept in her car. It was rainy, but I'd liked the saltiness to the air. It was soothing, I guess: Even you stopped crying when the rain started. A few days later, Mom brought us to the park. She made me promise to sit with you on the bench until she got back, but she didn't come back. I cried a lot at first, but over the years, I've forgotten what she looked like, except she had golden hair like yours." Jen said everything so calmly, but when Lizzie looked up at her, there were tears on her cheek. She wiped it away before she noticed Lizzie was watching. "So, do you like the bracelet?"

Lizzie nodded and jiggled it on her wrist. She hugged her sister tightly, feeling as though she had her family again and, for the moment, that was all she needed.

Chapter 21

Brian Matthew

August 2009:

B rian Matthew's reaction to Ms. Martin was just as strong as Francis's, but he was cautious of any attachments. Rejection would be imminent when you're one of three different people in a body and at least one of those personalities was an ill-tempered ticking bomb. He kept waiting for her to get sick of their mood swings, but she was persistent, talking with him every day they walked to the center and even going out for ice-cream with him after her dance class. She was caring and even affectionate to him sometimes. Francis never noticed when she touched his arm or whispered closely in his ear. He thought that was normal in a friendship, but Brian Matthew knew what that meant.

She was fond of them. Although he was reluctant to have anyone close to Francis, Brian Matthew couldn't help but adore her too. Even Brian had met her at one point when they were out for ice-cream one day. Brian Matthew had thought about intervening before he scared her, but Brian never seemed to be confused anymore. He'd awoken in so many strange places that he was relieved when he had some interesting company. Brian Matthew always wondered why Brian wasn't more afraid. Sometimes, he thought Brian could sense his presence, but if he did, he didn't say so. Nevertheless, he took to the girl as much as the others.

Everything was going well for them, but one week she didn't come to the center. Every day when her ballet students came through the doors, Brian Matthew rushed to his seat at the piano and tapped his foot impatiently as the clock ticked down its minutes before class started. Each second of anticipation became greater, swelling like an enormous balloon in his chest, waiting to be popped so that all the cheery, sparkly confetti could fly out. For a week, that moment of sweet relief never came, and Brian Matthew and Francis worried.

Did she move? Brian Matthew said.

Is she really sick? Maybe we should see if she's at the hospital, Francis thought.

The following Monday, she was back for her class, looking as vibrant as ever. She smiled, noticing him at the back of the room, and, for some strange reason, he couldn't help but smile back. The corners of his mouth had inadvertently flipped upside down into a complete grin. Brian Matthew was a bit confused about the feeling, but decided just to ignore it instead of going through a lengthy investigation in his mind.

"Missed you." He felt the words slide from his tongue in a gruff voice like some unfamiliar language.

Will you let me handle this, he said, disliking the sound of Francis's voice coming from his mouth.

Just thought she should know, Francis replied, not caring that he had invaded Brian Matthew's body time.

"I missed you too," she said. It was hard not to stare into those exotic eyes—amber with a strange tint of garnet when the light reflected from them, but then they dropped from him, staring aimlessly at the ground. She bit absentmindedly at her lip. "Do you think maybe we could get a burger after my class?"

"Sure. I would love to," he said. Was this a date? *Since when do we go on dates?*

He could hardly focus on his meal with her around. Her smile and laugh were infectious. Every time she looked away, he would just stare in amazement. Then he'd quickly avert his eyes before she could notice.

I have found my match, Brian Matthew thought.

She's absolutely perfect for me, Francis corrected, feeling a little grumpy that her first date wasn't with him.

She stared at him for a brief second and then reached over and pulled the hair back from his face. Brian Matthew waited to hear that compulsive explosion in his head of Francis's voice because he dreaded even the slightest movement of a single follicle, but it didn't come.

"There. Now I can see your eyes." She beamed as Brian Matthew tried to remember what they looked like this time. He noticed his reflection in the window behind her, ice blue like his mother's. He hadn't changed them.

"Most people don't like them because they're too blue. It creeps people out."

"That's what I love about them. They're unique, like you." She leaned in and her lips caressed his, and then he was consumed in her lips and mouth. The feel of her silky hair slid through his fingertips as he skimmed them down the length of her back and around her waist. Suddenly, she yelped and pulled away. Afraid he did something wrong, he backed away, quickly getting up from his chair and heading for the door.

What did I do? What if she thinks I was trying...? I shouldn't have kissed her, Brian Matthew said. He had never felt so unnerved in all his time in the body.

What did you do? You better not have ruined this for

me, Francis yelled so loud that he was giving Brian Matthew a headache.

"Francis."

She was behind him jogging to catch his long strides. She managed to catch him, turning him back around to face her. His heart still thumped loudly in his chest, half in longing and half in fear.

"You don't have to go. I'm fine."

"I'm sorry. I didn't mean—"

She held her finger to his lips, derailing every train of thought he had been developing.

"You didn't do anything wrong. It's not that. I—I just—I have to—Can we sit down for a minute?" She ushered him to the bench beside the restaurant door.

"Okay," he said with some confusion.

Before he could fully get the word from his mouth, she had him by the arm pulling him toward the bench. "First, you have to make me a promise. Promise me you won't tell anybody," she said, taking a deep breath.

"I promise. What is it?"

Slowly, and with a slight groan, she raised her shirt up to her stomach. Along the sides of her toned hips and abdomen were yellow blots of bruised skin. She winced a little as she covered them back up, trying to avoid the attention of anyone passing by.

Brian Matthew pulled her to him, trying to hug her without pulling her waist in. He cupped her chin in his hands and brought her face up to his. "Who did this to you?"

Whoever it is, I'm going to rip them apart, Francis said.

"It's not important. Don't worry about it," she said, looking away from him again.

"They can't get away with this. I won't let them. Tell me wh—"

She had him again. Those strawberry lips tingled on his mouth and, for a second, Brian Matthew felt completely calm. He'd even forgotten that Francis was still watching them, as annoyed as ever.

"Hey, girly, what are you doing here?" a slurred voice said and her body tensed. "I thought you was coming over to help yer mother clean."

"No, I'm not. She's not my mother and you aren't my father. I'm an adult now, so you can go away."

As she spoke, Brian Matthew felt her hand shake in his.

"Oh I'm not, am I? Well, who took you in when you didn't have anybody, huh? You could've been a little nothing orphan on the street, but we took you in, and this is how you repay me? By talking to me like this?"

"You got paid to keep me. It wasn't out of the goodness of your hearts, for sure. You're a miserable old drunk and I can't even—"

He held up his hand as if he was going to slap her, and she winced, going silent.

"You watch your mouth, girl, or I'm going to have to slap you in. You were always an insolent one. Did she tell you you were the first?" he asked, turning to Brian Matthew. "Did she tell you what a big slut she was in high school, waving her pom-poms around and shaking it for the entire football team? She gave them a bit more than cheers, I'll tell you."

Brian Matthew jumped up at the same time that she did, but she connected with him first, smacking him hard across the face. He pushed her, knocking her back into Brian Matthew's arms. He raised a fist, but noticed that he was out in the open and decided not to make a scene.

"You're lucky you're not home, girly or so help me, I'd beat some sense into your head. You're an ungrateful little bitch and you'll be coming crawling back, begging to come home when you fall on your ass." He started down the path before she could get another hit in.

"You go to hell," she yelled, moving forward to chase him. Brian Matthew grabbed her arm and pulled her back onto the bench. She sat next to him, wrapping her arms around his neck and crying into his shoulder. "I'm so sorry about this."

"It's okay," he said, rubbing her back and brushing her hair. "It'll be all right."

"Thank you," she said. "You've been so sweet."

"I actually have something for you. I was hoping you'd be here today." He pulled out a charm bracelet and latched it around her wrist. "It's to show you how much I care about you. As long as you have this, you'll be safe, I promise."

She hugged him tightly, kissing his cheek.

He's not going to get away with this, Francis said, not giving Brian Matthew any chance to object.

I know, Brian Matthew said, as ready to kill again as he was.

Chapter 22

September 2009:

He had done it. Somehow, he had managed to find that man again. The man hadn't made any more appearances while they were out and he didn't visit her at the dance studio, but the fear in her eyes never wavered. Brian Matthew knew that he still had a hold on her, so he followed her one day, keeping a minimal distance so that she wouldn't notice him. After weeks of this, she had led him to her old childhood home, picking up a few things before hastily leaving the place.

Now, Francis said, eager to get inside.

It's still daylight, Brian Matthew said. *All good things to those who wait.*

What a bunch of crap that is. Good things come to those who go after what they want, and right now I want to kill them.

Well, I'm waiting till sundown, Brian Matthew said, shaking his head.

Francis grumbled a little, but, for once, he obeyed Brian Matthew. He concealed himself in the bushes, watching people as they came and went, until at last the day grew dark and quiet.

Are you ready, he asked Francis.

I've been ready, he grumbled as Brian Matthew slipped out of the bushes.

He looked around to see if anyone was around and, when he found that the street was vacant, he knocked on the door.

"Get the door already," a woman's voice yelled.

"Well, who the hell is knocking at a time like this?" The sound of footsteps reached the door and the man opened it. Brian Matthew was relieved to find it was exactly who he was hoping for. He looked Brian Matthew over, recognizing him from their chance encounter. "What are you doing here? If you're looking for that little slut, she don't live here anymore, so you might as well go back to where you came from, do ya hear me?"

Brian Matthew was unresponsive until the man tried to shut the door on him. He grabbed the top of the door and pushed it back open. The man went to speak again, and Brian Matthew punched him in the mouth, causing him to stagger back into the house. He entered, closing the door behind him, and punched the guy again.

My turn, Francis said, pulling himself forward.

Fine, but I want the last part, Brian Matthew said, allowing him to take control.

Francis threw his whole body into the man, pushing him to the ground and beating at his face. It grew red as blood came out of his nose, eyebrow, and lip, but he continued to beat him. In front of him he heard a scream as the wife entered the room.

I'll deal with her, Brian Matthew said, pulling back to the forefront.

The man was unconscious on the floor, so he got up, kicking him before running down the hallway. The woman was hysterically crying as she ran for the backdoor in the kitchen. She tried to unlatch it, but her fingers fumbled. He grabbed her by the hair and wrenched her back onto the floor. He pulled a knife from its holder on the counter.

"Please, I don't deserve this. I haven't done anything to you. I won't say anything, I swear," the woman said, scooting back away from him. "You don't have to do this."

"Yeah, I do," he said and he came at her.

She screamed, and he slit her throat. He watched the shocked look in her eyes and listened to the gasping sound until he heard a groan in the next room.

Brian Matthew moved back down the hallway and stood over the man. He groaned again and tried to move, but found it difficult. Brian Matthew didn't give him much opportunity to try. He drove the knife into his chest, and the man let out a loud moan.

Francis's thoughts grew wild with excitement and Brian Matthew smiled. He remembered the night he killed his father, the rush of energy that built inside of him. He'd missed the feel of a knife in his hand, and now he remembered what he'd loved about it. Francis had been right all along. They were monsters, but he didn't care anymore. In that moment, he was taking control. In that moment, he was at peace again.

He stabbed the man several more times in the chest and stomach before heading back into the kitchen. He grabbed a washcloth and wiped the knife down, wrapping it in the cloth when he was finished so he wouldn't touch it again. He unlatched the back door and stepped back into the darkness. The air was cool, and a few raindrops were starting to hit the pavement. On his way down the street, he stepped into a neighbor's driveway and disposed of the knife in their trash bin. As he moved around the corner, he started to hum "Mockingbird" and didn't stop until he arrived home, hours later, at Michelle's apartment.

He fumbled for paper towels as he rinsed his hands in the sink. Francis's attack on the man had bloodied his knuckles, and he had blood smeared on his arm. He rubbed water on it, trying to scrub it off when he heard someone clearing their throat.

"What are you doing?" Michelle asked, watching him scrubbing vigorously. "Is that blood?"

"Go back to bed, Shelley," he said, wiping his hands dry. His knuckles stung, but his adrenaline was still high and the pain was easy to ignore.

"Did you kill someone else?" She tapped him on the shoulder, but he didn't look at her. He didn't respond at all. "Is that why you're out all the time? Did you hurt somebody?"

"Just leave it alone, Shelley," he warned, sensing Francis's anger start to build.

"How many people, Brian? How many innocent people have you been hurting? Answer me!"

He tried to walk away, but she grabbed his arm. He spun around, giving her a glare, but she gave him an equally painful one.

"There's no such thing as an innocent person, Shelley. Do you think anyone cared that we were innocent? Did Dad care when he almost beat you to death? Or did the nurse at school care when we happened to fall down and bruise a lot? Nobody would've missed us. It's not like those people are any better than us."

"Mom wouldn't want this," she said, gritting her teeth.

"Well, Mom's dead, so it doesn't matter what she wanted. We could argue about this all night, but it's already been done, so let's get our stuff together and head out before people start poking around. I don't think there's any way to trace me here, but I'd rather be on the safe side."

"Of course! You're just going to run off again. How typical of you." She waved her arms around like mini propellers as she spoke. "'Cause staying and dealing with the consequences is far too complicated for you to handle."

"Not me, Shelley. Us. We can go together this time. I would never leave you behind again. You're my sister, and I love you."

"I'm not going with you." She crossed her arms and shook her head. "I won't be a part of this."

"You already are," he said. "And you're coming with me, one way or the other."

I've had enough of this, Francis said.

Brian Matthew's arm jerked forward and he lost control. Francis grabbed Michelle, but she shoved him off, trying to storm away to end the argument. He grabbed her around the torso and lifted her off the ground.

"You're coming with me, Shelley, even if I have to make you," he said, as he tried to keep a firm grip on her wriggling body.

"Let go of me right now." She stomped on his foot and he dropped her to the floor. She got up and slapped him across the face. The impact startled him for a second before he released a loud growl.

"Don't you ever do that to me again, Brian. Now I'm going to bed, and you'd better be gone when I wake up."

She tried to leave the room again, and he grabbed her arm, twisting it around until she screamed. He knocked her to the ground and smacked her across the face. She squealed and burst into tears, rocking back and forth on the ground. He balled his hand into a fist, but it wouldn't move again.

Don't touch her again, Brian Matthew said.

Francis looked at the fist he had made. He looked at Michelle on the ground, and he became afraid of himself.

He released the tension in his hands and shook out his arms, trying to dissipate what little anger was left.

"Get packed. We're leaving tonight," he said, walking out of the room. He needed to breathe again, to feel the cool night air on his skin, and exhale into the darkness. He pushed open the door and received the relief he had hoped for.

Do you think she'll come with us? he asked Brian Matthew, looking into the darkness as the sun began to rise.

Definitely. Now that you've scared her to death, Brian Matthew said.

I almost killed her, Francis said, feeling fear in his chest again.

I know you would've. That's all we are anyway, monsters. You told me so once and I didn't believe you, remember?

Yeah, I do. I guess a tiger really can't change his stripes. Monsters we became, and monsters we will always be, Francis said, watching the dawn as it appeared across the horizon, illuminating the frown on his face.

Chapter 23

Lizzie

April 2012:

Lizzie had stayed with Jen for a couple weeks before her parents realized how much they missed their baby girl. They thought that, with more time, they could just start over, a fresh start was best. She thought so too, until she had realized what that meant. She hadn't been prepared to forget.

"Mom! Mom, where is my picture?" Lizzie ran down the stairs to where her mother was baking pies in the kitchen for Easter. Her mother looked up at her, kitten oven mitts on hands, holding her famous apple pie.

"What are you hollering about? There's no need to be upset." She placed the pie onto the counter to give her daughter her full attention.

"James's picture. You took it. Give it back. Where are all his things?" Lizzie could feel the rush of energy shooting through her like a rocket.

"We put them away, sweetheart. The doctor thought it best for you not to have all those awful things lingering over you." Her mother touched her gently on the shoulder, but Lizzie brushed it away.

"No. I want it back. Give it to me. He's still my brother. He's still my brother." Lizzie felt panicked. She needed to have it back. She didn't want to forget him. His hair color, the roundness of his face, she couldn't lose her brother. He kept her safe.

"Sweetheart, it's unhealthy to dwell on this. We need to move on, okay? You can have it back when you feel better. Now run along and—ow!"

Lizzie pulled one of the knives from the drawer and sliced her mother with it. Her mother recoiled in fear as Lizzie waved it around in her face.

"I want that picture back now," Lizzie said as calm and softly as possible. "Give it to me."

Her mother cracked, a soft sniffle escaping her, and tears fell down her cheeks. She held her arm tightly to her chest as blood started to escape between the gaps between her fingers. Lizzie looked at her mother and then looked at the knife in her hand. It clanged as it crashed to the floor. She moved toward her mother, trying to embrace her, tears pooling in her own eyes.

"Mom, I'm—"

Her mother pulled away from her embrace, fear and anger locked inside her irises. "Get away from me!"

The door swung open as Lizzie tried to grab her mother again, her father stepped through its entryway. Her mother was shaking, huddled in a corner, as her arm continued to ooze blood. Her father looked at them and then looked at the knife on the floor. His face tightened around his jaw and turned a reddish hue.

"Go to your room," he said through gritted teeth. "We'll deal with this later."

Afraid of what was to come, Lizzie hurried up the stairs to her bedroom. Her father had never hurt her, but Lizzie couldn't shake the uneasy feeling that something awful was about to happen. Before she could even make it up there, her father was dialing. She could hear his voice in the background, "Jen, I'm taking my wife to the emergency room. Come stay with Lizzie. We'll talk when I get back."

Lizzie sobbed into her pillows, feeling all the weight of her actions hitting her like cement blocks. *I just wanted the picture*, she thought.

When Jen arrived, she heard Lizzie crying and got into bed, creating a nest around her like a protective mother bird. She stroked her hair, as Lizzie continued to sob, and sang songs to her until her tears dried up.

Jen went downstairs when they came home, and Lizzie listened in on the staircase, hearing bits and pieces of what seemed like a fairly decisive argument on her parents' part. Suddenly, Lizzie heard the words "grandmother" and "Maine," and she saw her father pull out his checkbook. He reached out to give it to Jen, but she was too proud to take it.

She could hear Jen saying she could get another job, save up for a few years.

And then what? Lizzie thought. She didn't have years. She had to escape now, to hide from the backlash of student attacks on her, to cope with the desertion of her own parents, and even worse, to leave before he could come back to get her. Lizzie inched closer so she could make out the rest of what they were saying.

"Please," Lizzie's mother said, her eyes welling with emotion. "Take the money. It's all we can do for her now."

"She still needs you. Maybe you should just be there for her," Jen said, trying to understand, but her skin flushed red.

"That's not our little girl anymore," her father said sternly, looking at his wife, her arm in a sling. Her tears erupted from her eyes and she sobbed into his jacket, breath heavy and forced as she sucked in air between wails. Her father's eyes looked hard from where Lizzie could barely make them out, but then they softened into a deeper pain than she could ever realize. The next week, she packed her things and disappeared from their lives.

Chapter 24

September 2012:

With August flying by, Lizzie skidded into September with every intent to put her plans on hold and just be a girl for once. Already her complicated conversation with Michelle was fading, and the idea of normalcy was coming back to life. The more time she spent back at school, the more she felt this normalcy and she embraced it with open arms, hoping that things were finally coming together in a positive way.

Arising from her bed, Lizzie grabbed her brush from her nightstand and went to her mirror. With all the chaos in her life, something as simple and constant as brushing her hair had become essential to her emotional state in the morning. She ran the brush through her hair, feeling it slip through the delicate strands, soft and smooth. She closed her eyes for a moment, taking in its calm rhythm. She thought about the waves rocking her back and forth, just like the motion of her brush.

When her eyes opened again, Lizzie was no longer alone in the mirror's view. She turned to look behind her, only to find the room empty. Still, when she looked back again, he was there, slate gray eyes, light brown hair, and mouth parted for speech, but with no words escaping his lips.

"James," Lizzie whispered, putting her hand on the glass as if she could really touch him. *You're still here*, she thought. He had always tried to take care of her, even when she had gotten annoying.

She remembered when she was a kindergartener, following around her second-grade brother. It had been Lizzie's favorite game, running behind her brother, in pink overalls and pink-ribboned ponytails, as James whipped around the playground, trying to avoid her, the sound of flying woodchips clipping Lizzie's ears. He and his friend Billy would try to hide behind one of the slides, shifting positions every time she got close, but she grew too smart for that.

"Go away," James would whine in her face, but she would just giggle, giving him a hug.

He would hold his arms close to his body and twist to shake her off, but she stuck to him like bubblegum, stretching out as far as his arms could push her, but then retracting around his shoulders again.

Since the boys couldn't get rid of her, they created a game just for her called Tornado Tag. Lizzie climbed into the center of the merry-go-round, knees pressed to her chest, eyes closed as the boys grabbed hold of the metal bars.

"One…two…three!" They raced around in a circle, the merry-go-round picking up speed. When they released the bar, they pushed with all their might, creating a whirlwind of speed, and ran off in random directions. Closing her eyes hadn't helped her as it continued to spin. The darkness of her eyelids spun, flashing streaks of light when rays of sun connected with the metal. Then it slowed and Lizzie wobbled off. Her eyes were racing, shifting the ground to the sky and back again. She started running toward the swings, her knees swaying with every step. She knew that James usually hung over there, talking to this little girl with big green eyes. Lizzie used to tease him about her.

"Ooh, who's that girl, Bub? Is she your girlfriend? James and girly sitting in a tre—ow!"

Her brother had thumped her head hard like she was one of those whack-a-mole games, and she decided not to bring it up again.

As she approached the swings, something large collided with her on the side, knocking both of them to the ground. Her butt landed hard against the dirt, stunning Lizzie's brain enough to stop spinning and focus on the pain.

"Watch it," a chubby boy yelled in her ear.

She turned to him and realized it was Freddy, a big, curly-haired boy in James's class. His nose twitched as his pudgy fingers balled into fists. Lizzie had met him before and was still reeling from the last encounter, which cost her entire box of animal crackers.

"Nice, pigtails. I bet I could pull those off."

Lizzie tried to jump up quick enough, but somehow his stubby arms were faster. He grabbed hold of her hair, tugging at it until it fell out of its ribbon.

"Ouch. Stop it!" Lizzie cried, trying to loosen her hair from his grip.

Suddenly, Freddy's grip wavered as he was sent tumbling to the ground, knocking Lizzie onto her knees. She felt her hand scrape against the dirt and tears built in her eyes as the stinging of her hand and head registered through her body. She looked up to see James standing above them. He reached down and pulled his sister up before looking at the kid, stunned, on the ground.

"Leave my sister alone," James warned, balling his hands into fists.

"Fine," Freddy grumbled, brushing himself off before running away.

"You okay?" James asked with a sigh.

Lizzie sniffled, tears still fresh on her face, and held up her hand, pointing at the scratches on her palm.

James rolled his eyes. He looked around a moment, to see if anyone was watching, then kissed it. "All better, just like Mom does."

Lizzie smiled, looking at her hand and she did feel better. She reached out for her brother, arms stretched as far as they could go, but he dodged them, running away from her, and she pursued as if nothing had happened.

It was a week later when Lizzie started to learn one of the most important lessons of her life—he wasn't going to always take care of her.

"What do you mean he's not coming with me?" Lizzie asked, stuffing her peanut butter and jelly that she had helped her mother make into her Barbie backpack.

"James is sick, honey. He has a fever and needs to stay in bed today," her mother said.

Lizzie had remembered seeing a sick girl in her class being sent home for being covered in spots. Lizzie snuck one of her markers out of its package under the table and ran into the bathroom. When she emerged, her face was covered in red dots. Her mother was at the kitchen sink, washing the breakfast dishes. She tugged at her mother's sleeve, saying sweetly, "Look Mom, I've got a fever, too."

Her mother put down the plates and scooped the child in her arms, laughing and tickling Lizzie, who quickly realized she was still going to school that day.

On the playground at recess, she pumped her feet half-heartedly on the swing. She wondered if fever lasted long. *I hope not,* she thought, kicking the dirt underneath her feet and playing with her favorite doll, Annabelle, who was sitting in her lap. Suddenly, she felt pressure on her back, and her body was knocked out of the swing. She face planted onto the ground, scraping her chin and getting dirt in her mouth.

"Hey!" she said, getting up and spinning around to find Freddy's plump face. He shoved her shoulders, knocking her back to the ground.

"Where's your big brother today?" he asked..

Lizzie glared at him, answering with a small growl. "He's sick."

Annabelle was lying beside her, her golden hair dusted with dirt, and he grabbed her. Lizzie's eyes widened as he shook her fiercely. She jumped up to Annabelle's aid, but he was taller than her and stretched the doll out of her reach. He pushed her over and over as she tried, continuously and unsuccessfully, to rescue her little friend. He spun Annabelle behind his back, taunting Lizzie, not realizing there was a scrawny kid behind him. He was about Lizzie's height, but beanpole thin with dark brown hair. He snatched Annabelle from Freddy and handed her back to Lizzie.

"Leave her alone," he said, trying to look Freddy in the face, but he was far too short.

"Out of my way, worm," Freddy said, pushing the boy.

The boy shoved him back, grunting at the force he exerted, but it did little. Freddy shoved harder, knocking the boy to the ground.

Lizzie looked around for a teacher, but no one was there, and then she heard the boy groan as Freddy kicked him in the stomach. Lizzie's eyes narrowed, a tiny flame flickering across her body and reddening her face. She stepped closer to the boys, the one on the ground crying with pain and Freddy laughing above him.

She lifted her left foot and wound her leg back and

forward as hard as she could, kicking Freddy in the shin.

He yelped with surprise, eyes watering, and Lizzie kicked again, this time connecting with the fingers that he rubbed his leg with too. He fell to the ground and Lizzie sat on top of him, punching his face with her tiny fists of fury, Annabelle rocking loosely in her grip. He caught her in the mouth and rolled on top of her, tugging at her ponytails. The little boy got up and started punching Freddy in the back, while Lizzie latched her teeth onto his fingers.

"Ow," he yelled, trying to pry her jaw away.

"You're not supposed to hit girls," the boy said, before he was suddenly scooped up by a rushing Mrs. Adams, the kindergarten teacher.

"What's going on here?" She tried to pull Freddy up off the ground, but Lizzie still had his hand clenched tightly between her teeth. "Lizzie, let go!"

She released him and got up off the ground, brushing the dirt from her purple pants. Mrs. Adams gave them a stern look and ushered them into the school. Lizzie brushed Annabelle's hair with her fingers as she sat outside the principal's office, her own hair frazzled and fallen to one side of her head.

The little boy sat next to her, swinging his legs with boredom.

"I found this on the ground," he said, pulling her other pink ribbon from his pocket.

"Thank you," she said, taking it from his hand. She grabbed a chunk of her hair and tied the ribbon around. She wasn't sure what it looked like, but she didn't care. "I'm Lizzie."

"I'm Nick," the little boy said. His face turned red and he looked away from her as he spoke. "You're very pretty."

Lizzie giggled, her fingers covering parts of her face,

and gave him a little hug. *Good thing Bub isn't here to see this*, she thought.

Now, standing at the mirror, Lizzie tried to think of all the things she wanted to say to him, but her mouth refused to say the words. She thought about her school days on the playground, the summers surfing at the beach house, and all those pizzas they made while their parents went out for the night, but still her voice was caught in her throat like a baby chick getting ready to say its first chirp. As she watched the picture in the mirror, it began to flicker like the fuzzy image on an old black and white television screen.

"I'm sorry," she said to the fading picture. She called to it. "No, don't leave me. Bubba, I need you. I can't do this on my own."

The image vanished, floating out of the mirror like the few glimpses of Lizzie's sanity. She banged her hands against the glass, a tear escaping her fluttering eyelids down her cheek. She started to pound on it harder, her heart racing with a fiery anger. She could feel it boiling inside of her, her actions stimulating the heat of her body. Then there was a small noise as a crack grew on the mirror, and still she kept pounding.

"Lizzie? What in the world is all that noise?" Joel asked, entering the room. His mouth grew heavy on his face, sinking down into a frown. "Lizzie, you're going to hurt yourself, stop it."

Lizzie kept pounding as the crack expanded, creating a web of little cracks like the stretching of a tree's roots. "It's not fair! It's not fair!"

"Lizzie, stop it!" Joel said, pulling her arms away from the mirror as her fingers turned red from the impact.

She turned on him, beating at his chest, the anger stretching from her belly into her limbs. He stood there watching her, face bound up into a concerned frown as she kept going.

Finally, she let out a large growl as her knees sank under her, and she dropped her head onto her carpet, its smell a sweet coconut from when her sister had accidentally spilt perfume on it. Joel knelt beside of her, wrapping his arms around her, and all she could think about was how much she wanted her big brother. She clung to him like a lost baby monkey and rested her head against his chest.

When she was done, she got up from Joel's grasp as if nothing had happened, her face tight from all the tears left unshed, and went to the mirror again. She stared at it for a minute, trying to find the image, but she saw nothing.

Chapter 25

A few days later, she was surprised one night by the sound of a vehicle in the driveway. She hurried down the stairs when Jen yelled up that Nick was there to see her. Nick would make her feel better.

She stopped by the bottom of the stairs when she saw him. He was wearing a suit and had a bouquet of pink roses in his hand. At first, he tried to look suave and debonair, but eventually his goofy smile crept across his face. Lizzie tried not to giggle, her heart flapping in her chest. He bowed playfully, giving her a wink.

"What's all this?" she asked, inhaling the flowery scent.

"Well, tonight is the homecoming dance, and I was hoping a certain blonde would be interested in going with me."

He smiled again and she took all of him in. *Oh my god, he looks good,* she thought.

Seeing all of them grinning at her, she quickly caved, developing a nervous excitement that she hoped she could utilize to her advantage. Minutes later, as she was getting ready, she looked in the bathroom mirror and caught a glimmer of her former self. When they left for the dance she was almost perky. Earlier that day, Nick had gotten a job at the local garage, and the owner was letting him work on an old pickup truck. Genevieve let him drive it for the night. It trumped along in spurts and he decided to name it Old Hector, because it huffed like an old man.

The dance had already begun to boom when they arrived. People stopped and stared when Lizzie walked through, not sure what to make of the girl in the sparkly pink dress that had appeared from the depths of her dark depression. Fiona's group was clustered in the middle of the floor. Her rouge dress was cut low on top with a slit as high as school regulation would allow. *She looks like she just came from a brothel,* Lizzie thought, putting on a nice smile.

"Watch out, girls, scrub alert."

Lizzie wanted so bad to slap her all the way to Kansas, but her thoughts were hidden by a shyness she didn't know had existed in her.

"There's no need to introduce yourself, Fiona. We all know you're here," Nick said as they passed by.

He and Lizzie settled into a couple of plastic chairs near the punch bowl and sat for several minutes in silence, sipping the punch that Nick had poured for them, before he rose again to his feet. His hands were soft from years of little hard work as he pulled Lizzie up from her chair.

The music was low, gentle with the sound of light piano and acoustic guitar. He tried to pull her into the crowd, but she tugged back. Instead, he took her arms and wrapped them around his neck, while his hand clung to the back of her silky pink dress.

She inhaled the smell of Polo on his skin, but laughed when he spoke and she smelled Doritos on his breath. Normally, Lizzie was considered fairly clumsy, but when she danced, a sense of elegance surrounded her. She floated along like a wispy butterfly, or lately, a delicate moth drifting towards the burning flame.

"Aren't you glad you decided to come with me?" His crooked grin made her grin too, but she couldn't find a logical reason why.

"Decide? More like taken hostage. I'm surprised you didn't tie me up and throw me in the back of Old Hector." She smiled at him, trying to figure out what this feeling was. Happy, that must've been it. She had forgotten it for so long that it almost felt foreign in her brain.

"You know, I don't think Jen would have let me in the door had I come with a rope and some duct tape saying, 'I'm here to kidnap your sister.'"

"Probably not. She probably would've beaten you up," she said, laughing.

"Then you would've missed me, right?"

"Hmmm...nope, not in the least." Nick's lip quivered and he widened his eyes. "Alright already, I'd miss you a little bit."

"I win," he said, giving her a hug and a small kiss on the cheek. It lingered on her skin and Lizzie struggled with the urge to touch it just once. She wanted him to do it again, but he seemed to move on to the next moment. "You look beautiful in that dress tonight. Are you having fun?"

"Yeah." She really was excited but she felt a slight uneasiness in his question. "I'm not the same as I used to be, am I?"

"No, you're not." Nick looked away for a minute, staring off into a corner of the room and suddenly Lizzie felt guilty. "But it's okay. I like you no matter how you act."

"You must be a little bit disappointed?" *Of course he is*, she thought. *I'm cuckoo for cocoa puffs.*

"The worst part is the distance. We used to be so close. I used to be able to read your emotions well, but now I don't see anything." He looked away again, shifting his jaw with the motion of his mouth and biting his lip. "I'm sorry. Let's just have fun."

"Umm…I need a minute." Lizzie tried to walk as calmly as possible to the door.

She let out a loud gasp as she inhaled quickly and exhaled the night air. Inside, she had felt like she was suffocating with the guilt of hurting Nick. She needed a friend. She wanted a friend, but what about Nick? What if she couldn't be what he wanted her to be anymore? She sighed deeply, breathing slowly in and out. She was just getting ready to go back inside when she heard a faint sound.

"Heeeelp—helllllp me."

Lizzie wanted to run away, but she had to help the person. She would want someone to do the same for her. As she moved closer to the football field the cries became louder and more urgent. She sprinted onto the field and all silenced.

The air was cool on her shoulders, and the darkness swallowed up all of the moonlight. She felt her heels dig gently into the grass and tried not to trip. Each step weighed on her mind, stomach floating into her chest as it rapidly thumped. She could feel it booming in her body louder and louder. Then something latched on to Lizzie's foot and she tumbled to the ground.

As she began to pull herself up, a hand snatched her heel and yanked her back down. The heel was pointed and the fingers quickly lost their grip, but they fumbled with her ankles instead. Frightened, she kicked out her legs to break them free. The hands pulled harder, dragging her towards them. She curled into a ball and held her eyes tightly shut. The last thing she wanted to see was those horrible, icy eyes. She felt hot breath on her cool ears.

"Boo," the voice whispered before bursting into laughter.

A thunder of footsteps followed with spurts of laughter. Lizzie opened her eyes to see a crowd of guys with dress jackets all around her. The air reeked of cigarettes. A slinky figure slithered from the darkness and a glint of sparkly red caught Lizzie's eyes.

"I told you she was a complete freak," Fiona sneered. "What? Did you think the Boogeyman was going to get you? Oh that's right—you really believe in him, don't you? Well my mother's a shrink, and she thinks you're a schizoid with hallucinations. Oh, Mr. Boogeyman, come out and play! Now, you see—nothing. Come on now, don't be shy. Lizzie wants to see you." She walked around in circles, arms outstretched in the cool air.

"Don't taunt him, or you'll pay," Lizzie said, trying to pull herself up off the ground, but her knees shook under her and she sat back down. She brushed the dirt from her dress as well as she could, looking around to see if maybe he was listening.

"What's your little 'friend' gonna do? Shave my head and slit my wrists? You're pathetic," Her grin was so wide it looked as if it would touch her ears, like a fox getting ready to pluck the feathers from a chicken.

"You guys are pathetic. It takes half the football team and one dumb bitch to pick on a defenseless girl." Nick rushed to Lizzie's side and scooped her up in his arms, carrying her away from the crowd.

Her brain felt like it would explode with panic. She never should've come. Now Fiona had teased the Boogeyman and he would be angry. What if he decided to come for her tonight? She looked around, but only saw the group of teenagers trailing behind her as Nick carried her to the parking lot. She was shaking a bit but tried not to have a nervous breakdown in front of everyone.

"I'm going to take you home."

As he set her in the passenger's seat, Lizzie heard it—the start of a raging storm.

"Well you take that little freak whore back to where she came from," one of the guys said.

Nick hit the guy square in the jaw, and he went down like a falling door. Three other guys circled him. He squared off with two of them, but the third snuck up behind him and grabbed him by the arms, while the others repeatedly punched him in the gut.

Lashing out like a deranged chimpanzee, Lizzie leapt onto the guy's back, freeing Nick's arms. She clawed at the guy's face with one hand while latching the other around his throat. He tried throwing her off by shaking his entire body, but with minimal success. She chewed on his ear as he yelped with agony.

Nick had broken one guy's nose, and he was rolling on the ground in pain. Meanwhile the other guy, who was quite a lot bigger than Nick, knocked him to the ground and beat at his face.

"That's quite enough!" The principal's voice echoed through the parking lot. "I'll deal with you all tomorrow. Now disperse, before I call the cops."

Nick pulled Lizzie off the guy. He jumped in Old Hector and bolted out of the driveway with as much speed as it could give.

For a while, things were silent and tense in the truck. Anger began to boil inside of Lizzie. *Why did I let Nick take me to this stupid dance? I need to get out of here.*

"Are you okay?" he finally managed to ask.

He had a cut on his lip, and his eyes seemed to bounce in his head like a pinball, taking in everything and nothing all at once.

"Do I look okay to you? Why did I let you talk me into coming? This whole idea was a huge mistake."

"What? Would you rather stay home and hide under the covers for the rest of your life?" Nick practically snarled at her, like a furious dog, his hand tightening around the steering wheel.

"At least there, I know I'm safe! You think this is supposed to be easy for me? A maniac is trying to kill me, my sister thinks I'm crazy, plus I have to go to school with kids who seem to find my situation funny. And now I've got you complaining and trying to force me to be happy. Well, I'm not happy and you're just going to have to deal with it." She desperately wanted to bolt from the vehicle, but it was going too fast to even consider it.

"You think I don't know you're unhappy? I'm not an idiot. I can see you're scared and miserable. I'm not asking you to pretend, but you could at least try. I've never seen you so defeated. I hate seeing you like this."

"Well, then maybe you should've stayed out of trouble so you could've gone to school at home."

Lizzie was infuriated. If she had been the one driving, she would have pushed Nick from the vehicle. Suddenly tumbling into the rushing road seemed more probable to her. She didn't ask for or need this right now. The Boogeyman might be on his way to strangle her tonight and she was arguing with a stupid boy.

"You're unbelievable. Do you have any idea why I'm here? I made a choice. I decided that being with you was more important than anything in the whole world. So I got myself expelled from school to move in with Genevieve and start all over because I thought you needed me. I see now that loving you was a mistake."

She didn't respond to his words, trying to pretend that she hadn't heard them. She was too scared to allow any other emotion in. She couldn't have been more relieved when they pulled into the driveway.

Jen sprinted through the doorway and down the path,

the minute she saw them. Out the corner of her eye, Lizzie could see Joel standing in the doorway, his arms tightened and face alert. Lizzie realized how awful she must look. Her hair had fallen out of its ponytail. It hung off her head like a frazzled ball of yarn. Her dress was torn and disheveled.

"What happened? You were only gone an hour. Are you all right?" Jen grabbed Lizzie into a hug before pulling back and brushing the hair from her face.

"I thought it would be better if I brought Lizzie home early because it's a school night. I probably should get home. Good night." Nick briskly walked back to Old Hector and spun out of the driveway.

Lizzie couldn't even mouth the words back to him.

"Did he hurt you?" Joel asked, eyes staring out into the darkness of the silenced driveway.

Lizzie shook her head, trudging up the staircase to her tower before she needed to respond to more questions that she didn't want to answer. A wave of realization knocked her right into her computer chair. She had just lost the only friend she had left.

Her heart poured onto the desk in streams. The paper on it sopped them up. She couldn't think of anything better to do so, she typed "Michelle Smith" into the Google bar, expecting to find a bunch of random things. Instead, the article came up from the other day, as well as another article from a paper in California called the *Sunshine Herald*.

Ignoring the first article, she clicked through the *Herald* archives to where the next article came up. The date was from three years ago. In it was a picture of teenage Michelle, all smiles, getting an award from the school for exceptional athleticism. Next to it was a picture of the whole team, standing in front of the school, its hard brick exterior and students in windows made for the perfect background. Lizzie skimmed the article and printed it off quickly.

Then she flipped through page after page of Michelle Smith's that didn't fit her girl at all. How was Lizzie supposed to find out about her when she had such an average name? Suddenly, as she was rushing through page fifteen, something at the bottom of the page caught her eye, *Local Woman Goes Missing*.

Michelle's parents called police after their daughter hadn't visited them in a few days. She had recently gotten a new job, but hadn't returned to work in a week. The Smiths said that their daughter had been in and out of foster care before they adopted her and had run away often in the past. Lizzie yawned mechanically, printing off the article. She wasn't sure if any of this would be any help, but she had to start somewhere.

She crawled into bed and fell into a dark sleep, darker than she had let her mind enter in a really long time.

She wasn't in her room anymore. The room was cold, and lit with one small ceiling light that rocked back and forth like she was in an interrogation room. As it swung around, she got a glimpse of James's face, sweat sliding down his nose into his upper lip. She reached out to him, but a pain shot through her side. She cried out and she heard movement in the corner. She tried to crane her neck, but she couldn't see them.

"Shh…don't move, Lizzie. It's going to be okay," James said, rushing to his sister's side.

Pain shot across Lizzie's arm and side, but she couldn't move her limbs to touch it. She peered down at her feet, and blood was beginning to pool on the floor. She screamed, wiggling as best as she could.

"Restrain her," a raspy voice screamed, and James gently covered her mouth, patting her hair with his other hand. Footsteps shuddered the wooden floorboards, and

Lizzie saw the light cast a large shadow onto the wall. "Finish it," the shadow said beside her.

Her brother gulped hard and he looked at his sister, reaching for a gun beside her. "I'm sorry, Lizzie," he said, the gun shaking in his hand. "But someone has to be punished."

Lizzie wriggled again and tears overflowed onto her face. She closed her eyes, waiting for it to happen, but changed her mind. *I need my brother.* She looked at him, his own eyes full of sadness.

"Do it!" the voice screamed again and Lizzie heard something else.

What was that? That whimper.

Lizzie knew what was happening next, but she couldn't make herself look away. She hadn't then, and her dream wouldn't let her now. She couldn't feel the gun at her head and her eye wouldn't register it against her brother's brain, but she heard the sound of it as it went off, and she saw the blood paint the air as he fell to the ground, his body so close that the blood had splattered on her pink shirt. The pain increased in her side as the world felt hot and began to spin.

On the ground next to her, James's face was completely gone, a hole gaped open, blood intermingling on the floor with chunks of brain matter. She felt lightheaded and suddenly everything went dark. She could hear, though, whispers from a raspy voice being scolded by a softer one, but then there was something in the background. Something Lizzie needed to know.

Singing. Someone was humming in the background, a soft hum, not like a man's at all. Then she was floating, lifted from the ground, sweaty skin touching her arms and legs. She tried to open her eyes, but everything was blurry until she saw them, those icy eyes glaring at something above her, but Lizzie wasn't sure what until she heard it.

"Pretty little doll. Let me play with her," a feminine voice echoed in her mind in stark contrast to the thrumming pain in her body and her hazy perception in this darkened world.

Lizzie shot up from her bed, and went to her desk to look at her articles again, but they were missing from her desk. She spun around the room, afraid that he was there, but everything still seemed in place. Her mind swirled in flashes as the images started to meld back together.

James had been looking for her, but somehow the Boogeyman found out. Lizzie never knew how, but he seemed to know everything. When he kidnapped her, he had locked her in his basement. She clawed at the door for hours, but with no success. Sometimes, she waited, her ear against the door, listening to him talk. One voice was raspy, and Lizzie was afraid of him, but another had slid bread under the door while the other was away. She had never gotten to thank him or even see his face because every time the door was open, she would see the raspy voiced man.

Then one day, he had tied her up, sliding his blade in thin slices across her skin and whispering in her ear. "You're an ungrateful girl. You should've appreciated what you had. Now you're stuck with us until you die. What do you think of that?"

She had cried, begging him not to kill her, promising she would be a good girl. He covered her mouth with a rag and left the room, returning later with James. But *she* had been there too, rocking back and forth in the corner, singing "Mockingbird" and muttering to herself.

Lizzie was amazed about what she had remembered. This woman, this crazy girl who knew about Jen and her life, was telling the truth. Lizzie wasn't crazy, and that meant more to her than any possession she had had in her formal life. She knew she had to get this realization out as soon as possible, so she did the only thing she could think of at four in the morning.

"Jen!" She ran down the winding staircase and pounded on her sister's door. She didn't care what time it was. She had to do this now. "Jen, I remember. I remember, Jen."

Jen slightly opened the door, eyes groggy, not even having time to put on her housecoat. "Sweetie, can't this wait until morning?"

"No, it's really important that I tell you now, before I forget," Lizzie heard a noise in the room. An idea clicked into her head as she glanced back at the guest room door, slightly ajar. "He's in there, isn't he?"

"Umm…let's just go talk downstairs. He has to work in the morning," Jen ushered Lizzie down the second staircase, and Lizzie burst into laughter.

Chapter 26

Francis

December 2011:

Francis struggled with the anger his personality was built around. He thought of Francis Matthew Robinson, the man he had refused to call father, and he swore he would never treat Michelle like that, but it never stopped his rage.

She had resisted running away every step of the way, so much so that they were forced to live in abandoned buildings to prevent her from going home. When he thought she was slipping away from him, he would lock her away in a closet or a basement until she repented her behavior. Over time, her appearance and voice had weakened. She was prone to muttering to herself and singing in a regressive, childlike manner. At night, her terrors grew, waking the boys until morning.

She thinks I'm a demon, Francis told Brian Matthew.

Can you blame her? Brian and I try to comfort her one minute and the next you're screaming at her. Why can't you just leave her alone?

Because she's my family, too, and she rejects me. She keeps talking about running home. Francis couldn't understand this need for people, but all of a sudden it had come to him so strongly that he was desperate for her approval. *I can't get her to like me and it makes me mad. I'm supposed to be her brother.*

I thought you said she wasn't your sister, Brian Matthew asked. He had been trying to guide Francis, but he was losing what little control he had of him. They had begun to argue more often, even out loud with Michelle in the room. *You said you didn't need anybody.*

Well maybe I do, all right? Are you satisfied? I'm lonely and the killing isn't helping anymore. You do it, or I do it. It's all emptiness inside. Not that they don't deserve it. Francis was pacing across a deserted room that he had made into a makeshift bedroom. *How do I fix this?*

The holidays are coming up. Buy her a gift. You did pick out a great gift before for...her. Brian Matthew didn't want to say her name. It had been painful for them to leave the love of their lives behind, but she had been better off without them. Brian Matthew wished that Francis would realize the same for Michelle, but he was too selfish.

I don't want to think about her, but it's a good idea, Francis said and, without another second to waste, he went to find a jewelry store to steal his sister a present.

When he got back, he could hardly contain his excitement as he presented the bauble to her after releasing her from an old linen closet.

"Merry Christmas, Sissa," he said, smiling.

She looked at the necklace with a startled expression. She held it to the light to watch it glisten before asking, "Where did you get this?"

"From that fancy store we found on Main Street. Do you like it?" His body tensed, feeling uncertain of the expression on her face.

"You stole it then," she said with a scrunch of her nose like she smelt something rotten.

"Well, we don't have much money, Shelley," he said.

"Take it back," she said, handing the necklace to him.

Francis' hand curled around the necklace. "But I got it for you."

Stay calm, Brian Matthew told him, but he knew Francis wasn't listening.

"I don't want anything you steal for me. I don't need it, and I won't take it." She was being sterner than she had been in a while and this scared Brian Matthew, who knew what would be coming if she didn't change her attitude.

"You'll take it and you'll like it. I'm still your brother and I got this for you," he said.

"You're not my brother, and I'm not going to reduce myself to your level by taking it." She folded her arms and took a couple steps back. She seemed reluctant to be within reach of him.

"You think you're better than me, don't you?" he asked, starting to growl.

Brian Matthew was watching helplessly from within.

"I don't need to think anything. I know," she said, looking past him. "I'm leaving, and you can't stop me."

She pushed past him to the door, and he grabbed her around the waist, lifting her off the ground. He shook her a little in the air and dropped her into the closet. He slammed the door shut and locked it. Standing outside it, he could hear her sobbing.

"You ungrateful little bitch, you think you can leave after everything I've done for you. I saved your life," he screamed, not sure what to do next.

"And then you took it away," she said between heavy breathing. "You should've let him kill me so I wouldn't have to see this."

"You think you're such a saint. His blood was on your hands too," he said, thinking of a plan. "I'll show you."

He slammed the door as he left the house, looking around to see if anyone noticed him.

What are you doing? Brian Matthew asked, feeling shut out of Francis's thoughts.

Teaching her a lesson, he said, crossing the road. *If she won't accept that she and I are equals, then I'm going to prove it to her.*

How? He had stopped at the house directly across the street, and Brian Matthew saw him pull out the knife. *No, you can't.*

"I can do whatever I like," he said to the air, twisting the knife so he could watch the last light of sunset reflected on its blade.

She can't handle this, Brian Matthew pleaded.

She'll be fine, Francis said, opening the front door without knocking.

Brian Matthew kept silent as Francis snuck through the room. A black cat was curled up on one end of the couch. Francis petted it behind its ears and the animal looked up at him groggily. He listened closely and heard the sound of running water coming from down the hallway. He slid his knife into his back pocket and picked up an ashtray from the coffee table. He crept down the hall, trying to make his steps quiet.

An older woman was singing to herself, hands wrist deep in dishwater. She didn't hear Francis come in, and he knocked her in the back of her head with the ashtray. At first he worried he had hit her too hard, but he saw her chest rise with struggling breaths. He slung the woman over his shoulder, having trouble maintaining a hold on her flopping limbs. With labored effort he managed to get her across the street, constantly hoping that no one decided to go for a walk. He dropped her onto the wood of his bedroom floor.

"You can still change your mind," Brian Matthew said.

"Stop me. I dare you to try."

The two were shouting out loud, and the woman stirred a bit. Francis kicked her in the head and she groaned. He walked down the hallway and unlocked the closet. Michelle was curled into the corner, arms folded over her body. He indicated for her to move, but she wouldn't budge. He yanked on her arm, hauling her to her feet.

"Leave her alone," Brian Matthew said. He tried to take hold of the body, and, for a minute he had his sister's attention. "It's going to be okay."

"Don't talk to her," Francis screamed and Michelle flinched. "You're not going to baby her. She's going to learn."

He brought her into the room and she tried to leave, spinning around the moment she locked eyes on the woman. Francis blocked the doorway, spinning her around to make her look at the woman on the floor. She had awakened and was on her knees, hands clasped together.

"What do you want with me?" she asked.

Francis pulled his knife out of his back pocket, handing it to Michelle. She tried to give it back, but he tightened her fingers around the handle.

"Kill her," he said softly in her ear.

"No," she said. "Please, Bubba, I don't want to do this."

"You just said I wasn't your brother. Well, you're not so much better than me." He pushed her forward toward the wailing woman. "You kill her right now, or I'll kill you."

"No," she said, throwing the knife on the ground. She sat down in the corner, rocking from side to side.

Are you happy now? Brian Matthew asked. *You've just proven that she isn't like you.*

"Shut up," Francis said, talking to everyone at once.

He picked the knife up off the floor and stabbed the woman in the stomach. She choked a little and slouched over, blood pooling where she lay. Michelle gasped, trying to slide away from the body.

Francis looked down at Michelle, feeling disappointment and rejection. *She hates me,* he said to Brian Matthew.

Let me go talk to her, Brian Matthew said, stepping forward.

This time Francis didn't resist. Brian Matthew sat down in front of Michelle as she rocked. He pulled her into a hug, even though she was reluctant. He rubbed her back and patted her hair.

"It's going to be okay, Shelley."

"Why did you do this? I don't understand," she said, wiping her face on her sleeve.

"I don't know," he said. He looked over at the dead woman on the floor. "I'll take her home. You get packed."

Chapter 27

February 2012:

Francis had been stalking this girl for weeks. He wasn't sure what it was about her that annoyed him so much, but he knew that she had to be punished for her behavior.

So she's a spoiled little rich kid, big deal. Have you heard of anything more stereotypical? Brian Matthew had endured Francis's obsession with this girl but he couldn't understand it. *Why is this so bad?*

Look at her. She's so perfect. Francis pointed to the woman standing in front of the window. Her hands were on her hips, lips curled with a frown and eyes fiery with rage. Beside her was a tall, thin-framed blonde who rolled her eyes as the woman yelled.

How could someone so wonderful get stuck with such a burden?

She loves the kid, Brian Matthew said. *Hurting the girl will make things worse.*

The door slammed, and Francis ducked behind a tree, hoping she hadn't seen him. He heard heels on the sidewalk and a phone rang. He slipped behind her, taking baby steps to give her space.

"I don't need to work it out. I'm leaving. I'll just

walk home." She flipped her phone shut and stamped her heels a little harder against the pavement. Francis moved a little closer, each step with quiet precision.

The brother's going to be a problem, Brian Matthew said. *He'll be looking for her. That won't give you much time with her.*

I'll deal with him if I have to. Pit him against her. He's not her real brother. He'll betray her like any sibling would to save themselves.

Are you speaking from bitter experience? You're going to punish this family because you've made Michelle so crazy that she doesn't like you anymore. Brian Matthew was growing so tired of this game, but he didn't know how to stop playing. He wondered what Brian would think of this, but he had a hard time finding him. Francis had overpowered them both so completely that Brian Matthew worried Brian was gone.

She never loved us, Francis said, watching the girl. She seemed to be going in circles.

She loves me, Brian Matthew said. *And Jen would fight for this girl? How do you explain that?*

I think we've already agreed that Jen is an amazing woman. Francis pointed to the girl. *She deserves better than that.*

She stumbled as one of the heels of her shoes broke. She pulled the shoe off and hobbled along on the other one.

Okay, but when does this end? How long are you going to continue this madness, Mr. Boogeyman? Brian Matthew had intended this as an insult, but Francis was proud of his new media title. He would be remembered after all.

This is the last one, he said, and this time he meant it. Francis had grown weary of this lifestyle. He wanted to be free of this monster, free of this bloodshed. He wanted to feel real and be loved again. *I just want to do this for her. So she can have a better life.*

Fine, but make it quick. I don't want any part of this.

She had stopped again, trying to center herself, but it was clear she had no idea where she was going. Francis looked around to see if anyone was nearby and saw no one. It felt too open to risk. He had to get her back to the new house they were staying at. It was only a block from here, and the girl would be easy to carry. She spun around again, and he tried to blend into the shadows. He stared into her eyes as she unknowingly turned them in his direction. His stomach knotted, and, for a second, he considered turning away. He took a deep breath and started to hum "Mockingbird," the most comforting thing he had in his mind.

The girl stared at him for a moment before he knocked her unconscious with his fist.

Minutes later he had set her down in the basement. Michelle had been sitting against the main support in the center of the room, hair matted yellow, nails nibbled down to stubs. Months of abuse had deteriorated her mind, but Francis didn't care. She wasn't innocent anyway. She crawled over to the girl on the floor, running her fingers through her hair.

"Pretty little thing," she said. "You've brought me a friend."

"Why would I bring anything for a bratty, little thing like you? You're an ungrateful—" His thought was interrupted, an annoyance that he was getting sick of. "Why don't you go stay upstairs? You don't need to see this."

Michelle nodded, stopping to get another glance at the girl before going up the stairs.

You shouldn't baby her. She deserves to see this, Francis said.

We're supposed to protect her, not cause her harm.

That was the whole point of being here, Brian Matthew said.

I'm the master, not the puppet. And why should I protect her? She hates me. She wanted to leave. I'm nothing to her and she's nothing to me.

Then kill her.

The coldness in Brian Matthew's thought startled Francis. *I need to take care of this girl first.* He hoped this would be enough to change the subject. Behind him, the girl groaned, and her legs moved. *She's waking up early.*

"Boy! A boy! I see the boy coming! He's coming to get the big, bad man. He's coming to get you," Michelle hollered down the stairs.

"What are you yelling about?" Francis walked up the stairs, ignoring the girl moving from the ground.

Michelle pointed. "See the boy in the window." She giggled. "He knows what a naughty thing you've been."

Francis peered out the window and James, the girl's brother, was standing in the doorway, preparing to knock. He rapped on the door, and Francis ran to the basement stairs. The girl was getting up as he slammed and locked it. There was more rapping on the door, and Francis wondered if he should answer. While he was deciding he heard a thump behind him and the basement door shuddered.

She's trying to get out, Francis said. He'd never had this problem before.

Imagine that, an active, hormonal teenage girl wants to try to escape her quick but violent end. Kids these days, they take their deaths personally, Brian Matthew said.

Don't be such a smartass, Francis said as a thump hit the door again. There was a moment of silence then scratching at the door.

"Let me out. Somebody please let me out," she screamed.

"Hello? Is anybody in there," her brother called from the outside door.

"Hello," Michelle said to the door, turning the knob.

"What the hell are you doing?" Francis asked, running for his sister too late.

She opened the door up, and the boy pushed his way into the hallway.

"I'm looking for my sister," James said, but then he heard the screaming coming from the other door. "Lizzie? Lizzie, is that you?" He went to the door.

"James? James, get me out of here," she said, pounding the door.

Francis didn't give him time to answer. He rammed him hard into the door, and James fell to the floor. On the other side of the door the girl screeched.

"What did you do? Don't hurt him. Please don't hurt him. Why are you doing this," she asked.

"Because you're a bad girl, and bad girls get punished," Francis sneered in his raspy voice.

"Maybe you should let her go before this gets worse," Brian Matthew said.

Michelle dropped a bottle she had been drinking out of, and it smashed to the ground. She looked at Francis and he shook his head.

"We can't just let her go. We worked too hard picking her." He dragged the boy across the hall and stuffed him into the coat closet. He turned on Michelle. "What the hell were you thinking? You stupid, useless girl."

Michelle burst into tears. She dropped to the floor in the glass and Francis tried to get her to stand back up. He brushed her arm and she wailed louder. Down the hall, the girl was doing the same.

Francis rubbed his temples, trying to think while his brain throbbed. *What a mess,* he thought.

So what do we do now, genius? Brian Matthew asked.

"I don't know. I can't think with all this crying," Francis said. "Shelley, please be quiet."

She rocked herself, humming nursery rhymes. Francis shook his head again.

Leave her be. She needs to escape, Brian Matthew said.

Don't we all? Francis said, sitting next to Michelle on the floor. He wondered what sort of place she went to when she got like this. *Must be nice. She keeps going back.*

Go get a gun, Brian Matthew said.

"What," Francis said, not able to read Brian Matthew's thoughts.

Go steal a gun. We're escaping, Brian Matthew said, showing Francis an image of the boy shooting himself.

Well that would take care of the boy, but how would—

You moron, do I have to spell out everything? You want out of this Boogeyman business. Pin it on the kid. Do I have to do all the thinking?

Okay, okay. Just stop making my head worse. I got it. Francis hopped up and was out the door in seconds, hoping Michelle stayed in her safe place while he was gone.

It didn't take him long. There were a lot of little stores in this part of town with easy access and minimum security. He had returned with what he needed within the hour. When he entered again, he was struck by the stillness of the house. Michelle got up as he approached, following him as if she were leashed. He listened at the closet door and heard the creaking of boards. He went to the basement door and heard sobbing.

"Okay," he said, taking a deep breath. "Let's do this."

He opened the door and pointed the gun at the girl's head. Shock flooded her face and words became incoherent as they jumbled with her tears. Michelle stood next to him, muttering under her breath. For some reason, she had spent more time watching him, even taking his victims back to their homes or coming on stakeouts with him. This didn't deter his resentment of her, though it helped his tolerance.

"Tie her up," he said, giving her a smile. "These are the last ones, Shelley. I promise."

She kept quiet but did as she was told. The girl refused to look. She scrunched her eyes closed between tears and whispered to the room. Francis pulled out the knife, tracing thin lines on her arms. He watched the trickle of the blood as it emerged on the surface of her skin. Then, with one swift movement, he stuck the knife into her gut. She choked a little like the others had, and let out a gasp of pain. He pulled the knife back out and watched a moment as the draining process began. He had to keep moving if he was going to use her as leverage. He dropped the knife on the floor and pulled the gun out of his back pocket. Francis went back up the stairs to the hallway and opened the closet. The boy shifted as if to attack, but hesitated when Francis pointed the gun in his face.

"If you do exactly as I tell you, I'll let your sister go," Francis said, face solid steel.

"Unharmed?" James's arms were raised, but he was looking past Francis.

"I'll make sure she gets to a hospital," Francis said. "Are we in agreement?"

"You've left me no other choice. Is she all right?"

"No, but she might be if we hurry," Francis said, and

he couldn't help smiling. *This might actually work,* he thought.

"You're going to kill me, aren't you?"

"This way," Francis said, feeling jolted by the boy's accuracy.

He led him down the stairs to his sister. The girl was bleeding out, head nodding up and down as she struggled to stay conscious. She peered down at her feet, where blood was beginning to pool on the floor. She screamed, wiggling as best as she could.

"Shh...don't move, Lizzie. It's going to be okay," James said, rushing to his sister's side.

"Restrain her," Francis screamed, tired of hearing so much noise, and James gently covered her mouth, patting her hair with his other hand.

Francis leaned in to James and placed the barrel of the gun against his head. "Someone has to be punished. Take the trigger and finish it."

Her brother gulped hard, and he looked at his sister, reaching up to touch the gun. Francis squeezed his hand over James's, not allowing him control of it.

"I'm sorry, Lizzie," James said, the gun shaking in his hand. "But someone has to be punished."

Francis felt the tension release as James's finger released the trigger against his brain. The girl let out a gargle, and he felt the weight of the boy in front of him as the body sagged. Francis and Brian Matthew had never used a gun before, and they disliked the feeling.

Francis saw the mess it had made, the gaping hole in the head, the spray all over the side of the room, and he felt nauseated. He grabbed his knife from the floor with a rag, hoping it would minimize his prints. He wiped it down some more for an extra touch before gripping it in the dead boy's free hand. He assessed the scene, wondering what else should be wiped down. He untied the girl, letting her body drop to the ground, and stuffed the rope into his pocket. He stared at the girl's body and saw a slight movement.

"Better leave her a little longer," Francis told Brian Matthew. "We'll dump her at her parent's house so Jen won't have to see that. Do you think this is going to work?"

"I don't know," Brian Matthew said.

"I need air." Francis walked out of the room, feeling queasy from the smell.

He needed to just go out into the moonlight, to smell the salty air and think about nothing. His head finally stopped throbbing as he stared into the sky.

"She left a few hours ago," a voice startled him as she walked past him on the sidewalk. She was so focused on her phone call that she hadn't noticed his presence. "Well, I think she was headed back to your house, but she might be at Nick's. I'm going to head back to the house in case she comes back. Call me if you find her."

He walked in the other direction, not wanting to see her upset, or for her to see him. When he got near the house he peeked around, afraid that she somehow knew to follow him.

"Better take care of this and get out of here," Brian Matthew said.

"I know," Francis told him, still feeling shaken.

He opened the front door and that shaky feeling amplified as he saw the smears of blood down the entire hallway.

"Michelle," he said, feeling panic. He ran to the basement stairs, taking them two at a time. Michelle was humming "Mockingbird" in the corner and playing with her hair. The girl's body was gone. "What happened here?"

"Boom, boom, down he went." Her laugh was un-nerving for both boys.

"And the girl?"

"Pretty little doll went home. I brought her there and tucked her in under her bed where the Boogeyman won't find her. The girl will, though." She tugged on her hair until she had tugged some of the strands out.

"What girl," Francis said, trying to process this in-formation.

She smiled up at him. "The beautiful one with straw-berries in her hair, the special one. I gave her your pre-sent."

"Oh no," he said and a siren went off outside. He looked through the window at the blackened street, won-dering if they would stop there.

Chapter 28

Lizzie

September 2012:

The next morning Jen let Lizzie stay home on the condition that she get some much needed rest, but sleep eluded her. There were too many things to think about. They swirled around in a complex twisting circle in her brain, creating an instantaneous mind boggle of images each with its own intense meaning and fear.

They had stayed up all night, trying to figure out what to do, and Jen finally agreed to call the police to see if they could speak with Michelle. Joel had made them coffee and went over the articles repeatedly with Lizzie once she found them in her disheveled room. So far, they hadn't gotten far, but it didn't matter. She had a name. She could barely remember the image. All she could focus on was those haunting eyes.

She had sketched out what she could remember of him, setting her picture in the small pile of articles. She could remember a bulky outline of a dark, large shadow that could never be mistaken for a woman, but she had Michelle's voice. That's all that mattered. Sleep would have to wait.

Joel made breakfast, scrambled eggs and toast, which he placed before Lizzie on the table before he hurried off to work. Joel didn't like the normal, corporate kind of jobs, but he was good with his hands, so he did a lot of fix-it projects for people in town.

His project today was installing cupboards for one of Genevieve's neighbors. It didn't make much, but he was happy. He kissed Jen softly on the lips, and without hesitation, kissed Lizzie on the head. He paused for a second when he realized what he had done. "Oops, guess I'm getting too comfortable here. Love you," he said, as he sprinted out the door.

"What the hell was that?" Lizzie said, touching her hair where his lips had been.

Jen laughed. "Maybe he likes having a little sister or a kid."

"I'm not a kid," she said, still rubbing at the spot. "And when did the 'love you's happen?"

Jen beamed, her face turning as red as her hair. "Somewhere between your doom and gloom time and now. Besides, it's just words. It's not like he's serious."

"Aww, you're so cute," Lizzie taunted.

"Be quiet or I'll punch you," Jen said, nudging Lizzie's shoulder as she sat down next to her.

Lizzie looked at her sister's smile and then back at the doorway. She thought carefully for a minute. He did make Jen happy, and Lizzie felt a little safer with him in the house. Maybe he wasn't so bad after all. "I kind of like him. You should keep him."

"Thanks, Mom, glad I've got your approval," she said. Jen parted her lips several times hesitantly before she spoke again. "Lizzie, Michelle was released. I told them I was her cousin and they informed me that her stepbrother had already come and got her."

"I didn't know she had any family. Are you sure they weren't lying?"

"Well, it is possible that they didn't believe me. They said that another cousin had come by earlier to visit her, but disappeared without signing her release form. You wouldn't know anything about that, would you?" Jen said, as she watched Lizzie choke on her orange juice.

"Oops," Lizzie said, trying to look as innocent as possible.

"You know I should ground you for this. I'm going to let this one slide, but no more illegal activity, or I'm taking you out of research mode permanently, got it?"

"Yes, ma'am," Lizzie said. "I still can't believe Michelle has a brother. They never mentioned him in the few articles I found. He must've taken her."

"Well, they did say stepbrother. I mean, you don't really have much to go on about her. It seems like this girl just appeared out of nowhere then disappeared. I guess the internet isn't as all-knowing as we thought. Is this the article from when she was a teenager?" Jen picked the paper up off the table, while Lizzie tried not to pull her hair out. How could she be so calm about this? *Another girl is missing. He must've taken her. She knew too much.*

"Yeah, she looked so happy there. She was kind of a pretty girl. I can't believe the police let this happen. I mean, if I told them I was the queen of England, would they just run out and buy me a tiara?" Lizzie laughed and waited for her sister's musical laugh to follow. Jen was staring intensely at the pictures, picking each one up repeatedly and quickly setting them back down. Lizzie nudged her a little. "Hello, Queen of England. You're missing some good material here. What are you looking at?"

"Do you have a magnifying glass?" Jen said, suddenly turning to Lizzie. Lizzie shook her head. Jen lifted the second article again. "You're sure about this sketch, right? The blue eyes, the shaggy blond hair?"

"Yeah, why? Do you know him?" Lizzie's lungs started to fill with air, but her nerves made it impossible to exhale. Jen was on to something. Lizzie could tell by the movement of her eyebrows and the wrinkle in her forehead, but Lizzie wasn't sure if she really wanted to know. Was she ready for this?

"No, I don't think so, but he was definitely watching Michelle. He's right there." She pointed to the back corner of the school picture at a boy in the background leaning against the brick building, watching the tennis team. Lizzie's eyes adjusted themselves several times before she could focus them. "That's him, right? He looks a little bigger, but there definitely is some resemblance. Lizzie? Are you okay?"

Lizzie could feel vomit rise into her throat. She ran to the bathroom, releasing all of her breakfast contents. Her sister came in, holding her hair out of the way and rubbing her back. She was shaking uncontrollably. She got up from the floor, without a word, and crawled into her bed. Jen lay down next to her, hugging her to her and stroking her hair.

"I'm fine, Jen. I just think I need a second to myself," Lizzie said, holding her chest, feeling her breathing constrict.

"I told you, you should've slept. This is too much for you. You just lay down for a bit. I'll be down stairs if you need me," Jen said, heading for the door. "Remember your breathing exercises—slow deep breaths until you feel in control again. I love you, kiddo."

Lizzie lay in bed for hours before her mind drifted to sleep, but her dreams continued to work against her.

She was at the school again. Loud cries came from

the football field. This time Lizzie wanted to ignore it, but the shrieks were echoing in her brain. She walked on-to the field, and it lit up like a stage. A shadowy figure was strangling a woman. Her heels dug deep into the earth and she kicked and gasped for air. When the sounds stopped, Lizzie watched her head hit the ground. The ol-ive eyes lay cold and lifeless. It was Fiona.

Then the hood slid back, revealing muddy brown hair. He turned around and Lizzie stumbled forward as she looked at his beautiful gray eyes. *Nick! How can this be?* Nick fell to his knees, clutching his neck. Blood spurted from it as he choked and sputtered, reaching out to her. Then she heard it, that menacing, blood curdling laugh. Someone knocked her to the ground and then she saw him as he jumped on top of her, the blade glinting in his hand. She closed her eyes and tried to claw him away.

"Lizzie. Lizzie, wake up. It's just a dream." Nick's soothing words broke through her terror. "It's going to be okay."

"W—hat are you d—doing here?" she managed to stutter.

"When you didn't come to school, I got worried and decided to check on you."

"What does Jen think of you being here at…two o'clock in the morning?" Lizzie had slept through another entire day. It was like her body didn't care about the meaning of time anymore, just bouncing her mind around at will. Lizzie felt a slight breeze glide across her arms and she curled tighter into her blanket.

"She doesn't know. You have no idea how hard it was to reach your window. I was really worried, but it turns out once you get onto the side of the house, it's pretty flat until you reach the tower top." She looked at him a moment, giving herself a mental note to lock the window from now on. It was so out of the way, she never thought anyone would bother.

"You stole your grandmother's car?"

"Borrowed. I've got every intent of returning it with as minimal damage as possible, but, yeah, I drove it here. For an old car, it runs like a champ," he said.

"I thought you were mad at me?"

"I got over it. Do you want me to go? I didn't mean to intrude on your sleep, but I had to see that you were okay for myself. I know it's totally creepy."

Lizzie seized his arm. "No. I want you to stay. Will you lie with me? Just until I fall asleep."

"Oh? You like the sketchy Edward types, do you?" Nick said, curling his mouth into a half smile, with one eyebrow following his mouth upward.

Lizzie rolled her eyes as he lay down beside her. He wrapped his arms around her fragile body as she laid her head on his toned chest. At first, she was still shaking from the dream, but his heartbeat became a rhythmic lullaby and for once, her sigh felt peaceful.

Chapter 29

October 2012:

A month of peace had done wonders for Lizzie. Her hair glistened with a golden shimmer. Her cheeks were kissed with rouge, and her eyes twinkled with joy. She strutted down the hall in her new mini-skirt, her fingers entwined with Nick's. Her old fire had started to burn brighter than ever.

"Nice skirt, Lizzie," Fiona jeered. "Did you get it down at the dump?"

"Nice nose, Fiona. Did you buy it for half price when you got your boobs done?"

"I hate to tell you this, but your investments are uneven." Nick chuckled, turning to Lizzie. Lizzie gave him a small frown and he shrugged. "Guys notice those things. Well, to change the subject before I get in trouble, have you gotten a costume for tonight yet?"

"I'm still not sure if I want to go." The thought of having another disastrous night with jerks just wasn't appealing to her.

"This dance will be better, I promise."

"I guess so. What are you going as?"

"Count Dracula—I vant to suck your blood. Muha-ha!" Nick hid his face in his coat sleeve except for his eyes. "Maybe I should've been Edward." He wiggled his eyebrows playfully at Lizzie. She laughed, giving him a kiss before heading into her class.

Art had been her sanctuary the past few months. Any angry or hurt feeling she had, she just splattered on to the canvas. It allowed her to get out all her negative thoughts and manage to be really happy. Today, Lizzie was painting a demented clown. Its smile covered most of its face. The grin made it look sinister, but it was the eyes that made her classmates do a double take. It was one of the pieces she had planned to showcase for a school-sponsored art exhibit this week-end, but she was struggling to get it perfect.

After school, she darted out to give Nick a kiss before hopping into the car. If she was going to finish the painting for tomorrow, she had to be quick in the costume shop.

"Hold on. Where's the fire?" Jen teased. She was happy to see Lizzie back to her usual self.

"I have only tonight to finish my painting for the show at the museum tomorrow, and I have to get a costume for the dance tonight. Stop gawking at me, woman, and go. Come on, I don't have all day." Lizzie gave her a little shove and mimicked a person driving.

"Okay, boss man. I am so honored to be working for someone as wonderful as you, your highness. When I get done with this how about I rub your feet and paint your toenails?" Jen smirked, shifting the car into gear.

Lizzie laughed. "Well…if you're offering, then I suppose I can allow you the privilege of touching the royal feet."

"I thought you finished your paintings for the show a couple weeks ago?" Jen said.

"I had, but I really like this one, so I need to finish it so I can add it or you guys won't get to see it."

"All righty then," Jen said.

Rummaging through the costume racks was a chore in itself. Either things were enormous or they were for children. There was a troll, a goblin, and a dowdy witch. Then she saw the perfect costume. It was a renaissance dress. It flowed out in a long, poofy gown with a bodice stringed up tightly around her bosom. It fit perfectly and the indigo color brought out the blue in her gray eyes.

Nick is going to love this, she thought as she headed out of the store. The next few hours were a mad race for Lizzie to finish the painting. She had one outlined, but then she didn't like the color and started all over again until it was the perfect shade of blue. She was so dazed that she almost forgot her shoes when Nick came to pick her up.

The whole gymnasium had lights spinning different colors. Candies and punch were to one side of the room. Nick's friend, Thomas, was the DJ, cranking up some crazy dance mix. Technicolor costumes flashed all over the place as people danced along to the rhythm.

Fiona's posse strutted up to Nick. At first, Lizzie was waiting for the war to start, but then she noticed something different about them. The brunette was very pale and her eyes seemed worried. She fidgeted with her fingers and rubbed her arms, looking around for signs of someone. Then Lizzie noticed something that hadn't quite registered before. They were alone.

"Nick, have you seen Fiona? She's not answering my calls," the brunette, Abi—if Lizzie remembered correctly—asked, looking and sounding genuinely worried.

"Maybe she got sick of you stupid people stalking her and decided to abandon you. Oh, how tragic," Nick sneered. Lizzie shifted uncomfortably. Why was Nick acting like this? It didn't seem normal. "Let's go, babe."

As Nick headed toward the center of the dance floor,

Lizzie turned back toward Abi and Erin. "I'm sure she's just running a little late. If I see her, I'll tell her you're looking for her."

As quickly as Nick had snapped at Abi, his mood changed. He became the crazy, goofy Nick that Lizzie liked. Twirling her around on the dance floor, doing the robot, and any other strange thing he could think of.

I must be exaggerating things. He's not a bad person. She jumped right in with him doing the sprinkler and the running man. After they had worn out their feet on the dance floor for at least an hour, they sat down in a couple chairs near the door. Nick brought her some punch.

"I'll be right back okay? Don't go anywhere. I've got a surprise for you." He gave his half grin and walked out the double doors.

For ten minutes, Lizzie sat there sipping her punch, but Nick still didn't return. Then the doors flung open and someone dropped at Lizzie's feet. A wave of gasps floated into the room, starting at the front doors and making their way to the teachers standing by the back doors.

Her crimson hair stuck out against her pale face. Fiona tried to stand up, but she fell back to the ground, her blood staining Lizzie's shoes where her arm touched them. Her arms and legs had been sliced in a long strip all the way down. Two strands of blood streamed like tears down her face, little punctures that barely tainted her cheeks.

Lizzie sat there paralyzed with shock. She could hear teachers running towards them and screaming from the students.

"Let's not panic. Everyone, please exit through the backdoors in an orderly fashion," the principal shouted over the panicked crowd.

"I have a message for you," Fiona gasped as blood from her cheek dripped into her mouth. "He's watching and this is only the beginning unless you stop looking for him. All bad girls need to be punished." A tear mixed with the blood and sweat of her face. "You were right."

Voices whispered close in Lizzie's ear and then everything felt like she was floating before she succumbed to blackness.

In the blackness of her mind, she was walking along a beach, a beach that she had been to a lot when she was with her parents, but they weren't there this time. Instead, Jen and James were there eating sandwiches on a big blanket. James kicked sand at Lizzie as she approached.

"Oh no, sis, wouldn't want to get sand in your hair," he teased.

"It won't matter when I'm done with her." Nick scooped her up and threw her out into the water.

She sputtered a little as she spotted her target. She torpedoed through the water toward him and dunked him under.

"Hey, anyone for football?" Joel asked.

Lizzie thought it odd that he would be in her perfect image of life, especially since they hadn't met him until they went to Maine. *I suppose Jen needs someone too*, she thought.

Jen raced over the sand, trying hard to tackle Joel to the ground, his body barely moving under her little shoves. He raised the football as high in the air as he could get it and Lizzie laughed hysterically as her sister struggled to reach it.

Nick handed her a board and they paddled out into the waves. This was the most wonderful place in the world for her. She lay out on her board as the waves rolled beneath her. It rocked her gently in its arms and she felt completely at peace again. She didn't want to leave her safe place, but the image began to fade and she recovered from her foggy state.

It wasn't the waves that rocked her,. It was the ambulance rattling into the hospital parking lot. As she fully awoke, she noticed that she had been resting in Nick's lap. She tried to remember when she had seen Nick return, but everything was a foggy mess in her head.

All she could remember was blood and Fiona lying on the ground. What had she said? *This is only the beginning.* Then who was next? Lizzie shivered and Nick wrapped his jacket tightly around her, but that was of no help. It wasn't the cold that made her shiver. She decided to pretend that it was okay. No need to worry Nick. She gave him the biggest smile she could muster but he saw right through it. He shook his head and ran his fingers through her hair.

"I'm sorry I kept pushing you to go. I think it's clear that dances just aren't that healthy for you. Everything's going to be okay. Don't worry. I'll never let anyone hurt you in any way without paying for it." The intensity in Nick's face made Lizzie's heart pound in her ears.

What did he mean by that? Fiona had hurt me, but he wouldn't hurt anyone—The fierce determination in his eyes seemed to say otherwise. That was definitely no threat. It was a promise. *No. That makes no sense.* Lizzie finally managed to justify Nick's speech in her mind and locked it in the back of her head with all of her other concealed thoughts.

"Is Fiona, okay?" Lizzie asked the EMT as he helped her out of the ambulance.

"They brought her in the ambulance in front of you," the man said. "She's lost a lot of blood, but most of the wounds were shallow. Your friend is very lucky."

Lizzie opened her mouth to tell him that she wasn't her friend, but felt that sounded too unkind and suspicious to blurt out. She looked at Nick's face, but his had hardened again.

"Lizzie, baby, are you okay?" Jen was running towards her as another emergency tech chased her down the walkway.

"Ma'am, you can't leave your car here. Ma'am." Behind him, Joel had run up next to the guy to assure him that he would move the car.

Jen caught up with Lizzie before Joel could catch up with her. Lizzie, Nick, and the two techs were all standing there, watching this crazy little woman in disbelief.

Jen grabbed hold of Lizzie tightly, shaking her all over and talking animatedly. "Lizzie, are you hurt? You look all right. They said a girl was attacked. It wasn't you, was it? Did you see him?"

"Babe," Joel said, finally catching up to her.

"Yeah, take the damn keys. Do you really think I care about that stupid car right now," Jen said, flinging the keys at him. Lizzie laughed, smiling at her. "You're okay, then?"

"I'm fine. I just fainted, I think," Lizzie said, looking at Nick, who nodded in agreement.

"We need to run some tests to make sure she doesn't have a concussion, but you should be able to take her home soon," the medic closest to Lizzie said.

"Okay, that's all I need to know." Jen turned around as the police sirens announced the cars moving up the driveway. "They're going to want to talk to you, aren't they?"

Lizzie nodded and they all walked into the hospital. The police were going to have to wait.

They did wait. The whole thing was like one big mind explosion: two fat guys coming at her at a rapid rate with impossible questions. One trying to play the good cop when she knew they were both equally confusing and evil, and neither of them were officers she had dealt with before, who knew what she'd been through.

They had cornered her in her room while Jen was out with the doctor looking for her test results, but Lizzie knew better than to answer without a guardian present. Sure, they probably meant well, but she didn't trust anyone new. Who knew what their real angle was, and when they asked about her relationship with Fiona as well as Nick, Lizzie didn't even protest anything.

"What do you want me to say? We went to school together. Nick is my boyfriend. That's it. I don't know anything else."

The doorknob turned and Jen stepped into the room, assessing the situation like a viper preparing to strike down a group of mice.

"I think my sister has answered enough of your questions for the night. She has been through a great ordeal, and if you need her to answer anything else, we'll be happy to do it at a more convenient hour. But for now, I don't think she can give you any insight into this horrible crime. We're going home."

Lizzie smiled. The poor officers hadn't stood a chance against a determined Jen.

"Miss, we still aren't sure if your sister was involved in the injury of this girl. I'm afraid we have to finish gathering our information before she can leave. Where are your parents? Why don't you go and wait with them?" Lizzie shook her head. Jen looked young for her age, but she made it clear that no one was going to get away with thinking of her as anything but an adult.

"Um, first of all Officer…Buckley, I'm not some little girl you can send off to her parents. I'm a grown woman and her legal guardian. Now, unless you have some evidence to keep her here, then I know my rights, and I'm going to take her home. If you have any more questions, you can ask them at the house at a more appropriate hour. So what's it going to be?"

Lizzie couldn't believe it. Jen grabbed her by the arm and they marched out of the hospital room. The officers didn't go after her. They didn't arrest Jen. They stood there in that room as stunned as Lizzie was. Joel was out there waiting, chuckling to himself.

"You guys wait here," Jen said. "I'll pull the car around. I'm driving home too, so don't even think about protesting."

"I hadn't even dreamed of it, babe." He chuckled under his breath as she strutted out the doors.

"She is more crazy than me. I thought she was going to punch them out," Lizzie said, still somewhat surprised at her sister's attack on the local police.

"She has a lot of fire in her," Joel replied with a smile. Lizzie noticed that it reached all the way to his eyes, giving them a little twinkle. "That's what I love about her."

"How much do you love my sister?" Lizzie asked. It was good to see Jen happy.

"Very much. She's my whole life. I have nothing without her."

Lizzie didn't know whether to be happy for him or sad. She reached over and gave him a quick hug.

He patted her on the head, not quite sure what to think of the situation. "Does this mean you're not going to get rid of me?" he asked, as she pulled back from the hug.

Lizzie just laughed, giving him a slight nod.

The next day, it took all the strength Lizzie had to get out of bed, but she wanted her art showcased more than anything in the world. It had been a long night and everyone could still see the sleep in her eyes, but all of that was forgotten as people walked around staring at the beautiful paintings.

Lizzie had received a mixed review from people. The

more eccentric people seemed to like them, but the more conservative guests seemed somewhat appalled at her work. The eyes attracted everyone's attention. They were the lightest blue Lizzie could find. Two icicles so light and piercing that some of the girls tried to avoid its stare as they passed. She couldn't remember his face, and that made it even harder. Instead of a solid being, Lizzie would dream of blue as a ghostly aura, appearing from the nothing and inhaling the life from her soul.

"Your paintings are wonderful, kiddo. I'm proud of you," Jen said, giving her sister a hug.

"Thanks. Where's Joel?" Lizzie said, noticing no one behind her sister.

"Well, Nick and Genevieve were having car trouble, so he's gone to pick them up. They should be here soon, I promise. I'm going to go speak with Ms. Fisher. I'll be right back." Jen put on her mom face and walked over to Ms. Fisher, who was entertaining many of the moms for the evening.

Lizzie used this opportunity to excuse herself from the crowd and went to get some punch. As she sipped it, she stared watchfully at the people observing the other paintings. The only one that didn't seem to have many observers was her clown. It seemed that people's interest had faded or were trying to ignore that glare and then— she saw it.

The clown's eyes, they moved. They were still that similar ice color, but Lizzie could have sworn she saw them blink. It happened so fast, she couldn't figure out if she had just imagined it. Her mind had been playing too many tricks on her for her to believe it and yet…

She calmly walked across the room to the painting, trying unsuccessfully to dodge people in the process. By the time she had managed to get across the room, they were gone. All that was left were two little cut outs of where they had been. Lizzie stood there in bewilderment, rubbing her eyes and blinking heavily. Then it hit her brain and her eyes became slits, mouth curving into a gritted frown that caused her nose to twitch. Her hand tightened around her cup and she could feel the liquid drip onto her shoe. *He had been right here*, she thought.

"Oh, Lizzie. I'm so sorry your beautiful painting was damaged." Ms. Fisher consoled her, thinking that was the cause of Lizzie's distress. She and Jen had walked over and Lizzie noticed that Joel, Nick, and Genevieve were coming in the doorway. "I can't imagine how someone managed to take it down and damage it with a whole crowd of people here."

"That's all right," Lizzie muttered still lost in thought. She had been so close. Of course there really was no way to figure out when he would be coming but there was something she could do. She could prepare. If he came after her again, she would be ready, she would fight.

"Lizzie," Jen said, looking worried again. "Is everything all right?"

"Fine," Lizzie said, feeling more determined than she ever had.

That next week was a total nightmare. Everywhere she went, people stared and whispered. Rumor was that Lizzie had hired someone to kill Fiona so she could be the queen bee. Most people were too scared to go anywhere near her. Those with enough courage to approach her were the worst. They kept asking her all these aggravating questions. Who attacked her? Do they do other requests?

How idiotic could they get?

Lizzie buried herself into her homework and Nick. When he was around, he kept most of them at bay, sending them evil glares from across the room. Then he would always say something silly and make Lizzie forget the whole mess.

In the back of her mind, there still lay that sense of not knowing. She decided that there was something she could do, something she hated the thought of, but might be helpful to her.

She had to visit Fiona in the hospital.

When Joel picked Lizzie up after school that Friday, he was surprised at her request to go to the hospital, but couldn't seem to think of any argument against it. He waited in the hallway when Lizzie knocked on the door of Fiona's room.

"Fiona," Lizzie said, entering the room. "I thought maybe you'd want to talk. Is it okay if I sit down?"

Fiona looked so small, huddled into herself beneath the white sheets. She nodded slightly, not saying much of anything, or bothering to look at Lizzie at all. She spent several minutes staring out the window before she played with the petals of her daffodil on her small table.

"Your flower is very pretty," Lizzie said, not quite sure where to begin.

"My boyfriend gave it to me. He's a senior," she said. Her bandages on her arms were wrapped all the way up to her shoulders, but the small dots on her face had begun to fade. Soon there would be only minor scars on her body, but Lizzie knew too well how hard it was for the inner scars to go away. "You think I deserve to be punished, don't you?"

"No, of course not," Lizzie said. "Do you think I'm that mean?"

"You were right about everything. I should've trusted you. I should've known better. He said I deserved to die for what I did to you."

"Nobody deserves that. He can't justify what's he done, and when he comes for me, I'm going to make sure he's caught this time, but I can't do it without you," Lizzie said.

"Me? What can I do?" Fiona finally turned to look at Lizzie, and Lizzie could see her face was wet with tears.

"Did you see his face?" Lizzie was hopeful. If she could prove to the police that Lizzie and Fiona had the same attacker, she could finally put James's good name to rest and have them searching for the real Boogeyman.

"No," she said, shaking her head. "He was wearing a thick mask, but some of his brown hair was sticking out."

"Brown? Are you sure?" Lizzie tried to hold in her surprise.

"Yeah, the mask covered his entire face, but there was a small cut in it that exposed some of his hair. I must've ripped it when he was dragging me across the field. Does that help?"

"Yeah," Lizzie said, hiding disappointment. "I better get going. My ride is waiting for me. Thank you for all your help, and maybe I'll see you back at school soon."

"All right. You know, your style isn't totally hopeless, I guess," Fiona said.

"You know, your bitchy attitude isn't totally hopeless either, I guess." Lizzie smiled, Fiona laughed, and Lizzie left her, feeling slightly satisfied, despite her investigative setback.

Chapter 30

Francis

July 2012:

*T*his is a stupid idea, Brian Matthew told Francis as they walked down Cherry Street. *There's no such thing as psychic abilities.*

She's a tarot reader, not a psychic. She might be able to tell us what to do next. Maybe we can get the kid to stop before she ruins our lives. Francis had followed Lizzie from California to Maine. He didn't know if he should let her go, but it seemed she was having the same problem with him. All of this was at the expense of her sister, who he had such a passion for that the whole thing caused him nothing but torment.

I think the damage is already done. This quack's not going to know anything, Brian Matthew said. He felt the same magnetic pull to Jen, but knew it was too late for them. He wanted to go home and start over. He had tried to pull Brian forward, to contact him for the first time, but received no response.

Well, I believe it's possible. We exist and people wouldn't believe us if we told them. This woman might know what she's talking about. Francis finally reached the purple house. He climbed the stairs and knocked several times before realizing there was a doorbell.

When the funeral march played, Brian Matthew groaned internally. *Jeez, who lives here? Wednesday Addams?*

An older woman answered the door and Francis thought she looked the part. She had flowy, colorful clothes, gold bracelets down her arms, and the smell of incense around her.

"Can I help you," she asked, examining Francis.

"Yes, I was looking for Genevieve." He pulled a pile of coins out of his pocket, what was left of his money. "I don't have much, but I could use some advice."

She eyed him, seeming to see something she didn't like. "Young man, I'm not a counselor."

"I know," he said, not sure what to say. "But I need answers."

"Come inside. I'll give you what I can." She swung the door open and he stepped inside. She took him to the living room and indicated for him to sit on the couch. Candles were already lit and smelled of something fresh and fruity. She pulled out an ordinary deck of cards, and he looked them over with surprise. She shuffled them and broke them into three piles. "Cut the decks twice, then put them back together and shuffle it until you feel you've done enough. Let the energy guide you to the right stopping point."

He nodded, doing as he was told. He shuffled them for quite some time before setting them back on the table.

I didn't feel any energy, Brian Matthew noted.

It's not your reading, Francis said.

"Now we're going to use the top three cards." She set them side-by-side, face down. "From left to right we have past, present, and future. Are you ready to begin?"

"I'm more interested in the future. Can we skip to that," he asked.

"No." She laughed, giving him a smile. "Our future isn't set in stone. We are products of our past and present. We try to leave them behind, but without them, we become nothing more. The flower cannot bloom without rain and sunlight. You must accept these things before you can look ahead. Do you wish to continue?"

"Yes, please," he said.

"Okay. Let's take a look."

She flipped over the card and saw the king of spades. He studied her reaction and didn't like what he saw. Her brows were furrowed and her eyes were wide, as if the card were possessed.

She pointed to the star on the top of the card and tried to get her mouth to move. "The stars represent the energy of a card. Balanced energy is at the bottom, and negative energy is at the top."

"Okay. And what does that mean?"

"Well the king represents strength or weakness. Reversed it shows that your life has been in turmoil. Instead of having a strong foundation, yours was weak and burdened. This weakens your mind, leaving you with conflicting ideas."

"Like having two minds about something?" Francis asked.

Holy shit, Brian Matthew thought. *How does it say all that?*

"Exactly. Now the spade is representative of your personality. Spades are usually cunning, intelligent, and charming, but on the reverse side they can be aggressive, impulsive, and ill-tempered. Your friends would be wise not to anger you."

She paused a moment while he picked up the card. Francis twirled it between his fingers to feel its connection to him. He wondered if Brian Matthew would've gotten the same thing. He wanted to believe it was special to him.

"Do you want me to continue?" she asked.

He set the card back down. "Yes, I'm ready."

"Okay." She flipped over the next card, the ace of hearts, star down. The woman smiled. "The ace is representative of romantic connections. This indicates that you're in love with someone. The heart is the highest bond you can have with someone. It also represents transformation. This woman will make you a better person."

"Will that continue into the future?" He tried not to turn red as he thought of amber eyes. She flipped over the third card and Francis sighed. It was the three of hearts with the star facing up. "That's bad, right?"

"I'm afraid so. The star point up indicates a reverse three, which is a connector. It represents close bonds— friends, family. A reverse three means you will lose yourself or someone close to you." She stared at the card, shaking her head. "I'm sorry."

"Well what happens to them or me? Do you mean they die?" His heart had slid down into his stomach. He had hoped that this would give him answers, not more terrifying questions. "And who is it? Me? A friend? My sister? I need to know what's going to happen."

"I can only give you what the cards tell me, but I can give you a clarity card," she said.

"Yes, anything. Just tell me something," he said, feeling lightheaded.

"Think of one question you want answered. Say it to yourself and flip the card over, but don't tell anyone what you asked. This will be all the information I can give you." She waited for him to respond.

He took the top card from the deck thinking, *Who am I going to lose?*

It flipped over and the queen of hearts appeared.

"This person who relates to your question is a heart personality. They are passionate and protective people, in both fault and strength. This woman will be the one for your question." She picked up the cards and started to put them back in the box.

"That's it," he said, a little surprised. "You can't tell me more than that?"

"I'm afraid not. No charge," she said. She smiled at him, but it dropped when she saw the look in his eyes.

"Someone protective? Like a caretaker type? Someone who puts others before herself and loves unconditionally?"

"That's right?"

What's wrong, Brian Matthew asked, feeling the distress.

Jen, Francis told him before turning on the woman. He flipped the table and cards went flying. "You got it wrong. Tell me you got it wrong. I wouldn't hurt her."

"I never said you did," the woman said. If she were shaken up, there were no visible signs. She looked Francis directly in the eyes without fear. "I told you that you would lose someone. This could be physically or mentally, and how is unclear."

"But I can't lose her. I need her. I can fix this. I can change. Tell me how." He sensed his eyes start to water.

Let it go, Brian Matthew said. *She can't help us. No one can.*

Francis shook his head, trying to rattle the thought away. He gave the woman a nod and headed to the door.

"As I told you before, the future isn't set in stone. It's created by our choices. I hope yours can bring you peace." She opened the door for him.

"Thank you for your time," he said and disappeared down the street.

Chapter 31

Brian Matthew

August 2012:

Brian Matthew was relieved to be in charge of the body again. Francis's choices were too dangerous, and Brian Matthew didn't like to leave things to chance. He watched from a distance as Lizzie continued her therapy sessions with Dr. Stewart. She had started seeing her since they first moved there and wasn't having success with her recovery. Brian Matthew had hoped that, with a little push, Lizzie would forget what he had done, but Lizzie refused to give up. She wouldn't be satisfied until she ruined his life.

He watched her knock a few things over as she shouted. He couldn't hear what she was saying, but it wasn't good for him.

She's going to keep telling her until she convinces the police to re-open the investigation, Francis said. *We have to do something about her.*

Yes, I'm thinking, Brian Matthew said.

You tend to do a lot of that, Francis said. *When are you going to stop thinking and take care of the girl?*

We might not have to, he said. *Killing the girl now*

would be suspicious and messy. Perhaps she just needs some persuading, a warning.

Like what?

Let's come back at nightfall, Brian Matthew said, watching as Jen burst into the room. He ducked around the corner.

Hours later as the last patient of the day left the parking lot, Brian Matthew entered the office of Dr. Marion Stewart. The secretary had gone and Dr. Stewart was writing at her desk. She looked up briefly when he walked in.

"I'm sorry but we're closed for the night, and I'm not taking new patients right now." She continued to jot down her notes.

"I think you might make an exception for me, Doc," Brian Matthew said, taking the knife from his pocket.

He'd hated leaving his old knife at his last crime scene. This one didn't feel as good as the last. The familiarity and satisfaction of its feel was gone. She raised her head and stared at the weapon. Brian Matthew could almost see the cogs in her brain turning, but she was trained better than most to control herself.

"You have my attention," she said, putting down her pen. "How can I help?"

Bet she's never seen anything like us before, Francis said.

"What do you call three people in one body," he asked.

"Are you saying you hear voices," she asked. "What is your name?"

He fiddled with the knife in his hands. "I'm not giving it, and no, I'm not hearing voices. I am one."

Just kill her already. What are you looking for, Francis asked.

Thought maybe she'd know what we are, he said. *I guess we're more special than I realized.*

"I'm sorry I don't understand, but if you give me your name, we can schedule a time to discuss it."

She glanced at the phone. It was intended to be seen as a casual gesture but Brian Matthew noticed it immediately. He moved forward and she grabbed it as he reached her.

He pulled it from her desk, throwing it across the room. "I'm afraid my schedule is booked right now."

He reached around the desk and stabbed her. As he moved, she moved around the other side of the desk so that his first swipe hit her arm. She fumbled out of her chair and fell to the ground. As she got up, he came around the other side and slit her throat. She grabbed at her throat as the blood began to pool around her.

What the hell was that? Francis asked. *A bit dramatic for you.*

Eh, Brian Matthew said, pulling out a pair of gloves from his pocket. He went through the stuff on the desk, not seeing much of importance. *There must be an envelope here somewhere*

For what?

We're going to deliver a message. He pulled a large envelope from the bottom drawer. He grabbed a piece of paper from a pile and jotted down a note. He shoved the note into the envelope. He stared down at the body, thinking of what to do next. He took hold of his knife again and, hovering over her body, sliced off her ear. He stuffed it in the envelope and closed it. On the outside, he wrote Lizzie's name in big block letters.

What's that going to do, Francis asked.

Hopefully keep her scared and quiet. I want her to let this go, he said, walking from the room.

Do you really think it'll work? Francis sounded uncertain.

It has to, Brian Matthew said.

Chapter 32

Lizzie

November 2012:

Weeks went by, and the trees remained abandoned and exposed. Then the wind danced around the little town, bringing chills to the air.

For Lizzie, the weather became harsh. Her tiny body was freezing in her enormous parka, but what did she expect? After all, it was Maine that they were in. She missed her California home. Right now she could have been sitting in the sun, dipping her toes in the sand, and drinking fruity drinks. Of course they were non-alcoholic, but she always made her mom give her one of those tiny umbrellas anyway. She used to think they were cute when she was little. There was no warmth here anymore on the outside. Inside, Lizzie never felt warmer. Every day became more and more frigid until it came: the first snow of the season, and the first snow of Lizzie's life.

When Lizzie awoke that November morning, frost had painted all the windows. She hopped into her boots and parka and rushed outside. The morning light twinkled off the sparkly new-fallen snow. It decorated every inch of outside in a glistening sea of white. It was still crisp and delicate, completely untouched by man. Lizzie almost had the urge to run back inside. It seemed too beautiful to mess up, but she changed her mind. She flopped down clumsily into the snow.

Nick came sprinting from the house and collapsed next to her. It was a Saturday morning and Lizzie had convinced Jen to let Nick spend the night—as long as he slept on the couch. They flailed their arms up and down, making two deformed snow angels.

"Yours has a big head," Lizzie teased, looking at his lumpy mass on the ground.

"Yeah, well yours is so messed up by your ears that you can't even tell what it's supposed to be. Did Dumbo help you make it?"

Lizzie gasped with horror. *Oh no he didn't.*

Wham! A snowball cracked Nick on the side of the face. Lizzie burst into laughter, but then another came at her. Wham! It smacked hard in her chest. Then a bombardment of snowballs came flying across the yard. Joel and Jen peeked out from behind a tree, matching sinister grins.

Then another wave of destruction flew down on the two helpless souls. Nick started piling up snow for a fort while Lizzie tried desperately to dodge the shots.

"Take cover!" Nick shouted as they jumped behind their little mass of snow. This was the most pitiful fort Lizzie had ever seen. A two-year-old probably could have done better. She tried to fix it a little before another attack came. Nick rolled up tiny snowballs as fast as he could. "We need more ammunition."

"Surrender foul, demon children or be forced to go without supper tonight." Jen cackled, thumping Lizzie on the head with her snowball.

"We shall never surrender to you, evil woman!" Nick

shouted as Lizzie burst into laughter, but Joel was the best sport of all.

"Meet your doom," he bellowed with the deepest voice he had. "Luke, I am your father."

"Boy, am I glad I'm not Luke," Lizzie shouted to him.

He laughed so hard that Lizzie was able to get a shot in. It bounced off his head, still intact. He swiftly picked it up and chucked it like it was a football. It slammed into their little fort, cracking it in the center. The snow tumbled to the ground, exposing the two helpless victims. Nick took off his white glove and waved it around like a flag.

"Uh-huh. Victory is mine." Jen elbowed Joel in the side. "I mean ours. Now let's eat."

Jen served up her famous French toast. Nick and Lizzie moped all the way inside and to the table.

Joel taunted them all breakfast, enjoying his gourmet meal and crowing with laughter. "The taste of victory, the agony of defeat."

"You guys cheated," Lizzie pouted.

"We did nothing of the sort." Jen smiled wryly. "A good soldier is always prepared for an attack. It's not our fault you guys don't know how to build a fort."

"It was Nick's shoddy construction," Lizzie accused.

Nick gave her a sad face and whimpered like a scolded puppy. She laughed and gave him a kiss on the cheek.

They spent the rest of the day watching movies in the living room and eating extra buttery popcorn. It had been one of those happy days, where everything just seemed to go right, where all her troubles went out the window, and she could feel happy and normal for a change. Lizzie wondered how long that would last, probably not even a full day.

As the days rolled by, she became more and more impatient. Any second someone was going to come back and drastically change her life. Would he just directly come for her? Or would he attack someone else? She thought of her happy group. The thought of losing any of them now, even Joel, was heart wrenching. She just didn't want to even consider it.

Lizzie felt sick and disheartened. What was this guy's problem? When would the never-ending nightmare be over? Pain shot through her head like someone was beating her rapidly with a hammer. *Too much confusion, too many thoughts, can't take much more of this, need rest.* Lizzie was sick of the entire thing.

She crawled into bed and rocked herself to sleep. It would all be over soon. In that moment, she began to hope that he would come to her tonight and smother her while she slept. *He will be back and we must be ready.* Her mind kept her in check so that she wouldn't forget. If she did forget, then she wouldn't be ready. He wasn't going to catch her off guard. Still, as the days passed by, the likelihood of his return began to fade in her mind, and suddenly her worries seemed to almost completely disappear, except for in her dreams. They wouldn't let her forget. Before she knew it, she had drifted into another nightmare…

There were birds chirping. Lizzie knew how strange it was to hear them. She had closed the window before she went to sleep and yet, they were there, singing sweet melodic songs. She sat up from her bed, searching for where the little voices had come from. On her windowsill, she spotted a robin, its gray head supported by its plump red belly, twittering away in the moonlight. She climbed from her bed, pulling back its covers and walked to the little bird, slowly at first, but picking up pace when she saw it jumping about. She held out her palms, hoping to corner it into her hands. When she had retrieved it, it settled into her fingers, its little claws brushing lightly on her palms. She adjusted it in one of her hands and stroked its belly with her fingertips. Its breast feathers reminded her of the smooth feather on her peacock hat, the one she had bought for her sweet sixteen party.

She looked out the window into the darkness, still stroking her little friend. It was the middle of October outside, even though Lizzie knew it was November. The leaves shined with darkened oranges and reds in the glimpses of the moonlight. The old tree with the lightning bolt split looked strange in the light, like a mourning woman, arms spread to the heavens, asking for more answers than the earth could give her. Beneath it, she saw a figure shift before tilting its head towards her window, the glow of the moon beams casting a ghostly sheen over his blue eyes. She blinked rapidly, hoping to make him go away, but he wouldn't.

Her hand suddenly felt wet on her fingers. She looked down to see blood pressed into the grooves of her fingertips. Her little friend in her palm, dripped wet and cold. Lizzie realized then that he had been quiet for some time now. She tapped it with her finger, eyes watering, and its body twitched. She screamed, dropping it onto her floor. The blood pooled around her fuzzy pink rug, inching its way back toward her feet. *How much can one little bird bleed*, she wondered, wiping the tear, that had escaped from her cheek.

Then the floor rippled, and she fell hard, landing against the tile floor of the kitchen. She got up slowly, trying to determine what had happened, but there was no longer a hole in the ceiling.

Wham! The sound of the front door slamming caught her off guard. Afraid, she grabbed a kitchen knife from the counter and peeked into the hallway. The doorway was desolate, except for something light, hanging on the handle. She inched closer, knife at the ready, and pulled it from the door. She gagged when she felt it in her hand, strips of skin delicately laid out like dried meats. With it, Lizzie noticed some small strands of hair. She pulled it off the strip, eyes wide when she realized they were red. *Oh God.*

Something smashed to the floor in the living room and she spun around, knife raised. She could hear footsteps coming toward her, but everything was going dark. She slashed blindly and she thought she scraped skin, but seconds later a hand was tugging on her arm.

Lizzie jolted awake to find she was staring into Jen's bedroom. Jen held her arm up, staring at a new cut that was lightly bleeding. Lizzie could feel the tight grip over her fingers. She looked up and saw the scissors in her hand, and behind her, Joel was standing in his boxer shorts. She looked back and forth between them in confusion.

"You were sleepwalking," Joel said, exhaling a large breath and removing his hand from hers.

Lizzie stared at Jen with fear, but Jen just shook her head. "I'm okay. I can't believe you made it all the way down the stairs without falling. Lizzie? What's the matter?"

Lizzie was looking past her into the room, mouth slowly opening with confusion, when she saw what was behind Jen. Her closet was wide open and in it, taped against the door, were newspaper clippings. She dropped the scissors to the ground and brushed passed her sister into the room. They were all Boogeyman clippings, except for one.

It was about a man and his wife, who had been brutally murdered in their home. Their foster daughter, Jennifer Martin, the last person to see them alive, was the only suspect, and the woman in the photograph was her sister, Jen. Lizzie pulled the clipping from its tape. She stared at it, shaking in her hand. It seemed too unnatural to be real.

"Lizzie, sweetheart, I know what this looks like," Jen said, pulling the paper from her fingers.

Lizzie looked at Jen, mouth wide open. *This can't be happening. I don't even know my own sister.*

Jen grabbed her arm. "It's okay, Lizzie."

Lizzie pulled away again, running up her stairs and locking the door behind her. She paced her room frantically, her mind exploding again. *My sister's a murderer. I live with a murderer.* The knock on the door pulled her from her panic.

"Lizzie, it's Joel, please let us in. Jen wouldn't hurt you. She wants to talk to you about this. Open up. You and I both know she's not a killer."

"Lizzie, we've got to stick together," Jen said, through the crack in the door.

"I want to talk to Joel," Lizzie said, pulling the door open a smidgeon. She watched the two of them looking at each other, and eventually Jen nodded.

"I won't fit through that crack," Joel said, tapping his finger on the door. Lizzie opened it, grabbing Joel's arm, and pulling him into the room. She locked it back up, hoping that Jen wouldn't try to barge in. Jen stood there watching her for a few minutes before she walked down the stairs. "You know she'll be back soon, Lizzie?"

"I know. I just need a minute to think," Lizzie said.

"You know she loves you a lot, kid. She was trying to help with your investigation to protect you. She would never let anyone hurt you," Joel said, patting Lizzie on the shoulder.

"Then why does she keep things from me?" Lizzie said, giving him a hug. He patted her head affectionately.

Lizzie always felt like a dog when someone did that, but she let it go. *At least he's trying*, she thought.

"Sometimes the truth hurts too much to share, or maybe she felt she was protecting you. Whatever it is, I'm sure she meant well," he said, releasing her and unlocking the door. "You going to let her in?"

"I guess so. Ummm…Joel." Lizzie shifted her feet. She felt really embarrassed that she would ask this, but it's really what she wanted. "My big brother is gone now, but I really miss him. Do you mind if I think of you like my big brother?"

"I'm sorry you miss him so much. You can think of me however you like," Joel said, opening the door so Jen could step in and closing it behind him. He looked back inside for a moment before trudging back down the stairs.

Jen sucked in a deep breath and began before Lizzie could say anything. "I wasn't as lucky as you growing up. My foster parents were the kind that collected kids for money, especially my father. He did a lot of bad things to everyone in the house, and even when I moved out, he was relentless. He followed me to work almost every day. It made life difficult for me. When they were attacked, nobody even missed them, so I just moved on with my life. I kept the article because I just wanted to remember what I had been able to overcome. I didn't kill them, but I'm not going to lie and say that their deaths were a tragedy either. I know you probably won't ever be able to understand, but sometimes things aren't always black and white."

"And the Martin thing? Last I knew you were a Moore not a Martin."

"Martin was my foster parents' name. They had me use it as a child, but after their deaths, I had my name legally changed back to Moore. It was our father's last name."

Lizzie was having a hard time understanding and she wasn't sure if Jen was telling the complete truth. "If you didn't do anything wrong why didn't you tell me about this?"

"There are some things in my life that I feel I need to keep to myself."

Jen gave Lizzie a small hug, but Lizzie couldn't reciprocate. Instead, she was already replaying in her mind everything her sister said. Jen left her there to think about it long after breakfast had gone by. Lizzie waited for her gray area, but she didn't find it. She didn't find black or white or gray. All she could see from her sister's talk was red.

Chapter 33

Francis

December 2012:

This is a stupid idea," Brian Matthew told Francis as he watched him finish wrapping up the box on the table. He had at least convinced him to wear gloves to cover his fingerprints.

"I know what I'm doing," Francis said, tying the ribbon around the box. He admired his work, deciding that he wasn't as challenged in the craft department as he thought. "How does it look?"

"Oh it sure is per-dy. We've already scared her enough. This is going to make things worse."

"She's finding out too much. She needs to know we're watching her." They had been arguing all morning. Brian Matthew thought this was too risky, but Francis was in control again, and he wanted to do this. Brian Matthew hated being an onlooker in his life. It made him more aware that this life wasn't just his own and that bothered him.

"What if they come home early?" Brian Matthew asked.

Francis hadn't thought of that. He had seen Lizzie

and Jen leave early that morning. It was noon time and they still hadn't returned. Here he was sitting in the middle of the kitchen having an argument with Brian Matthew out loud. He got up from the kitchen table, moving through the hallway to the front door. He opened it a bit and peeked out. A chill hit his arms as the wind picked up. It was snowing again, a constant here since November. Everything was barren and white. The road and driveway had been covered and not a car could be seen for miles. A blackbird flew down, landing on one of the tree stumps in the yard. He thought it strange for a bird to be out in this weather. He watched it sitting there, black against the pure white of the snow, and thought of its resilience.

"It's not supposed to be here, but chooses to be anyway," Francis said. "Just like us."

"There are lonely blackbirds inside of everyone," Brian Matthew said. "Nobody ever feels like they belong in this world."

"It's a pity they don't sing," Francis told him.

"Not every bird can have the same song. They'd no longer be special," Brian Matthew said, a little surprised at his friend's reaction.

"I think we're good for a little longer," he said, placing the box under the tree.

Chapter 34

Lizzie

December 2012:

It wasn't until Christmas Eve that she heard from the Boogeyman again. It was the most perfect little thing she had ever seen—wrapped in beautiful silver paper with little white snowflakes all over it, and a red ribbon dangling from its top. It was neatly wrapped to perfection and had caught Lizzie's attention the minute she saw it under the Christmas tree.

Jen didn't know who it was from, but Lizzie knew it must've been from Nick. He must've snuck it under as he went home to spend Christmas Eve with Genevieve. As tradition had gone with her parents, Lizzie was allowed to open one present on Christmas Eve, and Jen decided that it was good for Lizzie to keep some of their traditions going to make her feel at home again. Unfortunately, she happened to choose the wrong one.

Beneath that gorgeous paper that she unwrapped gently not wanting to rip it, laid a picture of James. It smiled up at her, taunting her in every way possible. A note lay beside it, *You'll be joining him soon, if you don't stop.*

Anger boiled up inside of her. *I'm so sick of this,* she thought. He was playing a game and she didn't like being his favorite toy. Screaming wildly, she tore the note into shreds. Then she stamped as hard as she could on the box, wailing with rage. Joel went to her and wrapped his arms around her in a comforting hug.

"We won't let anyone hurt you. It'll all be okay." He picked up the half-mangled box and handed it to Jen. "Take that down to the police station. I bet there'll be fingerprints on it."

This Christmas Eve was the worst she had felt since James died. Jen drove the evidence down to the police station immediately, while Joel stayed to keep an eye on Lizzie. She had been silent on the couch for several minutes, face red and hands balled into fists. Joel was watching anxiously out the window for Jen to return, but it had started to snow, so she would be longer than either of them anticipated.

Joel turned away from the window and sat next to Lizzie. "Are you okay, kiddo?"

Lizzie shook her head. She wanted to say more, but she wasn't sure what to say. She was angry, really angry, but it was boiling so deeply within her that she didn't know where to begin to express it. Joel seemed to sense all of this while he was sitting there and came up with a better course of action than patting her on the back for comfort.

"Get up," he said, rising from his seat. He tugged on her arm a little when she just stared at him. "No more moping. I'm going to teach you something. Get up."

"Okay," Lizzie said, getting up. "What is it?"

"Basic self-defense techniques. All right, when you throw a punch, put your weight into your swing and ro-tate your wrist for maximum impact like this." He swung into the air with a steady speed that probably would've bruised whoever it connected with.

Lizzie swung in the air, but it looked more erratic and flimsy. Joel stood behind her, balling her hand into a fist and swinging her arm to show her how hard and fast to move. She jabbed the air a couple times then Joel had her practice by using his hands as a target. When he shook his hand because it had received instant pain, he moved on to the stance for an attack from behind.

Halfway through the lesson, Jen walked in through the door. She watched a few minutes with curiosity as Joel gave Lizzie pointers about hand holds before participating herself.

"And if all this fails and they're a man, just knee 'em in the groin," Jen said, winking at her sister.

Lizzie laughed, but Joel wasn't amused.

The night had ended on a high note, but Christmas morning quickly turned into a disaster.

"May I come in, ma'am?" Officer Buckley asked, slightly pushing his way into the doorframe. Officer Perry was right on his heels.

Jen looked somewhat agitated at their presence. They had just started opening gifts. Nick had half a guitar unwrapped. He watched the gleam on its green finish tantalize him while everyone waited. Jen saw the urgency in the officer's eyes and reluctantly let him in.

"Sorry to have to come on Christmas, but we had no other choice." Officer Perry apologized.

"To what do we owe this visit?" Jen asked, politely hiding agitation.

"I'm afraid we're going to have to take the boy here downtown for some further questioning. Is his grandmother here with him?" Officer Perry said.

Nick looked stunned and Lizzie clung on to him firmly.

"What for?" Joel snapped. "You can't just take him without a warrant. He's only a sixteen-year-old kid."

"We have a warrant for his arrest. We believe that he was involved with the attack on Fiona Applebee and may be responsible for these anonymous letters to Lizzie. We're also going to contact his grandmother so that she can be present for the questioning," Officer Buckley said.

Lizzie gasped with horror at the same time as Jen shouted, "That's the stupidest thing I've ever heard! Nick wouldn't hurt Lizzie in a million years. Let me see that." She snatched the warrant from the officer's hands as confusion lit across her face. "It says that you have substantial evidence to suspect Nick of these crimes. What do you have for evidence? Since this case is concerned with Lizzie, we have the right to know."

"Ma'am, I'm really not supposed to discuss that with you," Officer Buckley said.

"Can you discuss it with me? Because I definitely have something to say about this," Nick said, fists curling into a ball.

Lizzie patted his arm to calm him, but with little effect.

Officer Perry pulled the paper away from Jen's hands. "We found your fingerprints all over the package that Ms. Moore gave us yesterday. No other fingerprints were found except for the victim's and the other residents of the house."

"I picked up all kinds of packages yesterday. I was trying to find mine so I could figure out what Lizzie had gotten me." Nick tightened his fists. "This is complete bullshit! Why would I hurt my girlfriend? And if I were the stupid Boogeyman person, do you really think I would leave my fingerprints all over the evidence?"

"Did anyone else rummage through the presents yesterday?" Officer Buckley asked, clearly getting annoyed.

Lizzie knew he really didn't even have to go through this process with them, but he was willing to hear them out.

Jen seemed completely stunned. She didn't believe this anymore than Lizzie did. "Well, not that I know of. I saw Lizzie and Nick playing with them for a few minutes, but no one else was here except for Joel and me."

"I didn't kill anyone! And why would I hurt Lizzie?" Nick rose in anger, his fists so clenched that Lizzie wasn't sure if he would swing at the officer.

"Jealousy, you want to keep her near you. Did you not just get kicked out of your last school for smashing the principal over the head with a chair, even though you had no previous record of violence?" Officer Buckley said.

"Yes but that was something completely different. I did—"

"And didn't you get into an altercation with some of the football players at school that also involved a Ms. Fiona Applebee?"

"Yes but that was—"

"And is it true that some other students witnessed you threatening Ms. Applebee on several occasions?" Officer Perry watched his partner speaking and seemed to have something to say about it but whatever it was he kept it to himself.

"She was driving Lizzie crazy, so I just made her shut up already."

"By attacking her?"

No. This can't be real. I'm dreaming again. I'll wake up soon and it will all be over. Lizzie couldn't wrap her mind around all of this.

"Absolutely not! I love Lizzie and I'll be damned if I let anyone hurt her, but I didn't attack Fiona." Nick's outburst was unnerving for even the greatest skeptic in the room.

Lizzie pulled away from him a little, not sure what to do now. Her own boyfriend might want to kill her. Joel was the first to speak.

"What about the doctor? How is Nick connected to her?" Joel seemed very deep in thought now. He didn't seem as outraged anymore, more serious and contemplative. He put his fingers over his mouth, rubbing his lip as if he could make the words spill out in Nick's defense.

"Nick's grandmother was friends with the doctor, and on the day of her disappearance after Nick returned home, from a visit to a friend, his grandmother sent him on an errand to Dr. Stewart's house." Officer Perry answered.

"And she wasn't there when I arrived. I told you guys that a while ago. This is ridiculous. Tell them Lizzie." All was silent. Nick looked at Lizzie, but she couldn't form the words. He twitched with anger, fists raised. Officer Buckley stepped forward to seize Nick, but Jen stepped in the way.

"Do you have any proof that Nick did more than threaten Ms. Applebee?" Jen said and Joel moved in next to her, taking her hand. "I mean, being angry is one thing, but attacking someone...I know you've indulged us a lot, but I can't just let you take him on such little cause as teenage hearsay."

"Which brings me to the real question I wished to ask. Do you recognize this?" Officer Buckley held up a mask, dark and black with barely any slits for the eyes. "We pulled this from your locker this morning, and Ms. Applebee identified this as the image she saw on the night of her attack."

"I think that you should go with him, Nick," Jen said firmly. "He has a warrant, and I don't want to hear any more of this interrogation in my house. Lizzie has suffered enough."

"This is friggin' stupid. What kind of girlfriend are you? You don't even believe me. This is bullshit, Lizzie, and you know it. You know I love you, Lizzie. Lizzie, look at me."

Joel wedged himself between Lizzie and Nick as Officer Buckley hauled Nick out the doors, still kicking and screaming. Officer Perry followed behind him assisting when Nick continued to thrash around.

How could this happen? When did Nick threaten Fiona? He had said that nothing would ever hurt me…no. This can't be right. She choked back her tears as she heard the car's tires squealing out of the driveway. It felt like her heart had fallen out. She felt so empty. She couldn't even comprehend what had happened. Nick was her life now and she loved him more than anything in the world, except for Jen. What was she supposed to do? That cold, empty feeling hit her hard in her chest. She ran up to her tower and sobbed for hours in her pillows.

Jen and Joel tried to comfort her, but she barricaded the door, screaming for them to go away. She curled herself into the tiniest ball she could fit on her bed. It felt so unnatural to be lying there alone. She had gotten use to the warm comfort Nick brought lying next to her. She fell asleep in his arms every night. How would she ever sleep again? *What do I have to live for now?* Lizzie tried to picture Nick there with her, his hands stroking her hair, his breath at her earlobe, the sweet scent of his cologne. That night she dreamt of Nick and how things were supposed to be.

Nick was released to his grandmother while the police investigated further. He would be tried in a couple of months, but until then he was most definitely suspended from school with a possibility of expulsion.

For the rest of Christmas vacation, Lizzie remained at the house. She was afraid if she left, she would see Nick, and she just couldn't bear that. It was hard enough seeing that stupid guitar sitting in the living room, still half-opened. It tortured Lizzie's mind for hours on end.

Nick should've been here now. He would be sitting down with Lizzie, strumming on his new guitar, trying hard to write her a song but getting frustrated every time one of the strings was out of tune. She could just imagine those beautiful gray eyes piercing her heart. Her body would be caught in some hypnotic sway that wouldn't quite fit with the rhythm of the song, but seemed to amuse him anyway. That would be the right thing. But nothing was ever right anymore.

The next day Officer Buckley came by with the paperwork for a restraining order. Lizzie stared blankly at the little piece of paper. It would remove Nick completely from her life. How could she do that? Her heart ached with agony just thinking about it. She looked to Jen for some kind of assistance, but Jen just frowned at her. This had to be Lizzie's decision. She pushed the paper away from her and shook her head. She couldn't do that to him, even if the police advised otherwise. She cared too much about him to hurt him. She still wasn't sure if he had anything to do with the attacks, but she wasn't ready to end their friendship this way.

Going back to school was one of the hardest things Lizzie had to do. Nick's friends tried to be comforting, sitting with Lizzie at lunch and talking with her during classes, but it didn't matter. He still wasn't there, and he still wasn't answering her calls. Not that it mattered, because Jen had banned him from the house until they could figure out what was true.

Lizzie hoped that the school board would change their minds and she would see Nick strutting down the hall again, but all she saw was Fiona, completely back to normal at this point, forgetting everything she had learned. Without Nick, Lizzie felt completely lost in the crowd, submerged in a sea of people all trying to go in random directions while chatting incessantly to the person beside them. It made Lizzie sick just thinking about him.

What have I done? I could always fix this. Do I really want to? Of course the answer was yes. The real question was should she? She could tell them it was made up. That she had done it for some reason. Maybe to get attention. Perhaps they would believe it but could she lie to them? Better yet, could she lie to herself? Lizzie made up her mind not to think about it again. It was done and she had to learn to accept it. She must trust her instincts.

Chapter 35

Francis

January 2013:

Francis had kept an even closer eye on Lizzie since Christmas. He had been just as surprised as Lizzie when the police arrested Nick. He had stuffed the mask from his encounter with Fiona into a random locker, not sure what would become of it, but it had worked to his advantage. It had taken Lizzie's mind off the Boogeyman, and Francis would be able to move on with a new life. He watched at a distance as Lizzie trudged through the school hallways, face down, eyes watery.

She looks so lonely, Francis said, watching her pick at her food in the cafeteria. She twirled some peas around the plate with her fork, but never scooped any up for a bite.

She seems to have forgotten you, Brian Matthew said. *I would think you'd be happier.*

She just looks so sad, Francis said. A twinge hit his chest, and he felt something he hadn't felt in a while. *I actually feel kind of guilty.*

It worked didn't it?

Yeah, but it's not that satisfying. I can't even get

what I want. He kicked a chunk of ice away from a tree trunk.

What's that, Brian Matthew asked.

To live, to really live, he said. *And be with her.*

And the girl? What are you going to do with her?

Leave her be, Francis said as Lizzie got up from the table. She dumped her food into the trash can and shuffled to the next class. *She's been through enough.*

Wow. Showing a bit of compassion for a change, Brian Matthew said. *I'm proud of you.*

It's not compassion. Francis thought of Shelley. He missed his sister, not the delirious woman he knew now, but the old one. He hadn't seen her since he signed her out at the police station. He had meant to take her to a safe place, but she ran away from him. He'd searched for her for months, but still had no sign.

He missed the girl who danced around her room in her tutu, the girl who made cupcakes for her Barbie dolls. The little girl that had curled next to him on the floor of his room when their mother had died. He missed her asking him to fix her shoelaces and put her hair in ribbons. He missed the innocent children they had once been. Even when they had found each other again, he missed those nights of sleeping on her couch, of staying up late eating popcorn and watching movies. He missed laughter and a sense of home. Looking at Lizzie then he knew he couldn't take all of those happy memories away from her. He'd already destroyed one girl, and he couldn't destroy another. It was then that he realized what it was.

It's love.

Chapter 36

Lizzie

February 2013:

February fourteenth, Valentine's Day, the most dreaded of days.

The whole day had been so terrible for her. Guys giving out candy and flowers all through the halls, girls gasping with surprise, as if they didn't know, and hugging their little boy toys gratefully. Not to mention all the other people backing each other into the lockers, unable to control their urges like some crazy dogs in heat. It was awful. How on earth was Lizzie supposed to enjoy the day?

The entire day she had everyone blocked from her mind. All she could think about was Nick. What was he doing right now? Was he thinking of her? The thought crossed her mind once or twice that he might not even miss her. He hadn't tried to make any form of contact. Maybe he had moved on without her. Then Lizzie came to the other horrible realization. She hadn't received any more mysterious messages since Christmas Eve. Was that really linked to Nick?

No. It won't be true. We'll be able to be together just

as soon as his trial is over and they find him innocent.
Jen had gone to the first hearing to let Lizzie know what
date they had decided on for the trial and, to her dismay,
they had extended the date to the beginning of March.
Lizzie wasn't sure how she would ever make it that long
without knowing what would happen to him.

After school was the same as it had been for the past
month. Lizzie went straight home where Joel was waiting
for Jen to get home from work. Tonight was extra special.
He was going to make her a beautiful dinner. He took
some strawberry-scented candles, Jen's favorite, from a
box, and set out some long stem roses. Not wanting to get
in his way, Lizzie ran upstairs to do her homework.

When Lizzie entered her room, she noticed something was different. A single red rose lay on her pillow.
She reached out and inhaled its aroma as the door creaked
shut. She jumped with surprise as she turned around to
see Nick in front of it.

Her mind raced with possible escape methods. She
could always climb out her window and along the edge of
the roof. It was slanted more towards the front, so if she
made it there she should be able to jump without hurting
herself.

Nick looked paler than usual, and his eyes had rings
around them with fatigue. If he were to attack Lizzie, he
looked like he wouldn't be able to do much damage. He
stood there motionless for a few minutes. Every time he'd
go to speak, the words would stifle in his throat.

"I'm not here to hurt you, Lizzie, I swear. It's just
that it's Valentine's Day, and I wanted to see you. It
would make the most sense to be with your girl on Valentine's Day, if you're even my girl anymore."

"I d—don't know what we are a—anymore…" Lizzie stammered.

"Well, apparently we weren't much to begin with,

because you seem to think that I want to kill you. Do you have any idea how much you hurt me? How could you do that to me?" His hands balled into fists, but when he saw her watching him, he released them, trying to relax the tension he was feeling.

"I don't know. I just wanted to make sure it wasn't true, then we could be together again, just like before."

"What makes you think I would come back to you? How could it ever be the same if you don't trust me? I love you so much, and you think I take some twisted pleasure out of torturing you. I guess you don't love me." Nick walked to the window, stepping one foot onto the shingles. It happened so quickly that Lizzie almost missed her opportunity to react.

"No, don't." Lizzie grabbed his arm. She couldn't bear it any longer. "Please don't go. I love you too. I was just scared. It's the biggest mistake I've ever made. I'll talk to the police, just don't leave me. I've missed you so much."

She fell into his arms and he gave her the warmest hug she could ever imagine. He ran his fingers through her hair all the way down her back, stopping around her waist. His scent enveloped her mind in some mystical daze. It was so magical that she didn't even notice his lips pulling closer to hers.

Their lips locked and that passionate feeling over-whelmed her.

Suddenly, Valentine's Day was a time of joy again, a day of passion, life, and true love.

"What the hell are you doing here?" Joel bellowed from the doorway.

It was so powerful that Nick looked terrified, his face turning pale.

"It's okay, Joel. I let Nick in. I realized that it's stupid for us to be apart." Lizzie noticed quickly that the tension in Joel wasn't going away. His face was gaining redness, and his jaw stayed tight.

"No, it's not okay. Do you think just because you say it's okay that it really is? This kid could be a stalker and a killer, and you still want to be together? This proves it. Your mind has completely gone. You have no rational thought whatsoever. Boy, you better stop staring at me, and get your ass down the stairs before I throw you out the window!"

Nick scrambled out the door, being careful so that he wouldn't bump into Joel. Joel rushed down the stairs after him. Lizzie, frantic and angry, followed right behind. She managed to reach the bottom just as Joel was slamming the door in Nick's face. Lizzie heard Nick's footsteps trudge off down the driveway and the truck drive away. She turned back on Joel as he moved down the hallway.

"What do you think you're doing?" Lizzie yelled in his face. "How dare you throw Nick out? This isn't your house, and you aren't the boss of me!"

"Would you have preferred me to call the police? That kid is a psycho, and you have the nerve to tell me that you want to be with him! After everything you've put your sister through, you should be grateful that this mess can be over, but you insist on putting yourself into danger!"

"It isn't your place to decide when I'm in danger or not! You can't do this! I'm going after him right now, and when Jen gets home, I'm going to make sure that she kicks you out of the house." She grabbed for the door-knob, but Joel slammed it shut again.

"Why would Jen listen to some spoiled brat? She loves me, and we're going to be together, so that's something that you're just going to have to accept. If you can't handle that, then run away: go back to California and be with your prissy parents. It would make your sister's life a hell of a lot easier. She doesn't need some selfish twit running around with a crazy boy trying to get herself killed just so she can have sex with him."

That did it. There was no way in hell that Lizzie was going to let dumb old JoJo talk to her like that. She threw her fist back and with one big swoop, punched him right in the eye. She watched as a tiny brown circle fell to the floor. She picked it up, all her focus completely drawn to that one little shape. *Contact lenses?* Lizzie lifted her head up to assess the damage to Joel's face. A strangled gasp lodged in her throat.

One very sinister, icy blue eye stared down at her, and it looked infuriated. Joel's entire mass seemed to swell up like he was some extreme hulk, but he took a deep breath, trying to release the tension from his body. He put his hands up in a surrendering motion, as if he was trying to reassure Lizzie that there was nothing to fear.

"It's not as bad as you think, Lizzie. Just give me back the contact, and we'll discuss this like two normal adults. I'll even call Nick up and apologize. Let's get you something to eat." Lizzie's heart stopped, his words hardly registering in her mind. *He was here the whole time. We invited him into the house.* "Lizzie, let's be rational."

Lizzie sprang forward and darted back up the stairs, but Joel was on her in no time. He was so tall that he bounded up the steps two at a time. He tugged at her ponytail, yanking her back onto the steps. She felt her head crack against one of them. She poked him in the eye and started climbing again, but he grabbed her around the ankle and she cracked her chin against the step.

She bled all over the carpet, and she could feel one of her teeth wiggling in her mouth. He pulled her all the way back down to the bottom rung. She covered her face with her arms to stifle the blows of each stair. At the bottom, he pinned her down with his body and began to choke her. Frantically, she pulled at his hands, but his grip was far too strong for her. She gasped desperately, feeling the wind being drained out of her.

"Do you really think I would let you ruin things for me? Huh? We could have had it good here. You could have made everything go away, and we never would have to deal with the evil Boogeyman again, but no, that wasn't good enough for you. You had to go searching for answers. You had to go talking to people like my sister. Well, little girl, how do you like the game now? Huh? Game over. I have won and you've failed, and now your little Nicky is going to rot in jail forever because you couldn't let things go." His voice was smooth and slick, not as raspy as Lizzie had remembered, but she knew that glint in his eyes.

Lizzie felt faint. She could feel everything going black and then an opening appeared. Bam! She kicked up her knee knocking him right in the groin. His grip loosened as he rolled on the ground in agony. Lizzie gave him another good kick for measure and tried to open the front door, but the massive, whimpering Joel was blocking it, so she tried all the windows in the living room, kitchen, and dining room. Someone had jammed them shut.

He must have known this would happen someday. He was just waiting for the perfect opportunity to destroy me. Lizzie heard a door opening. *Was he leaving?* Then it hit her. *Oh no, Jen.*

"Hey, where is everybody?" Jen called. Lizzie peeked out from the living room, scared Joel would attack Jen, but Joel wasn't at the door. Then where was he? Jen came into the living room and casually put her coat down. "Lizzie, there's blood on the stairs, did you trip and fall?"

"Jen, look out!"

Joel came out of nowhere, whacking Jen in the back. But what Joel didn't realize was that Jen was tough. Lizzie had seen her take down a guy twice her size once for grabbing her butt in public. A little dazed, she shot up, feeling mad as a honeybee. She punched him right in the gut, still unsure of what was going on.

"What the heck? Why did you just hit me?"

"Because that bitch sister of yours had to go and ruin everything," Joel growled and Lizzie recognized the raspy voice. What she had thought were two voices were really different aspects of one.

"What do you mean?" Jen turned to her sister. "What is he talking about?"

"He's the one who attacked me," Lizzie said, backing farther away from him.

"No!" Jen cried, mouth agape, staring at his one blue eye. "You did this to us? You tried to destroy my family? You killed all those people?"

"I was trying to do you a favor. That little brat has caused you enough problems." As he spoke, the space between him and Jen shortened.

Lizzie didn't know how to respond. She held her stance ready to do whatever Jen told her.

As he spoke again, his voice changed back to the slick tone. "Don't you see? Once she's gone, everything will be good in your life. Let me make everything perfect for you, and I promise you you'll be the happiest girl in the entire universe."

"If you think that I would ever let you hurt my family, you're dead wrong."

Now he was right on top of her. Jen tried to back away, but he pulled her closer to him.

"It doesn't have to be like this, Jen. I don't want to hurt you. I'll make it all go away. I'll make him go away."

Lizzie noticed that something in his eyes really meant it, but Jen would fight for Lizzie, no matter how he really felt.

"You can go to hell." Jen slapped him so hard that Lizzie thought his head was going to roll around.

Anger burst from him and he threw Jen against the wall. Her head cracked against the family portrait, shattering glass all over the floor. He paced beside her body, shaking his head and running his fingers through his hair.

"What did you do?" he yelled, his body was shaking.

Suddenly, something shifted in his body. It tightened, his mouth curling into a sneer, and Lizzie heard it. The voice she faintly remembered, his raspy tone.

"That bitch had it coming. Love is weak. I'm doing you a favor."

Then he charged at Lizzie again. She flew out of the room into the kitchen. They danced around the table a bit and then he bolted across it. At the same time, Lizzie tried to dive under the table and, luckily, she was quicker, but unfortunately not smarter.

Trying to run from the room, she smacked straight into the wall. Her head started to spin and she swore she saw all those little Tweety birds like a cartoon character would. Unfortunately that gave enough time for a furious Joel to come back around the table. He grabbed her by her hair again, pulling her along to the cupboard as he dug around in the knife drawer.

Crack! Jen flew through the door in a fit of fury and whacked Joel in the head with a frying pan. He crumpled to the ground, but her swing was too gentle. He shifted lightly and the girls ran from the room.

"Go, Lizzie, go to the door, baby. Hurry, hurry," Jen said close behind her.

They sprang to the door, but the lock had been jammed with something Lizzie couldn't make out. Jen shook it fiercely but it wouldn't open. *We're trapped.*

Footsteps thumped from the kitchen. Jen grabbed on to Lizzie's arm and practically hauled her up the stairs. They climbed all the way to the tower and immediately started barricading the door with everything they could find. Another sound of footsteps alerted the girls of his presence, and then all was silent.

"You girls open this door right now or you'll be sorry," Joel said, but no one answered.

Thunk! Joel's body collided with the door, causing the girls to shriek with fright. Suddenly the hamster dance broke the girl's hysterics. *Nick.* Lizzie scrambled into her bag and pulled out her cell phone. She had almost forgotten that it was in there.

"Hey, I'm really sorry about what happened with Joel. I won't be over to bother you any—"

"Nick, I really don't care about that right now. I need you to get the police and come over as fast as you can," Lizzie whispered frantically, not sure if she wanted Joel to hear that she was calling for help.

"What's wrong? Are you in trouble?" Nick's worry could be heard in his tone. Genevieve spoke unclearly to him in the background. "Genevieve wants to know if she should call the police."

Before Lizzie could respond, Jen had started to shove her toward the window. Joel had made quite a bit of progress while Lizzie was distracted and was now climbing over her desk. Lizzie dropped the phone and monkeyed her way out the window. She reached out to help Jen up, but was intercepted when Joel pulled Jen back through the window. She could hear the tortuous screams burning in her ears.

"Run, Lizzie, go! Get out of here!" Jen shrieked and so, hesitantly, Lizzie made her way across the side of the roof. The tower was the hardest part. It was so slanted it made it nearly impossible for Lizzie to pull herself across, but once she reached the part of the roof by the porch, it allowed her to gracefully land in a bush. The cold stung her body at first, but the adrenaline was rushing so fast to her brain that it quickly disregarded everything irrelevant to the moment.

She sprinted down the driveway slipping and sliding on the black ice as she went. She thought if she could cross the unplowed area, she would find herself halfway down the road and closer to her neighbor's house. Unfortunately, Joel was bounding down the drive after her, and the snow was still so deep that Lizzie sank down to her knees with every step.

This was slightly advantageous, due to the enormity of Joel's body. It made it nearly impossible for him to reach her. She reached the shed in quick pace and realized what she had to do. She had to shut him down. She grabbed for the nearest thing she could find, James's baseball bat. He had loved that bat. It was one of his favorite possessions. It was the only thing her parents let her keep besides the photograph.

"Are you sure you want that old thing?" her mother had said, trying to make mild conversation all morning so that she didn't have to acknowledge the fact that she had given up her child.

"Yes," Lizzie said, trying to find a good place to stuff the bat in one of the boxes. She had said very little to the two of them and, when the time came, there were hardly words of good-bye. She hadn't needed them, after all. Everything that mattered to her had been packed into that car, including that old baseball bat.

She charged out of the shed, heading straight for Joel, who had managed to find a solid patch of snow to steady himself with. She raised the bat over her head, but he noticed her coming, and with one quick snatch had the bat firmly out of her reach. He knocked her to the ground again. By this point, all the blows to the head were beginning to take their toll.

Her head seemed to spin around, and she thought for sure that she would vomit on his feet. He threw the bat to the ground and pulled out a steak knife, apparently his preferred weapon of choice.

Lizzie struggled with him, even managing to cut him down the right side of his face. He growled with irritation and stabbed Lizzie in the arm. She yelped in pain and punched him in the face again, causing the knife to slip out of his hand. She kicked it and it slid across the ice, moving a few inches away. Then she gave him another swift kick to the groin, and she had him on his back.

Seeing her opportunity, she picked up the baseball bat and started pounding him with it, over and over. Even after it was clear he was unconscious, she kept pounding him. *This one's for James. This one's for Jen. This one's for Nick, and this one's for me.*

"Lizzie, Lizzie, stop." Nick came running over, screaming, but Lizzie kept on. She had been so distracted that she hadn't heard the sirens. "You're going to kill him."

Nick reached Lizzie and tugged at her arms until, finally, she released the bat. She let out a long groan as her body gave out, and she collapsed on the ground next to Joel. Behind them, the ambulance and police rushed in to assess the situation.

"I need a medic over here," a voice shouted.

"Patient seems to be still breathing, but heart rate is low. I need a gurney," a medic said. Seconds later, they were lifting the unconscious man onto the gurney and pushing him down the driveway.

"Is anyone else injured," an officer asked Lizzie.

"I'm not sure," Lizzie said, trying to remember everything, but her head was throbbing. "My head hurts. It all happened so fast. He pulled me down and Jen."

She let out an agonizing cry and tears poured all over her face. Nick pulled her into his arms, rocking her calmly and trying to soothe her with his words, "It's okay, baby. It's all over with now. It's going to be all right. I'm here. I won't leave you, I promise."

"I think he killed my sister," she sobbed.

"I need another medic in the house. We've got another one upstairs, injured but conscious," someone shouted from the house.

"I'm going to need a set of handcuffs for the ambulance and I'll ride with him," another officer, who Lizzie recognized as Buckley, said. "Lizzie, you're going to have to go to the hospital to get your head examined. There's not much room in the ambulance, so one of my officers will take you."

"What about my sister?" Lizzie said, feeling that sudden rush of vomit come at her again, but she didn't get sick.

"She's been badly wounded. She needs to ride in the ambulance," he said.

"With that animal? There's only one ambulance. You can't put her in there with…" Her head was really spinning.

Nick caught her as she planted her butt in the snow. He lifted her back up, supporting her against his body.

"Let's just get you to the hospital, okay," Nick said. "Officer Buckley will make sure Jen's safe."

Lizzie nodded, following Nick to a police car and getting in. She felt dizzy and it was getting hard to stay awake, but Nick wouldn't let her fall asleep. He tapped her shoulder or whispered in her ear, keeping her as aware as possible. She could hear the sirens ringing in her ear, hurting her brain, and in front of them she saw the ambulance, but she still had a hard time recalling what had happened.

"It all happened so fast," Lizzie said over and over. "He was here all along."

"It's okay," Nick said. "It's all over with now. They got him."

A few hours later, the doctor had concluded that Lizzie could go home with a minor concussion and stitches in her head and lip.

"Good thing you've got a hard head," Nick teased.

Lizzie gave him a little whack, laughing for the first time since the whole mess started.

Jen wasn't released for several days. She had a single knife wound to the abdomen, but luckily, no internal organs had been hit. She had lost a significant amount of blood, but the doctor had reassured Lizzie that with a few transfusions, some stitches, and some pain medication, she would fully recover with little effect. Lizzie was surprised to find that he had only stabbed her once, but she was very relieved.

"What happened?" Lizzie had asked her.

"He couldn't do it," Jen said, sitting up in the hospital bed. That was all she would say. She stared off into space and Lizzie saw her try to wipe her eyes without Lizzie seeing.

Lizzie stayed with Nick for the night, not wanting to be alone in her house. She cuddled up next to him, soaking in his warmth and shelter. When she woke up in sweat, he caressed her hair and rocked her until she felt safe again.

Chapter 37

Brian

B rian lay in bed, tossing and turning with his haunted memories, glimpses of scarlet with the sweet, sickly smell of copper. Suddenly, his mind settled on the too-familiar golden locks, the ones he had seen just before his head had hit the icy snow and his life had been destroyed.

He jolted upward, escaping what he feared. Heart thundering loudly in his chest, he tried desperately to focus, to remove the disappointing image from his mind. He shouldn't have this memory. It wasn't his. He hadn't been the man that hurt those people. It was these others that the doctor had told him about, but they had slowly lost control of some of their memories, slipping them into his thoughts like sand through a sieve.

His memories of her had been happy, had been love, but now she lingered in every nightmare like a soul-altering vampire ripping out the good parts of his soul and replacing them with pain. *It's just a dream. It's all just a dream. She can't be here. You're lying in a hospital bed, feeling sorry for yourself. You probably won't ever have to see her again*, he would tell himself.

Adjusting his eyes, Brian noticed something peculiar

about his room. The walls were painted sky blue and the sweet aroma of strawberries filled the air. He looked to the oaken bureau, where he knew the last remnants of ember would be glistening from the candle's wax. His body shook with surprise as he felt outstretched arms wrap around his waist.

"Bad dream?" Jen asked, kissing his earlobe, and then his neck. Her breath gently whispering in his ear soothed his mind, and he couldn't help the temptation of playing along, even though he knew he would never know the feeling of her touch again.

"You could say that," he said, turning back around to face her. He pulled her in as close as possible, trying to surround her with his body. He gently kissed her forehead, lying back down to allow her to rest on his chest. He stroked her hair as soft as fleece and whispered into her ear, "I love you no matter what anyone tells you."

"What do you mean?" she asked.

"I don't know. I'm just afraid of losing you. I feel like you're going to disappear." *I know you're going to disappear,* he thought.

She sprang away from him, eyes darting around the room then back at him. She started to screech at him, waving her arms around and pointing at him, "Monster! You inhuman creature, I know what you have done! Demon!"

His breath rose from the depths of his stomach into his throat and released out his mouth in a billowy cloud, as if the souls he had killed were trying to escape from his own body. The images of his world went black. It wriggled around, smothering him, sticky, black, and smelling of melted plastic. He desperately tore the substance from his face, but it clung to him. He ripped harder, gasping for breath, and a light crept into the corner of his eye. Moving toward it, he pulled away from the blackness. As he walked towards the light, he turned around to see if the monster was following him, but his stomach churned when he saw himself behind him. He had never felt more afraid and more self-loathing in all of his days.

He woke up in a sweat, still remembering the look of madness on the monster's face, on his own face. For the past few days, his head had gotten worse and worse, startling him from his comfortable place next to Jen, in fear of what may be coming, but it had never felt like this. It had come and cost him one of the only things he had left to cling to in his life. He had stabbed her. He would've killed her, but he didn't. No, not him, those other two, the others he hadn't known about. They had been running his life in spurts for so long that he didn't bother finding out what they were, or maybe he had been too afraid to know the answer. Either way, it was too late now. He had to endure their constant bickering.

You should've let me do it. I could've eased your pain, the one called Francis grumbled. He was always growling about something.

You think that would make it better? You ruined me! No more, just shut up, Brian Matthew said, as heartbroken as Brian was.

You can't make me. I am you, remember? We are one. You are the monster. Monster. Monster.

Brian pulled on his head, trying to get the throbbing pain to stop. He got up from the hospital bed and the alarm went off to alert the nurse, but he didn't care. The pain was excruciating, and Francis was screaming in his ear, over and over. One of the officers guarding the door peeked in cautiously to see what the prisoner was up to but that didn't stop him. He felt bile rise into his throat as he staggered into the bathroom. He emptied himself into the bowl, wishing the monster inside of him would just come out with his half-digested vegetables and make the screaming stop.

He went to the sink to cleanse his face and splashed the water against it, letting the coolness of the water and sink top soothe him, but it still didn't calm his thoughts. Slowly, he lifted his head from the sink and looked into the mirror. It had been a long time since he had paid attention to the reflection, for fear of what he may see. He searched within the glass for the man, but all he could see was the monster.

Chapter 38

Brian sat on a hard seat in the courtroom, his palms sweaty and his heart strumming faster than his mind could count. His mind felt a little fuzzy from the prescription the doctors had given him, but for the first time in thirteen years, his mind was quiet. The others that he had been told about had said little after the initial dosages, and Brian soon realized that they had no interest in communicating with him.

A firestorm of media had arrived just to get a glimpse at his notorious face, their shouts echoed in his brain from outside the courthouse.

"Will the defendant please rise?" the judge said, raising his voice so that all could hear. He stood, towering over his lawyer, who was a mere five foot seven. "Would you please state your full real name for the record so that the court may decide on a trial date?"

He scanned the room, hoping that she might be there. *Just one more time*, he thought. *I just need to see her one last time.* His eyes landed on a mass of purple fabric and a strand of silver hair. Genevieve sat between her grandson and Lizzie, her lips shut tight and her eyes squinted, adjusting to the light.

"Would you please state your name before I hold you in contempt of court?"

"Brian Matthew Robinson, your honor, born August 23, 1990."

His eyes stayed on the trio and found Lizzie's face. He tried to use his expression to ask her the question, but she just stared at him sullenly. Then she blinked, realizing what he wanted, and a smile crept across her face, a smile so poisonous to Brian's being that he had to look away.

"Are you aware of the charges that are brought against you and the severity of these crimes?"

"I am, your honor, and I understand that I should be punished for what I've done. I just—"

"Your honor, my client is asking that the charges against him be dropped due to mental defect. My client was clearly incapable of controlling his actions at the time of the incidences, which were beyond his mental capacity," his lawyer said, cutting off Brian's own argument.

He towered above her like a darkened shadow. Her body was slender and secure in her navy jacket.

The district attorney was a demon in a suit. "Your honor, the defendant has proven to be clever and manipulative to a point where even those closest to him didn't know his identity. The state will argue that this proves his capability to understand and control his actions." His gleaming eyes and booming voice gave him the highest win rate in the entire state, and Brian was sure that today would be no exception.

"My client is suffering from a rare form of mental disorder that causes violent delusions. Even psychiatrists have yet to truly understand the functions of the disorder and how it may be prevented. Since he has been arrested, he has been making a quick recovery to become a useful part of society. A specialist for his condition is being flown in to evaluate his situation. I recommend the court withhold their decision until he is further evaluated."

"The defendant has already been evaluated by two of our top psychiatrists, who insist that his faculties are fine. This is just a ploy my colleague is using to manipulate the system. We clearly have a serial killer on our hands, and setting him free without a trial would be a great injustice to all the families who have suffered under his rage."

"Neither psychiatrist has any expertise in this type of mental illness and, therefore, don't know what to look for in my client. How can my client be responsible for all these people's sufferings if, at the time of incidences, he wasn't aware of himself?"

"The defense has three days to gather this information," the judge said.

"Your honor, I would also like to request that my client be released to the hospital for care during this extension."

"Absolutely not. Your honor, the hospital is ill-equipped for a case of this magnitude and will put the other patients at risk."

"I agree with the councilman," the judge said, directing his attention to Brian. "Mr. Robinson, you will receive psychiatric care at the state penitentiary until your evaluation is completed, at which time it will be determined if you're fit for trial. Court adjourned." The judge's gavel rapped against the bench, ending the sentencing for the day.

The officers escorted him from the room, back into the crowd of reporters flashing cameras in his face. It happened so fast that he didn't know what to do. He pushed forward through the crowd, wondering if he'd ever get his life back, not even sure what his life had been.

Chapter 39

Lizzie

The day the girls came home to the disaster zone, everything was in complete disarray. Since Jen's release from the hospital, they had been staying at Genevieve's until the court date, not wanting to return to the memories of their home yet.

Now the first court appearance had occurred and the girls reluctantly agreed to move home. Jen had the hardest time, taking hours to pile the clothes that Nick had brought her from the house back into her suitcase. She picked up each item, folding it several times before putting it in place.

"Are you okay," Lizzie asked when she noticed that very little had gone back into the suitcase.

"Yeah," she said. "It's just so…I just don't…The whole thing seems so unfair. I just don't know what to think, or what I feel. The man I knew loved me and not just me, he loved you too. I know he did."

"Yeah," Lizzie said, not wanting to argue. "I almost miss him too."

Jen nodded, stuffing her clothes into the pack without bothering to fold them again. Lizzie watched her hands shake and she gave her sister's hand a squeeze, trying to do anything to make the pain better.

"Well, he's gone now, and that's that," she said, pushing Lizzie's hand aside.

Pulling into the driveway, Lizzie felt a turning in her stomach. There were just too many memories floating around the yard like dandelion seeds in autumn. They had built their snowball fort down by the trees, Joel had stood on the porch with concern on his face as Lizzie had come home from dances and art shows and other activities.

Lizzie always thought it was funny. He had been so protective, so loving. For a moment, a fraction of that ache that Jen was feeling hit Lizzie, and she realized what she had lost. She was brother-less again. After the initial pain, she remembered the night everything fell apart, images flashing across her brain like a horror film: the escape on the roof, the wading through snow, the baseball bat. All those things hardened whatever sympathy she had been building.

Jen had already gotten out of the car and was standing on the ice, not willing to move closer to the steps. Lizzie got out of the car, walking up to her sister, and taking her hand. She gave her a smile, determined to be the brave one for once.

"Are you ready," she asked.

"I don't think I'll ever be, but we have no choice, do we?" Jen started up the steps, Lizzie following behind her, not letting go of her hand.

The girls went into the kitchen and sat at the table. Rose petals and candles showered the floor. Jen sighed, a deep sigh that Lizzie could sense traveled to her core. There was a loss there that Lizzie couldn't possibly understand, an ache that wouldn't go away with the reminder of a few painful memories.

Lizzie wasn't sure what to do or say. She didn't have that same feeling looking at the mess. She felt empowered, strong. She had survived, and that meant more to her than the loss she had suffered, but she couldn't tell Jen that, not when she was still mourning.

Jen picked up a tiny box that had been lying on the table and opened it. A diamond twinkled innocently from within the box. Inside the ring was the inscription, *Love is eternal*. Jen bit at her lip, but one tear escaped her eye and trickled onto the table. This time, it was Lizzie that sighed, but with relief. It was finally over.

Saturday night she and Jen had stayed up late, discussing the future. Jen was going back to work on Monday. Lizzie wasn't certain about the decision but Jen reassured her it was for the best.

"The best thing I can do is keep busy and move forward with my life. If you're not ready to go back to school we can wait a few more days," she said.

"No, I need to go back. I told Nick I would be there to support him on his first day back." As she spoke her cell phone rang. Lizzie checked the number and it was her parents. She stared at it for a moment, unsure of what to do. "Hello?"

"Hi Lizzie, it's Mom," Her mother hesitated on the line, waiting for Lizzie to respond but she didn't say anything. "Lizzie, are you there?"

"I'm here." Lizzie said trying to choke down the pain that was coming up into her throat.

"Your father and I saw the news and, honey, we're just so sorry. We weren't there for you and you were telling the truth. You cleared your brother's name and you caught the murderer and, sweetie, we're just so proud of you. We miss you so much."

"I miss you too, Mom." Lizzie looked at Jen. Jen was frowning.

"We were hoping, your father and I…well, you see, without your brother this house just feels so empty, and the way we treated you…We weren't there for you, Lizzie, but we would like to be. We want you to come home to us." Her mother's voice sounded so hopeful.

Lizzie looked at her sister. Jen was pretending like she wasn't watching. She stared out the window but Lizzie could see her eyes water. "Thanks, but I am home. Maybe you guys could come to Maine for a visit soon?"

"Umm…okay. I think that would be nice. We will do that soon. And your father and I will call you every week, okay?"

"Okay," Lizzie said, giving Jen's hand a squeeze. She had relaxed when she heard that Lizzie was staying. "I love you, Mom."

"We love you too," her mother sniffled, hanging up the phone.

"Starting new, okay?" Lizzie said, hugging Jen.

"Okay," Jen said, holding her tightly.

That Monday she was back at school, walking the halls with Nick. They held each other's hand tightly, not willing to put any distance between them ever again. With Joel's or Brian's—as she found out at the trial that was his real name—full confession of all the murders and terrorizing Lizzie, the charges on Nick and her brother, James, were dropped. Lizzie was relieved to know that they could all finally have some closure. Of course, the knowing wouldn't bring any of those people back or take the pain away, but she wasn't crazy. She was a survivor and now the world knew it. Walking the hall, she felt resurrected again.

Fiona walked up to them, arms folded and foot tapping. "I see you're back finally."

"Yeah. They finally caught him," Lizzie said.

"Good. Thank you," Fiona said. She hugged Lizzie. Lizzie didn't know if she should hug her back. She patted her back and they pulled away from each other. The other students in the hallway were watching them. "What are you losers staring at?" Fiona snapped. "Don't you have better things to do."

Lizzie watched Fiona wave as she walked to her first class. "You don't see that every day."

"I guess hell froze over, after all." Nick laughed. He hugged Lizzie close to him. "Ready for the next chapter?"

"Yeah," she said, inhaling his cologne. "You bet I am."

Chapter 40

Brian

Brian didn't have to wait long for the expert to arrive. After his first night in prison, Dr. Collins had arrived promptly the next morning. She was a stout, short woman with curly gray hair and glasses that she had to push up over and over because they didn't quite fit her face. When she saw Brian, she smiled at him, talking quickly with the police officers before sitting down at the table.

"Hello, I'm Jeanine Collins. You can call me Dr. Collins," she said, pulling out a folder and a pen. "I've been hearing a lot about you, Brian. Why don't you tell me a little about yourself?"

"Umm...okay. What do you want to know?" Brian gnawed on his bottom lip. He felt uneasy with everyone watching him, too exposed and distressed.

She put her pen down, placing her hands on the table and looking into Brian's face. "Well, why don't you tell me a little about yourself? Where did you grow up?"

"Umm...in California. I grew up in the suburbs. I have a sister Michelle, but she's not with me right now—well, obviously. I mean, I am here and she's out there, but umm...my parents were happily married, I believe.

My dad worked in an office, and my mom was a kinder-garten teacher and piano teacher. She gave lessons to kids at the house."

"Do you know how to play too," Dr. Collins asked, not bothering to write anything down, just keeping eye contact with him. He noticed from time to time that she would look away for a second or blink rapidly, but she never moved for her pen or even bothered reading what was in the folder.

"Well, duh, I'm not a friggin' idiot. I'm sorry, what was the question?" Brian had felt fuzzy for a second, feeling something reaching into his mind and creating confusion in his thoughts.

"We were discussing the piano. You said you can play?" Dr. Collins leaned her head on her hand. He thought it an odd gesture from a psychologist.

"I did? I used to play a little, but I didn't really keep up with it after my mother died," he said, a little surprised that he couldn't remember telling her he could play. "I thought they said this medication thing's supposed to work?"

"Has it been working for you so far," Dr. Collins asked.

"Well, I'm not sure. It's been really quiet, and I ha-ven't had any blackouts. The first couple days were hor-rible with them shouting all the time, but they don't fight with the medication."

"I see. Perhaps the medication is working better than expected. You said your mother died? That must've been difficult for you?"

"Yeah, it happened so fast. We got into a car acci-dent and she didn't make it. It hurt a lot at first, but it got easier for me." Brian looked down to see he was picking at his fingernails and one of them had begun to bleed.

"Is that when you started blacking out or did you

black out when she abused you," she said it smoothly, lips barely moving with a vocal motion.

"What did you say?" he said, feeling an uneasy shift in his mind. Someone was unhappy, and, for the first time, Brian could feel the rage that had built up inside of him. His hand automatically balled into a fist.

"I asked you if you blacked out when your mother abused you or after her death?"

"My mother didn't abuse me," he said, starting to growl, then the rage burst forth and his fist hit the table as he jumped out of his seat. "Who told you that? My mother loved me. Who the hell told you that?"

"Well, your behavior when speaking of her suggests that you don't miss her very much, and, from my professional opinion, it would seem to be stemmed from some bad memories of her."

"No, my mother loved me. He's the idiot that doesn't miss her because he doesn't feel anything, ever. He spends all his time hiding, but I'm not like him. I miss her, and she never laid a damn finger on me, you hear? It was that scumbag, piece of shit she married. He beat them, so we took care of it." He paused, realizing he had said more than he should have.

"We, huh? Can I ask your name?" she said, a curious glint in her eyes. "Would you sit down, please?"

"It's not important. I'm not real," he said, sitting back down.

"You seem to voice your opinion quite strongly for someone who doesn't exist. What are you then?"

"I'm Francis. I protect them," he said, feeling unsure of what to do. He felt very lost again.

I'm still here too, Brian Matthew told him, making him smile a little.

"Does Brian know you're talking to me right now?" she asked, noting the shifting of emotion in his face.

"I don't know. I don't like talking to him. He's weak," he said, looking away from her. "Will you take back what you said about my mother?"

"Of course. I'm not unwilling to acknowledge my mistakes. Are you?"

"I fix my mistakes," he said. He suddenly didn't like where it was going and curled back inside. Brian looked around for a second, feeling confused again, but he didn't speak this time.

"Very well. I think my time here is probably close to up." She closed the folder, clipping the pen to the top and rising from her chair.

"That's it? You don't want to know anything else," he said, watching her go to the door.

"I think I have enough to make my report," she said, smiling at him again. He wasn't sure why she kept doing that. What made her so happy to be talking to a crazy person?

"What's going to happen to me?"

"The charges have been taken against Brian Robinson, and I feel confident that you weren't involved in these crimes, so I'm going to recommend they transfer you to my facility in California for treatment. How does that sound?"

"I'm going home?" he said, looking stunned that this woman would even consider trying to make him better. He wasn't sure what that meant or how he felt about it, but it wasn't jail or worse, so he decided not to protest.

"Yes. I think you and I will become well-acquainted. I have already had the pleasure of talking about you a little bit with your sister and think I can be of some assistance to you both."

"Shelley's okay?" Brian asked.

"Yes, she's been moved to our facility for recovery. It was nice to meet you, and Francis as well," she said, giving him a nod. Brian wasn't sure who Francis was, but something about the name made him cringe. "Perhaps you and the others will know a normal day soon."

Brian watched her go with a slight awe. This woman was to be his salvation, to fix this strange mess that had become his life. He thought about what she said about being normal. He wasn't sure what normal was or what it had ever been, but he was anxious to find out.

About the Author

Katie Marshall lives and works in Dover-Foxcroft, Maine. She is a graduate of the University of Maine at Farmington and has three self-published books. When she's not writing, she enjoys reading everything she can find and spending time with nature.